SOUL SACRIFICE

COURTNEY DAVIS

5 PRINCE PUBLISHING

Copyright © 2024 by Courtney Davis, SOUL SACRIFICE

All rights reserved. Smashwords Edition

This is a fictional work. The names, characters, incidents, and locations are solely the concepts and products of the author's imagination, or are used to create a fictitious story and should not be construed as real. No part of this book may be reproduced in any form or by any electronic or mechanical means, including information storage and retrieval systems, without written permission from the author, except for the use of brief quotations in a book review.

Published by 5 PRINCE PUBLISHING & BOOKS, LLC

PO Box 865, Arvada, CO 80001

www.5PrinceBooks.com

ISBN digital: 978-1-63112-380-1

ISBN print: 978-1-63112-381-8

Cover Credit: Marianne Nowicki

F072324

As always, I am thankful for the support of my family. If I didn't have that, I couldn't dedicate my time to creating. Thank you for always listening to my half story rambling ideas and encouraging me when I feel like I've written myself into a hole.

ACKNOWLEDGMENTS

Thank you to the staff at 5 Prince Publishing for all you do to help me make my stories the best they can be.
I would be lost without the dedication of my amazing editor Cate! She takes my story and pushes me to make it better.

ALSO BY COURTNEY DAVIS

The Atlantis Series
The Vampires of Atlantis

Aristotle's Wolves

Descendants of Atlantis

Stand Alone Titles
Butterfly Kisses

The Serpent and the Firefly

A Spider in the Garden

Princess of Prias

Soul Sacrifice

SOUL SACRIFICE

CHAPTER ONE

It was after the last great war, and the Gods had descended from heaven, cursing the earth with souls. Like a disease, it spread unhindered, and the consequences weren't known for generations...

Lark Duport stood alongside his two men, with fifty or so members of this small town in north Montana as they watched the two soulbrothers engage in a soulbattle to the death. The town was much like many scattered across the country; a few neighborhoods of houses in disrepair, and a school, a post office, and a bar. There was a grocery store, and a police station of course, that had to keep order among the masses. No real industry existed, aside from what the citizens could provide for each other in services like small farms or crafts. No one here was making good money, but they were surviving mostly because of the rations that the government provided.

Government rations were given in the form of bank credits, linked to the chip that was implanted in every registered baby when they were born. The right wrist could be scanned, and it would show the person's status and the number of ration credits they had. It was a great way for the government to keep track of where everyone was, and for business owners to discriminate. They could scan you and kick you out for not having the available rations they saw fit to be in their establishment or, more likely, for being a halfling, despite the possibility of being able to pay in cash, which was still an acceptable way to pay for things.

People around him were whispering with excitement at what they were about to witness; one of their own had a chance at a full soul. Looking around he saw a lot of dull eyes meaning most of these people were halflings themselves. Today's battle might motivate some of them to go looking for their own other half, if they were lucky enough to have one out there. Not every soul's other half was ever born.

The pair circled each other, sizing the other up. They were unmatched physically, there was a clear favorite to win and it wasn't the man Lark had brought here. It didn't matter to Lark who won, he'd done what he had been paid for without any guarantees about the result. He had found the client's other half and brought his client here for this battle. Only one of them would survive, and that one would gain the other half of their soul. In this world of halfsouls, fullsouls and very unfortunate nosouls, nothing mattered more to a halfling than the chance at finding the other part of their soul and to join through the death of one; becoming a whole person in the eyes of the government and society. Lark wondered for the millionth time what the end of all this would be, was this all just a slow descent into hell for the world or was there actually some redemption for them all somewhere? He was inclined to think the former, but he knew plenty of people who had hope.

"That was a rough trek. The amount of dead space through

Utah and Wyoming has gotten worse, don't you think?" Stone said.

"Yeah, I remember a few more settlements there that were mainly halflings," Granger agreed. "I hate to think anything is ever right about what the government says, but we know that halfling settlements often lead to nosoul issues, could be what is driving a lot of those halflings back to the city settlements, it's a little safer."

"Or the government went in and moved them out forcefully," Lark grumbled. He wouldn't put it past them to break up a halfling settlement that was surviving well. It was harder to control people when they weren't dependent on government rations.

Granger nodded agreement.

Lark looked at the two men who were still circling each other and posturing for attack and wondered why they weren't just getting to it already. It didn't surprise Lark that the smaller man was hesitating, perhaps rethinking what a great idea this whole journey was. Lark had learned a lot about the man on their search. He was a halfling who had grown up with a single mom, common for halflings, and currently worked at a tire shop his fullsoul grandfather owned. He was lucky by halfling standards, many were completely abandoned by their families, unwed mothers forced to raise children with no support or give them up to the orphanage. This guy didn't know how lucky he was to have a good paying and respectable job. He just wanted more, wanted a wife and family and the only way to get those things was to get the other half of his soul. Now he was staring down a man twice his size and almost guaranteed to lose everything. Lark shook his head, sometimes he almost wished he failed to find his clients' soulsiblings for them.

"I wasn't sure we'd find the soulbrother this time, honestly," Lark said. It had felt like they'd already exhausted all their usual methods and then they'd heard of this place tucked up so far north it was almost in Canada. It reportedly had a large population of unregistered halflings living off the land in a fairly self-contained town.

"We rarely fail," Stone said, clapping Lark on the back. "That's why we can charge so much," he added with a laugh and Granger grunted nearby.

It was true, they'd learned how to track when they'd left the orphanage in LA as young men, barely adults. They had worked together to find their own soulsiblings and all of them had been victorious, claiming the other half of their souls. It had been the only goal they'd had growing up. The only thing three orphans could imagine wanting to do with their lives after living in such destitute conditions with so many other unwanted halfling children. One good thing that had come from growing up like that was they'd found each other and now considered each other brothers; something they never would have had otherwise. Lark was sure he'd never heard of a fullsoul woman having more than one halfling child, the regret after the first was enough to stop any further mistakes.

Lark had connected with Stone first, he'd been so easy to make friends with, a happy kid with blond hair, he was big and muscled now but had been just a tall, scrawny kid once upon a time. Lark had to step in more than once to save his ass, growing up, which is how they'd initially become friends, Stone decided hanging out with one of the physically stronger kids who didn't seem to be annoyed with his constant chatter was a safe bet. Lark hadn't minded the company. Then they'd met Granger. He had always been intimidating, the only orphan of obviously Native American heritage that they'd grown up with. He had dark eyes and long dark hair which had given him a mysterious air that none of the other boys had wanted to mess with, especially combined with his quiet demeanor. Granger had been drawn to Lark and Stone because of their bond against the other assholes in the orphanage. By the time they were all seven years old they'd been inseparable. Now they were all big and muscled, Granger still had the long hair and had added tattoos that covered everywhere except for his face. He was good for intimidating silently, while Stone tended to try charm first and was a whiz with the computer, doing a lot of the research for their jobs.

In front of them, fists finally started to fly as the two soulbrothers engaged in their fight. It was all Lark needed to see; this job was done. "Let's go," Lark told his brothers and started to walk away.

He couldn't help remembering his own soulbattle, always did when they were at the end of a search like this. His own search had taken seven months, they'd searched and traveled, following the small spark inside of himself that indicated he had a soulsibling, Granger and Stone by his side the entire time. When he'd taken the man's life Lark had felt the partial soul surround them both, searching for where to go. If Lark hadn't been close enough to touch the man, the soul would have just drifted away, to wherever souls that weren't claimed went, but he *was* there. He had his hands on the man's bleeding and limp body and the soul had clung to him and soaked into him and he'd felt it through every cell in his body, a burning that turned to a tingle and then a new strength. And then the memories came, a high-speed slideshow in his mind of what this man's life had been, now stopped, cut short by Lark.

Lark was pulled from the memory by a small boy, maybe nine years of age running up to them as they passed by a row of dilapidated shacks.

"Hey, sir," the boy said with a confidence that came from being too young to know better. "Is it true what they say? Will Big Jim get a full ration after this?"

Lark's stomach twisted at the big, dull eyes staring out of the child's dirty face. His cheeks were hollow and his lips pale. Lark squatted down so he was eye level with the boy. Lark ran a hand through his own dark hair as he considered his answer, and the boy's eyes widened a bit when they spotted the deep scar that started at Lark's right ear and disappeared below his shirt line below his collarbone.

"If Big Jim wins, then yes, he can get a full ration from the government," Lark said.

"Wow," the boy said, licking his lips. "I hope he keeps coming to visit my mom at night, maybe he'll want to share his rations," the boy said and ran off to join the crowd around the fighting pair.

Lark stood with a grimace and pushed down the urge to give the child and whoever his mother was some cash. It wouldn't solve their problems, but neither would Big Jim having his full soul. The man was more likely to leave the small town and try to find his soulmate than to stay and share his newly-gained ration status with the woman he was sleeping with, and her halfling child.

Everyone thought gaining a soul would fix everything for themselves and the people around them, but Lark knew better. It just presented them with a new set of problems, a new set of expectations and rules. It presented them with a new goal they thought attainable; a soulmate and fullsoul children, the new American dream.

What people didn't realize until it was too late was there was no way to win in this new world they were cursed into. There was only survival, and Lark was skilled at that.

It helped that he had access to records and files that no one outside the government was supposed to have because the government needed people like him to do their dirty work. Ever since discovering that the only way to heal the destitute halflings was to unite soulsiblings in a soulbattle, it had become the government's main goal. They wanted to strengthen the country and stay on top as a world power, which was hard to do when most of your population was weak and dying. Death was such a touchy subject for the upper class, the born fullsouls in charge, so it opened an opportunity for men like Lark, Stone, and Granger. And they made a great living doing it without the need for Government rations.

"Raise the prices when we get back," Lark said as they reached their vehicle. They'd been so busy lately, it was a sign that they could charge more, do a little less and still profit. "As always we can send those who can't pay the new price over to Stan and Terri." Lark and his men weren't the only ones in the business, but they were the best. "I wouldn't mind a couple weeks off," Lark admitted as he slid into the driver's seat. This search had taken three months and they'd been to some of the deepest, darkest pods of humanity that the country held. If you were a halfling and you weren't in a government-subsidized encampment within a city, there was almost no chance of living in safety, or any kind of sanitary conditions.

Lark didn't understand why the halflings would choose life in the run-down towns over the alternative, but he did know that the government-established districts within cities were barely better.

And even worse, was being a kid growing up in a halfling orphanage like they had been.

"A break sounds nice, I need to get my dick wet," Stone said with a groan. "Even taking suppressants on these trips isn't enough to keep my man down."

"Maybe if you took them more than once a week while we were on a job," Granger pointed out.

"No way. That shit will fuck you up. Last time I took it as

prescribed I couldn't get it up for a week after I stopped. Wasted a whole week of not satisfying the ladies of LA"

"You're ridiculous," Granger said, and closed his eyes in the backseat, obviously done with the conversation.

Lark knew Granger didn't take the suppressants no matter what. Lark didn't either. But neither of them complained as much as Stone when they weren't jumping from willing bed to willing bed. When they were in LA and surrounded by other willing non-suppressant-takers, suppressants weren't a consideration for any of them because despite what the government would like people to believe, sex wasn't going to be the downfall of society.

The government didn't want anyone having sex outside of sanctioned fullsoul marriage, so they encouraged suppressants for their citizens and outlawed sex outside of marriage. Problem was, it was a voluntary program to take the suppressants. It hadn't started that way, but the uproar and near-toppling of the government over it had the president at the time backing off quickly with lots of propaganda about the evils and risks of having sex outside of fullsoul marriage. After that there was an increase in the halfling population and nosouls, proof that people were still fucking, despite the risks. It was nearly impossible to convince the poor and depressed that free entertainment wasn't worth taking a chance on.

Lark drove away from the small town in Northern Montana, his thoughts already on the next possible job. Even though he planned to take a break, he knew that as soon as Stone checked the business email, there would be a list of people pleading for assistance.

At least the desperate halflings' desire for a better life gave him a purpose, because the Gods knew he wasn't going to take on the duty of finding his soulwife and having fullsoul babies as his purpose on this hellscape of earth.

They drove for a day without passing another town large enough to have a hotel. Most of the dwindling United States population had crowded into a few main cities after the initial cursing and civil uproar had settled down. The small places scattered about beyond them were usually nothing more than a few homes and farms. Enough to keep those that lived there alive, barely. But the farms provided a necessary service to the rest of the country, food production.

It was eerie, some of the places they drove through looked like the earth was trying to reclaim the territory after a nuclear war. Destroyed buildings, abandoned cars and everywhere nature was crawling over it. Plants and animals encroaching back where they had once thrived before modern humans decided to pave and plow and build over it. Lark liked the idea of the earth gaining some of its power back in these places, even if it was a reminder that their world had been forcefully changed and had yet to really settle since. There wasn't civil war currently, at least not here in the United States, but there wasn't a lot of freedom and choice most places.

Around the world, things were worse in a lot of countries. Places where the governments hadn't been able to quash rebellions as quickly, hadn't been able to give out suppressants and get their citizens in line with the new rule of law to keep the nosouls from becoming rampant.

When two halfsouls chose to chuck caution to the wind and indulge their base desires, a pregnancy was disastrous. A child with no soul was born, an evil that the world wasn't equipped to handle.

Pulling into Boise, Idaho, they all sighed with relief to see signs for businesses. This was the second largest city in the northwestern United States next to Seattle, which had continued to thrive because of its port which still received many things that got shipped off all over the country for use. Lark had heard stories of before, when every store and every town was so full of things that it was impossible to even choose sometimes. Now you were lucky to go in the store and have two options for anything you might need, from batteries to shampoo, choice was limited. Lark didn't mind, he wasn't sure that having to glance over a hundred different soaps would in any way make his life better.

It was the same for food. Mostly you could get a good selection of things grown locally but anything that wasn't manufactured in your town or nearby, was limited in supply and limited in choice. It was one reason most people congregated in large cities, the ability to grow, manufacture and support the population was better. Partially because the government helped fund a lot more infrastructure for large cities, keeping the trains and trucks moving things from one to another with all the comforts its citizens demanded.

Lark couldn't help feeling it was just another way to control the population, making it seem so good and comfortable to be where the government had a good watch over them, and hard to survive outside of it. But people made it work somehow, he'd been to plenty of small towns that survived with very little.

"Looks like we can take a shower and sleep in a bed tonight," Stone said happily.

"Good, I am tired of smelling you two," Granger grumbled.

Boise being the largest city left in Idaho had a sectioned-off halfling district, not allowing them to mix freely with the fullsouls who lived in the medium-sized city. It was surrounded by farmlands and also had a large industrial portion, making it a popular location. Halflings could often get jobs at those farms and factories doing the work fullsouls wouldn't do, hard work picking and planting. A job like that could get a halfling a small house outside of the government funded housing neighborhoods.

They'd stopped here often, looking for soulsiblings and knew of a good hotel where they could get a bed and a shower.

When they were settled into a small room with two beds and a pull-out couch, Stone got to work on the laptop looking for their next job. Lark knew he'd start by deleting anything that started with pleading for free help, they didn't do that. Stone would then narrow down the possibilities of clients to a few that sounded like they had cash ready and send them to Lark. Lark opened one and read a short and to-the-point paragraph from a woman stating she had cash and wanted to find her soulsister ASAP.

Women on the search always intrigued him more. It was usually harder for them to be bloodthirsty enough to kill another person and it was also easier for them to find ways to make money to live well, outside of the government rations. Highly-illegal prostitution was big business in this new society of illegal sex. He replied to her email with a date and time to meet at his office. Maybe she'd be the last client before the price increase went into effect.

CHAPTER TWO

Ebony Landry was aware from a very young age that she was missing a vital part of herself, and society made sure she never forgot it. She also knew that, unlike most of the others in the halfling district of LA, she had a soulsister out there. The likelihood of two soulmates who were unable to find each other, both having children with other fullsouls was slim, and so most halflings never even had the chance to find their other half and try to win a soulbattle.

When she was five, she'd felt it, a sudden burning in her heart. She'd thought she was having a heart attack, and being a little on the hypochondriac side, she'd made her mother take her to see a doctor even though they could barely afford to feed themselves. The doctor had acted like he was giving them wonderful news when he explained that the burning sensation was an indication that Ebony had a soulsister out there.

No one talked about the kind of pressure that puts on you, what kind of torture you put yourself through thinking of taking another life, the kind of fear you live with knowing someone else could be coming for you at any time.

Everyone thought she was so lucky.

She was supposed to feel blessed that she had the chance to kill. That she had hope of one day being whole and accepted in the upper class. Until recently, she hadn't been tempted at all to go find her soulsister.

That's what had brought her here tonight, that's why she was standing in this low-lit office, waiting for this man to consider her desperate plea. She was out of time, and he was her best hope.

"Ebony Landry?" Lark Duport asked with a raised eyebrow.

She nodded nervously; her future hung on his next words.

He sat behind a huge mahogany desk in a plush leather chair. The room smelled of sweet tobacco and dust, the scent unfamiliar but not unpleasant. There were bookcases along two walls filled with more books than she'd ever seen in her life, more books than there were in the entire halfling district, she thought. What could someone like him be doing with so many books? He looked like the type who was mostly interested in smashing things with his fists, not sitting down to read the lives and adventures of others. She wondered what kinds of books they were, did he read history or fantasy? Was he a poet at heart? She almost laughed at the thought, the guy looked like he preferred violent physical expressions, not verbal. The books were more likely just a decorative element, not actually something he indulged in, during his free time.

She had always loved to read, had read everything she could get her hands on as soon as she'd learned how to. Unfortunately, halflings were schooled by whoever in the community was best suited to a subject and mostly done without supplies like extra for fun books. She was willing to bet this man had learned in a proper school with everything available to him. He'd likely grown up in a house filled with everything his little heart could have desired and spoiled rotten by two parents with great jobs and every opportunity to offer their son.

She grew up with half portions of rations allotted to her by the government and whatever small amounts of food and necessities her mother could buy with her earnings as a waitress. It hadn't been a bad life, it certainly could have been worse, she could have grown up in the orphanage where many halflings were abandoned to try and cover up their parents' indiscretion.

Ebony had grown up with her mother who loved her deeply and who had reminded her every day that Ebony was as good as anyone else, no matter what the government said.

Lark's eyes assessed her critically and she had to stop herself from crossing her arms nervously.

She'd put on her nicest T-shirt for this meeting and despite the cool night, had left her jacket behind; it was far too past its prime. Now she regretted having nothing to hold around herself as she stood before the man feeling exposed. But she tried to keep her mother's words in her head and dared to meet his gaze with her own.

She may live in a one-bedroom home in the halfling district of LA, but she wasn't trash.

She held her head high and bit her cheek as she faced him. She tucked a lock of black hair behind an ear as an excuse to move. She'd never felt so seen and it made her want to fidget, to fix and try to be something more than she was. She didn't wear much makeup usually, but she'd put a little on for this and her hair was loose and clean around her shoulders. She knew she looked fine, she wasn't trying to date the guy, just hire him. That reality wasn't enough to stop the feelings of inadequacy however, as she looked across the obviously expensive desk at the dangerous man that she needed to help her.

The curtains were drawn over the windows keeping his face mostly in shadow, but his eyes were the bright green of a fullsoul. The cool night air drifted in, this was a pretty nice part of town and she couldn't even smell the river here, it made her uncomfortable. This was the air that fullsouls breathed, it wasn't meant for her, and on the walk from the bus station she'd felt like everyone she passed could see it when they looked at her in her worn jeans and dirty shoes.

Lark would gather just as many looks, she was sure, but for a different reason, he was sexy as hell. Even she could admit it, despite the fact that she tried very hard not to recognize such things in others, it led down a path that destroyed so many. Some called halflings lust-babies; implying that their mother had been an idiot or a slut. You were only born with a half soul if your parents were not soulmates and the government wanted everyone to believe that sleeping with someone who wasn't your soulmate was sinful.

Ebony didn't take the suppressants that so many did, had never felt the need. She knew she would never risk pregnancy for a few moments of pleasure that she could give herself safely on her own.

But Lark Duport's dark looks intrigued her, and she couldn't help studying him as he considered her proposition.

He had dark hair, long enough to get messy but not long enough to look unprofessional. He had a dark stubble on his chin and his lips curved slightly while he took his time looking her up and down again. His skin was darkened by the sun and if she had to guess, she'd say he was in his late thirties. He was dressed in all black; jeans and T-shirt, fitted enough to show off lots of muscles and his arms were covered in tattoos that she wished she could get a closer look at. He had a scar on his neck that started at his right ear and ran across his chest and below the V-neck of his shirt, she couldn't help following the line with her eye and bit her lip when she caught a hint of a hard nipple there.

"You don't have enough money," Lark finally said.

"I was told five," Ebony insisted, panic tightening her throat. This was her only chance.

He shrugged and leaned back in his chair, sliding his hands behind his head dismissively. "You were told wrong; I don't take jobs for less than eight anymore. Things have gotten a little more dangerous lately and I'm very good at what I do."

"I don't have eight. You can't imagine what I had to do for five," she grumbled as all her hopes collapsed inside of her.

"With a face and body like that, I can imagine," he said with a grunt.

Heat erupted on her face, and she glared. How dare he insinuate that she was a whore? She pushed the money that she'd scrubbed toilets for and starved herself for, across the desk at him. "I need you to find her," Ebony demanded.

He looked at her with a cocked eyebrow that did something unfamiliar to her stomach. But he did not seem impressed with what he saw before him. "You have what it takes to kill?" he asked doubtfully. "You look like you can barely carry your own weight around. You are better off hoping your soulsister never finds you," he said with a frown.

Ebony stiffened and resisted wrapping her arms protectively around her thin body. "It doesn't matter," she said quietly and met his green gaze with her own dull blue eyes. Why did he care anyway? His job wasn't to guarantee her a win, it was to find her soulsibling.

He raised an eyebrow and he assessed her again with a smirk, this time there was a hint of curiosity that she could only hope would get him to change his mind.

Self-conscious under his scrutiny, she clenched her teeth and fisted her hands so she wouldn't touch her hair again. Her gaze was drawn to his mouth, and she found herself wondering things she'd never wondered about someone before. Things like, what would those lips feel like pressed against hers, what would they feel like on her neck or her wrist? She shuddered at the images and scolded herself. Rumor had it he wasn't just a searcher, but he was a fullsoul who didn't take libido suppressants.

Taylor had warned her not to fall for his charms, they were epic, or so she was told. Taylor had never met the man either, but rumors of him flowed through the halfling community as if spoken about a superhero or a god perhaps. Ebony could see why, just looking at him was making her feel things she thought she'd been born without.

He stood smoothly, his chair sliding back with a low scrape. She was pulled from her lecherous thoughts as he towered over her. He had to be over six feet.

"Doesn't matter?" he asked, a new gruffness in his voice. "You want the benefits, the improved health, the place in the upper class, you want the better job and a full ration? You want to find your soulmate and have little fullsoul babies and get the rich rewards from the government?" He paused but she didn't say anything, "Then it matters," he continued.

"I am not paying you to ask questions or judge the results," she said with surprisingly little shake to her voice. He was very intimidating.

He put his hands on his trim waist and she flicked her gaze down, then immediately back up, embarrassed to note the tight pants and obvious bulge. He was the kind of dream that would have a girl waking up shivering with orgasm.

"You aren't paying me for anything, darling. I don't search for less than eight anymore no matter how cute the client. Now, unless you want to work off the other three with that delicious little body, I suggest you leave."

The laughter behind her made her back stiffen and her resolve tighten.

"If you succeed, I can get you more," she said firmly,

knowing it was a lie but also knowing it wouldn't matter in the end.

"Bullshit," the man behind her spat, one of the searcher's lackeys. He was just as large, just as intimidating too, but she ignored him.

"There is no *if*. It's an almost guarantee, that's why I charge what I do, it's why you're here isn't it? I'm the best," Lark said darkly. "You expect me to believe you can give me more after, when you say you can barely afford five? Do I look like an idiot? Even when you're newly souled you'll have a hard time making a quick three grand. It's not like the soul comes with education or job qualifications. Just the opportunity to get those things." He leaned forward slightly and she had to stiffen her body to keep from stepping back. "Just because something is within reach of your social rung, doesn't mean you'll have the balls to grab it, or the brains to keep it." He tilted his head and raised an eyebrow. "You don't even live in the halfling neighborhood within the city proper, so that means you don't have a fullsoul parent with money and connections. Are you an orphan?"

"I grew up in the halfling district, my mother was orphaned as a teen," which was probably what drove her mother into the arms of Ebony's father at seventeen, "it is all she could afford."

"But you expect me to believe you'll have the money after? *And* that you'll win the battle?" His eyes swept over her again, full of doubt. "You must also think your soulmate is just around the corner, and rich, too." The way he said it was telling. How many people had he helped and how many had been disappointed with the ultimate result? Ebony had never known anyone who'd become a fullsoul; but she couldn't imagine it not solving every problem *she* had.

"Yes, that's what I expect you to believe," she said with a confidence she didn't know she had.

"With no explanation? I just have to hope you're right?" he

said with a touch of amusement now in his voice that surprised her.

"Yes," she said. If he challenged her on it, she might break down and tell him why she was doing this, but it was none of his business and she doubted it would help her case.

His eyes narrowed and she thought he was about to kick her out, but then he started to laugh, shocking her with the deep rumble of it. It filled the room. "Lark, at your service, sweetheart," he said with a grin that did little to detract from the air of danger he projected. "If for no other reason than to see you through to the mysterious reasons, and find out where your confidence comes from, I'll take you on for five."

She reacted slowly, reaching to take his outstretched hand, a little lightheaded with the shock of his agreement. She couldn't believe this was actually going to happen, it scared the shit out of her, if she were being honest.

When his palm touched hers, it was like an electric shock, a bolt of hot lightning rushed through her body. She gasped, eyes wide and mouth gaping. *What the hell was that?*

"Fuck," he hissed and pulled his hand away so fast he almost took her down with it. "Get out," he ordered as she wobbled to keep her footing.

Her mind reeled at the sudden change of attitude. "What?"

"I changed my mind. Get out." He took a step back, as if he couldn't stand being near her.

"But—"

"Now!" he bellowed and leaned over the desk, green eyes flashing, his big hands fisted, and she feared he was barely holding back from grabbing her and tearing her apart.

Large hands grabbed her from behind, his blond lackey taking her from the room and before she knew it, before she could demand answers or beg for another chance, she was dropped on her ass in the street.

Small hands were on her in seconds.

"Oh my god, are you okay, Ebony?" Taylor shouted.

Ebony huffed and stood, brushing the dirt of the street off the back of her as shame and betrayal flared inside of her. "I'm okay, Taylor, thanks," she whispered, barely holding back tears.

Her friend's eyes assessed her quickly and decided she was physically fine and that the meeting had not gone in Ebony's favor. "Was he as hot as everyone says?" she asked with a wink to cheer Ebony up. "That one who just threw you out was damn cute."

"Lark was intriguing, though not really my type." It was a lie; he was hot as fuck and had attracted her like no one ever had before. Not that it mattered, he was an asshole and she'd never be attracted to that.

"Yeah right, as if you have a type. I think you were born without a libido," Taylor teased. "Maybe your soulsister got that half."

Ebony ignored the jibe as usual. She definitely had a libido, and for the first time, she wondered what it would be like to break that law, to give in to lust. It wasn't just illegal to have sex, it was dangerous, depending on your beliefs about nosouls, and she'd never been much of a risk taker.

Taylor was patiently waiting for an explanation, and Ebony frowned. "He turned me down, apparently it's eight now."

"Eight! Who the hell can afford eight? Halflings can't make that in three years of starving and saving."

"Right, so let's get out of here." Ebony glanced behind her at the large brick building she'd been thrown out of. A light flicked on upstairs, and a broad-shouldered figure stood there watching. Somehow, she knew it was Lark and a shiver of something unfamiliar crawled up her spine. "This place creeps me out."

"It's a nice neighborhood," Taylor said with a frown, not

understanding Ebony's rush. "A few lucky halflings live around here I think."

"Not us, let's go." Ebony grabbed her friend's hand and pulled her down the street toward the bus station. Was he watching to make sure she left? Was he worried she was going to come back in begging for his help?

She hoped to never see the asshole again.

And the weight of hope leaving her body started to crush her. What was she going to do now?

CHAPTER THREE

Lark watched Ebony walk down the street, seething. But it wasn't anger that was boiling his blood and prickling his skin.

Lust, unlike anything he'd ever experienced in his life, and all because of that spark, that fucking spark that never should have been there. How the hell could she be his soulmate? He rubbed his hands together furiously, trying to get rid of the remaining tingle. He didn't want a soulmate; it had never been a part of his dream.

"What's up, boss?" Stone asked carefully as he walked back into the room.

Lark glared at the window as thoughts of punching Stone's pretty face for laying a hand on Ebony filled him. It's what Stone was supposed to do. he was Lark's main muscle when Lark didn't feel like doing it himself. And he had clearly indicated that the meeting was over, so Stone had done his job.

So why did he want to break a bone in Stone's face for having laid a finger on the woman?

Because she was his.

"Follow her, make sure she gets on a bus safely, then contact any other searchers in town, make sure they know that if she knocks on their doors, they are *not* to take her business."

Stone looked at him with surprise but didn't question him. Lark was sure he would later, but for now Stone had been given an order and he'd see it done. They owned the business as partners, the three of them, but Lark was the official face and the unofficial boss. Stone didn't have the practical discipline to be in charge and Granger didn't have the patience. Stone turned and left the room.

Lark went back to his desk confident in the knowledge that Ebony would safely make it back to her part of town. Somehow the thought wasn't as comforting as it should have been. Anywhere but by his side felt wrong.

And yet he'd sent her away.

"Fuck," he growled and swiped a hand over his desk, crashing everything onto the ground, then he fell back into his chair and stared at the spot where she'd stood. He had too many questions and no answers. He pulled out his laptop and quickly typed in the passwords needed to access the government-run database that listed the halflings and everything on record about them.

Ebony Landry, no birthplace listed, no registered anything until the age of five. She'd been implanted then with a tracking chip that usually went in at birth, registered to a fullsoul mother, Henrietta Landry. No father listed, no living family listed for Ebony or Henrietta. Henrietta died of breast cancer five years ago.

It was a little odd that Henrietta had been able to survive with a halfling for five years without registering her and taking the half rations for the child. It wasn't unheard of, though, for a fullsoul to hide their halfling child from the government for a time, it just usually meant they came from a wealthy family or had a decent job or home they didn't want to lose.

In Ebony's original email inquiry about hiring him, she had said that she worked at a hotel, but according to the government database, she was unemployed. Ebony claimed she had been cleaning rooms there since she was sixteen and was still employed. Lark clicked on the link to pull up a fuzzy employee badge image. It looked like it was a few years old but it was definitely her. It didn't prove that she was still working at the hotel though.

Was Ebony lying about her employment and how she had made that money? Knowing how some women were forced to make money hadn't bothered him much in the past and when she'd walked into his office he hadn't judged her for what she might have had to do, even if he had teased her about it. But now it was all different. Now he wanted to murder anyone who might have taken advantage of her while she was desperately trying to survive.

Unfamiliar feelings of anger flowed through him as he pulled up the hotel's database. After a few minutes he'd easily hacked into their employee files. Ebony was listed there as a current employee but the badge image was the same old one on the government database but less fuzzy.

"Why are you hiding Ebony from the government?" Lark wondered aloud as he pulled up a picture of her boss. He looked like the usual born-fullsoul idiot. Fat and lonely. Edward Glick had been the manager of the hotel's restaurant and housekeeping for the last thirty years, it said. He would have hired Ebony's mother as well as Ebony.

Something wasn't adding up and it just increased his frustration. He clicked back to the image of Ebony.

"How can she be a halfling and spark with me?" Lark mumbled to himself as he eyed the picture critically, trying to find anything that would hint at deception. But it was her, same beautiful eyes, same smooth skin, dark hair and proud chin. He stared at her lips and licked his own, thinking about how they must taste. So soft and supple, so inviting. Had she ever pressed them to anyone in lust? Did she have a halfling lover? The thought sent a jolt of jealousy through him so strong he nearly threw his laptop off the desk.

He had to get ahold of himself.

He closed the picture and started searching medical facilities in the area he knew dealt with halflings often. It was easy enough to find one that she'd been to. It said she didn't take suppressants, but that didn't mean she slept around, he reminded himself as his body tensed again to kill anyone who might have touched what was his.

What he read next was like being doused with ice water, his body going from fight to fear in seconds. He didn't move, just stared at the screen in disbelief.

She was dying. That must be why she'd come to him, she needed the other half of her soul to survive the cancer.

"She's on the bus back to the district and no one in town will even think about helping her," Stone said as he walked into the room. "Her friend was hot."

Lark wasn't sure how long he'd been staring at his screen, but he quickly closed it, wanting to hide what he'd just found; from Stone and himself. "Forget her," he said.

"Want to tell me what's going on?" Stone asked, sitting in the chair opposite him.

Stone was one of his oldest friends. They'd been through everything together, they helped each other deal with the guilt of murder and survival afterward, but somehow, he didn't know if he could share this with him, didn't know if he could face this with him.

"No," Lark said simply and stood, grabbing his computer

and coat. He strode from the room, leaving Stone to follow and think what he'd like about the situation.

He'd tell his friend when he figured it out for himself.

Ebony settled into the bus seat beside Taylor and breathed a sigh of relief when no one got on behind them. She hadn't been able to shake the feeling of being followed as they'd made their way to the bus stop. Of course every time she'd looked back, she'd seen only shadows.

"Okay, well if you aren't going to blow your money on finding your soulsister, what are you going to do with it?" Taylor whispered excitedly. She'd been pushing Ebony to splurge on herself for years and now it would seem to Taylor like no reason not to.

Ebony had always known she should save up for an emergency, her mother had instilled that in her. She hadn't ever thought this would be that emergency. She didn't need to keep saving for the future though, so she knew exactly what she was going to do with the money if she couldn't hire a searcher. "Donate it to the halfling orphanage, those kids never have what they need."

"You are too sweet," Taylor crooned. "I'd go on a shopping spree!"

"That is a close second, but where would I wear new clothes? Certainly not to clean toilets all day."

"Ugh, yeah they'd probably disintegrate in your closet waiting to be worn," Taylor agreed. "But still, a few nice things, just in case you wanted to feel pretty sometime, that would be fun."

Ebony didn't disagree, and if she had more time, she might do just that.

Taylor was Ebony's best friend and the only person who knew that Ebony was interested in finding her soulsister. Taylor didn't have a soulsister. Her mother had actually found her soulmate when she was a young teen, but he'd died before they could grow up and have children together. When she'd sought comfort in the arms of his brother, she'd gotten pregnant with Taylor. Taylor's father had enlisted in the army immediately to try and save face, it was one of the only respectable places for a halfling parent to make money. His plan was to send home support for his daughter.

Unfortunately, Taylor's father had also died shortly after enlisting, never meeting his daughter. Taylor's mother had moved to the halfling village after that, her family disowning her, she had no other options. Taylor had grown up next to Ebony and her mother.

They'd all been great friends and really it could have been worse. They had both seen worse, growing up; kids abandoned by their desperate mothers, adults who had lost all hope. It wasn't the sort of place anyone would want to live, but they'd been able to make a life of it. Against the odds they were given, they had grown up and gotten jobs. They had survived despite the government's best efforts at neglecting them.

Ebony smiled at her best friend as she chattered on about all the things she would buy if she had a chance. Taylor had bright red hair she kept short that curled around her face, pale skin, and green eyes. She had freckles she hated and slightly crooked front teeth. There was no fixing that sort of thing on a halfling salary. She was a bright spirit, and whenever Ebony had let the weight of the world bring her down, Taylor had been there to lift her up.

Ebony had returned the favor the only time Taylor had needed it, when her steady halfling boyfriend had lost a battle with his soulbrother. Though Taylor couldn't have been the guy's soulmate, it was still a hard thing for her to get over. She'd seen an out with him, a way to step above the station she'd been born into. Ebony never told Taylor what she really thought would have happened if he'd won the battle; the guy would have taken his full soul and left Taylor and the halfling camp as soon as he could. Maybe because it was too depressing to look back at all the people you couldn't possibly help, or maybe because the pressure to conform as a fullsoul was just too much to ignore. Either way, she didn't think anyone with a full soul would stick around for long if they didn't have to.

Taylor got over it eventually and found comfort in friendships and the occasional one-night stand. Ebony took strength from her friend's ability to accept what the fates had dealt her. She supposed she did too, in a way. But unlike Taylor, she didn't try and cheat the system.

She also wasn't a big fan of going along with the system. Ebony tried to imagine a scenario where she had a full soul and found her soulmate, only to bring a child into this mess of a world. It seemed selfish and insane, what kind of punishment would that be for a child? Forced into a world where they may never be able to have a real life with a spouse because their soulmate might never be born or only half their soulmate's soul might be born. It was a torturous life they all lived, fullsoul or not and she didn't agree with perpetuating it.

The bus took them to the outskirts of the city, it wouldn't go beyond the fence that separated the halfling district from the rest of the city regardless of the fact that no halfling could afford a car. Ebony and Taylor had to walk half a block to the entrance, which wasn't the safest thing this time of night, but they weren't worried as long as they weren't alone and neither of them went around completely unarmed. Both had a bottle of pepper spray close at hand, it was something every halfling girl got used to from a young age. The world wasn't kind to the less fortunate and if you were also a female, it thought you were made for the taking. More female halflings were missing and murdered than any other demographic, orphan children were a close second.

"Do you think you'll try someone else?" Taylor asked as they walked. Her tone serious after all the shopping talk.

Ebony sighed heavily, "I suppose so, though if they all charge eight now there's nothing I can do."

Taylor nodded sympathetically.

The fence that stood between the halfling district and the rest of the city wasn't a real barrier, just a chain-link marker. Los Angeles had such a large population of halflings without support of fullsoul families that it needed to dedicate an affordable housing area to it. From what Ebony had heard, some cities merely dedicated neighborhoods loosely marked to their halfling population. And some small cities and towns around the country had chased out all the halflings with high priced homes and unaffordable food so they didn't concern themselves with making a space available at all. These were places that the halflings in her district told her about, places they'd come from, been kicked out of when they were children, or their mother's had been forced to leave, pregnant and alone.

Las Vegas was the last completely open city in the country with no designated barriers and from what she'd heard, freely-interacting individuals of all status. Ebony wasn't sure how she felt about that. A few countries in Africa and Asia hadn't regulated their populations at all after the cursing and their halfling populations had exploded, now it was considered a humanitarian nightmare and it was what the most recent war was being fought about.

The U.S. claimed to be so fair and reasonable with their separation solution, yet by looking at the dark dirty street beyond the fence, Ebony couldn't understand how anyone could really think that this was an equal and deserved way to live based on who their parents were. No one asked to be born, no one chose to come into this world with half a soul, yet they were punished for it. Of course, the ones in charge were all fullsouls and they paid high prices to find their soulmates and breed lots of fullsoul children and find them their soulmates and on and on. They were working hard to keep other countries' halflings from seeking refuge in the U.S. too. If the U.S. government couldn't convince the government of the foreign country to regulate their population to the U.S. standard, they were trying to invade on the basis of doing *god's* work.

Of course she had her own theory about it all, and it had a little more to do with the rise in halfling populations that weren't regulated and them breeding massive amounts of nosouls who could take out large populations of people in the middle of the night. The U.S. government knew about it, and they were going in there bombing large sections of cities to try and kill them off.

Ebony couldn't even be sure that wasn't a good thing. Nosouls were more demon than human, from what she'd heard.

CHAPTER FOUR

Ebony and Taylor walked through the fence and onto the familiar streets of the halfling district. The scents of outdoor fires and the river drifted on the wind, pulling Ebony to the here and now.

"Looks like Jimmy is hosting a party," Taylor pointed out.

"Well, we'd better not miss that," Ebony said with as much enthusiasm as she could muster, which wasn't a lot.

Jimmy was an older halfling who worked at a bar stocking liquor and doing some prep in the kitchen. Sometimes his boss would send him home with near empty bottles as a tip and he'd hold a party when he acquired enough to get a few people drunk.

Ebony grabbed Taylor's arm and pulled her along faster. "I think I could use a drink. Don't tell anyone where we were."

"Duh, secrets come to me to die, remember?" Taylor said with a wide grin.

Ebony loved this redheaded ball of energy. "Thanks."

By the time they joined the party, it was already hopping, the alcohol was almost gone, and quite a few people were drunk.

"Ebony and Taylor!" Jimmy yelled when they entered the

light of the small bonfire. "Hurry before there's nothing left to drink." Jimmy was about fifty and he looked closer to seventy. Gray hair, wrinkles and a sadness in his eyes that comes early to the halflings. Ebony knew he hadn't expected to live this long and was enjoying what he could of life while he had it.

"Thanks, Jimmy," Ebony said when he handed her an empty cup and poured in a shot of vodka.

"We already ran out of mixers so it's straight shots, sorry."

Ebony laughed and slammed the liquor, enjoying the harsh burn and cleared her throat. "I think straight shots is exactly what I need tonight," she said, holding her cup out for another.

"Of course, my dear," Jimmy said. He didn't ask why, it didn't matter. They all knew life was hard and sometimes you just needed to forget it.

"I didn't think you two were going to show up," Maralynn said as she walked over with a huge smile. Her short brown hair was newly-shaved up one side and she'd styled it so it swept over to the other side. She was about the same age as Taylor and Ebony, but she'd grown up in an orphanage and it gave her a harder edge.

"We wouldn't miss a Jimmy party," Taylor said, coming up and putting an arm around Maralynn's shoulder.

"You wouldn't miss a party. Period," Maralynn teased.

"Of course I wouldn't," Taylor agreed enthusiastically, then dragged Maralynn into a conversation about a new arrival. A boy had just turned eighteen and was kicked out of the orphanage. On an orphan's eighteenth birthday they got a bus ticket to the halfling district and a garbage bag for their things. Maralynn was the resident caretaker of the newly aged out. But everyone in the district tried to pitch in where they could and support a newcomer.

"I think there's an opening at the hotel in maintenance. If he knows the difference between a screwdriver and a plunger, I bet they'd give him a shot at least," Taylor offered.

"Great, his name's Peter. I'll have him ready at your door in the morning. He can bus in with you two."

"Of course," Ebony said, and Maralynn sauntered off to deliver the good news.

The halfling district was a tight community, they watched out for each other. Ebony thought maybe if she told them what she needed, they'd come through for her. Maybe she could have the eight within six months if everyone pitched in.

It was something to consider, at least. Ebony rubbed absently at a spot high on her chest where a familiar dull ache was pushing through the haze of the alcohol, the buzz from the two shots was fading with the pressure of reality and she decided she didn't really want to party after all. She looked around, no one was paying attention at the moment, so she snuck away.

Tomorrow was supposed to be the start of her final adventure but instead, it was going to be just another day.

Ebony's one-bedroom home was comfortable, it was her safe place, full of memories of her mother and her happy childhood. She touched the afghan that still hung over the back of the floral print couch. Her mother used to throw it over their laps as they'd cuddled. They'd spent many a night staring out the window and talking about the stars. Her mother had known a lot about the stars and constellations. She probably would have gone to school for an astronomy degree if she hadn't become pregnant with Ebony. She could have found a job at an observatory perhaps, talking about stars for hours every day. She would have been so happy. She would have been able to afford proper healthcare.

Tears stung Ebony's eyes as she moved past the couch and into the tiny bedroom. She had one bookshelf here that held every book she'd ever owned, a few she'd borrowed but hadn't yet returned, and a picture of her mother as a young woman. Her mother was standing in the desert wearing hiking gear and a huge smile. That girl hadn't a care in the world. That girl hadn't lost her parents yet, hadn't become pregnant yet. Hadn't fled to a community that would accept a fullsoul who was pregnant with a halfling.

Ebony picked up the small image next to it, it was herself at about three, held in her mother's arms. Her mother smiled in this picture too, but it wasn't as bright. It was the smile of someone who knew what the world could do to those who didn't conform. It was the only image she had of herself and her mother. Cameras and photographs were a luxury they'd not spent money on, which made this one even more special.

Ebony carried the photograph to the bed she'd once shared with her mother. Now that it was just her, the small home felt too big, too empty. She couldn't imagine spending the next forty or more years here by herself. At least she could be thankful that wasn't the fate she was looking forward to. She pressed a hand against her chest where a near constant ache served as a reminder that she was living the end of her life.

She stripped down to her underwear and crawled under the covers, falling into an emotionally exhausted sleep.

That night Ebony's dreams were full of Lark. She dreamt of his large hands covered in tattoos and flashing silver rings, and his sinister lips that sneered at her while begging to be caressed. She dreamt of his intense green eyes staring at her and she swore he was looking directly into her soul. She wanted to cover herself, hide from his scrutiny and at the same time she wanted to rip herself open and reveal everything for him, beg him to really see her and accept her as she was.

He only stared, eyes narrow and lips turned down. "You're not enough," he hissed in her dream.

Ebony woke up before the sun, devastated and aroused. She slipped a hand under the blankets and arched to meet her fingers. It wasn't unusual for her to wake from a dream and feel this need, but the intensity was unlike anything she'd ever experienced and the very real person who had instigated it was definitely new. She bit her lip and arched her back as Lark's face filled her mind and she shivered at the memory of the spark that had shot through her when they'd shaken hands. She gasped as her body exploded, feeling it all over again.

She settled back into her blankets and drifted back to sleep wondering what it had been, why there had been that spark, why was he invading her dreams and why her body reacted to him with such eagerness?

Mostly she wondered why he had sent her away with so much anger.

CHAPTER FIVE

Lark sat in a dark bar; a familiar place filled with people looking for a brief moment of pleasure in an otherwise lonely life. He came here often with his men, looking for just that, always successfully, but tonight he didn't see anything he wanted.

"Hey, so what's hitting your fancy tonight?" Stone asked as he returned to the table with two beers.

"Nothing," Lark grumbled.

"Nothing?" Stone gasped and looked around the room filled with attractive women and the men who hoped to take one home.

"Boy's been moping since we got here, so who's going to tell me what happened at the office tonight?" Granger asked.

Lark glared from one to the other. He considered these men brothers, but he didn't trust them with this knowledge. Not while he was still figuring out what it meant. "Just some chick who couldn't pay for the service," Lark grunted.

"And she's keeping you from wanting any of this fine ass walking around?" Granger prodded, not buying the excuse. He took a sip of his whiskey as he waited for further explanation.

Granger was a tough man, an expert at getting unwilling

people to give up information, violently when necessary, and that stare would have worked on Lark if he didn't know him. The threat of violence was palpable in his hard glare and his whole look screamed that he was tough.

None of them were strangers to physical violence. It had been a necessary skill growing up in the orphanages and knowing they were going to have to go out and kill to live a full life, they'd all taken to training with a seriousness that they still held onto. No use getting soft even if they did have full souls now.

Stone was less intimidating to look at, but still a muscular man. His shaggy blond hair made him look like a playboy out for nothing more than a good time. It was useful too, getting information from the softer gender as well as blending into society where Granger would be too noticeable.

They all had their talents and no trouble with the ladies. Lark saw a table full of willing women looking their way and whispering. Soon the women would get brave and walk over, it had happened a million times. It was usually exactly what he wanted when he walked in here.

But not tonight. Tonight when Lark looked at their heavily made-up faces and skimpy outfits, he only saw what they weren't. They weren't a too-skinny woman in an old T-shirt and ripped jeans. They weren't Ebony. She hadn't been wearing much makeup, but she hadn't needed it. Ebony's natural beauty had been obvious. Her long, black hair was surprisingly shiny and healthy, and there'd been such a determined light in her eyes he'd almost given her the service for the old price.

Until Lark had touched her.

That spark, that impossible, wonderful spark. It had touched his soul and his world had collapsed into a single point. Ebony.

So what had he done? Sent her away. Because he didn't

want that, he wasn't interested in a soulmate. But how the fuck was Ebony his soulmate when she didn't even have her entire goddamn soul?

Lark realized he was hissing in frustration when Stone told him to knock it off before he scared the dames away. Lark downed the beer and stood up. "I'm out of here, nothing good tonight," he said quickly and walked through the bar before either man could ask him any more questions.

"Hey baby, looking for company? Wanna buy me a drink?"

Lark shrugged off the woman's touch, feeling only revulsion for the petite blonde with full red lips and a low-cut dress.

"No," Lark hissed and walked away. "I want my goddamn soulmate," he muttered too low for anyone to hear.

The next day Ebony was nursing a slight headache as she cleaned hotel rooms at a place far enough inside the city that it catered almost exclusively to fullsouls, and employed exclusively halfsouls. It wasn't a bad job for a halfling, and she got to work alongside her best friend most days.

Ebony was trying very hard to not think about Lark today though, and she wasn't doing a good job of it. He invaded her thoughts constantly and made a thrill shoot through her body even as she was filled with anger at his dismissal of her request. Maybe she should start taking suppressants. Desiring someone who had treated her poorly was definitely a sign of an overactive libido and that was a problem she didn't want.

Taylor didn't seem to be having any problems after drinking last night and likely staying up far later than Ebony had. Taylor chattered on and on about the latest news. Apparently Shine Buchanan, the foremost proponent of separation, was on the morning news shows talking about all the good her family was doing for the halfling districts, really beautifying and updating them.

"That bitch has never set foot outside of DC and you *know* they don't let halflings set foot across *those* city lines. It's the most heavily guarded fullsoul city in the world," Taylor snapped.

"They say it's because they were attacked by halflings trying to kill everyone in the government and take over the country. But I think it's because they're afraid the nosouls will get in," Ebony said conspiratorially.

"Yeah, right. Have you ever even seen a nosoul?" Taylor rolled her eyes as she fluffed a pillow. "I'm not sure they actually exist. It's just another way for the government to not give us rights and keep tabs on what we do with whom."

Ebony didn't disagree with parts of that, she didn't believe the government had the halflings' best interests in mind and she didn't think they would let one walk into the capital and demand more rights. But she definitely believed in the nosouls.

Most halflings just lived lonely lives and died young, never marrying and definitely never having children to perpetuate the suffering. There were two beliefs on halfsouls breeding, one was that the babies, on the rare occasion they weren't immediately spontaneously aborted, died shortly after birth. The other was that the ones who did survive, had no soul at all. It was said that they had black, lifeless eyes and pale skin, they were allergic to the sun and often resorted to drinking blood to survive because the government didn't give them even half an allotment of rations. They were stolen from their mother by other nosouls immediately after birth and raised in cities below ground, coming out at night and killing to slake their thirst.

Most believed that was just a scary story invented to keep halflings from breeding with each other; Ebony felt differently.

She'd seen one born and it had been the scariest thing she'd ever experienced.

The mother hadn't believed the rumors either and had risked the pregnancy. Ebony's mother was the woman's friend and helping her through the birth and Ebony was learning a little about life by watching. The baby was born deathly pale with huge black, soulless eyes, and sharp teeth.

Ebony's mother had tried to convince the poor woman to mercifully kill the thing, but the woman had refused to let her child die, assuring them that she could care for whatever it needed for however long she might have it. They left her alone, promising to return in the morning with some food, but the next morning the mother was dead, the baby was gone, and no one, except Ebony and her mother, had any idea what had happened.

"They come in the middle of the night to take the newborns and kill the mothers so there are no witnesses," Ebony whispered, knowing it would rile up her friend.

"Oh pish, that's ridiculous. Patrice died because she didn't have proper medical care and the danger of a halfling giving birth is so extreme no one should do it. The stories of nosouls are just a government-propagated conspiracy to keep us under control and taking their suppressants, god forbid we have a little fun in our lives that doesn't cost money," Taylor said.

Ebony shrugged; she knew what she'd seen. "Then where did the baby go?"

Taylor ignored the question. It was a familiar argument that led nowhere. There was no proof that either of them could bring forward for their side and neither of them was willing to change their minds about it.

"You're sure you don't want to buy a new dress or a pair of cute shoes?" Taylor said to lighten the mood.

Ebony laughed. "And wear them where? I come here to

clean up other people's crap, then I go home and sit with you by the river. What do I need a dress or fancy shoes for?"

Taylor held up a glittery red gown that had been tossed on the floor of the hotel room. "Sometimes a girl just wants to be pretty," she said as she held the slinky dress up to her body and twisted to make its skirt flow.

"And sometimes a girl just wants to eat," Ebony said with a sigh, staring down at the remains of a large steak with potatoes and apple pie. She had never had a meal as big as the leftovers she usually found in the rooms. She wasn't too proud to admit she'd sampled bites before, most of the housekeeping staff considered it a perk of the job.

"Well then, how about you treat us to a nice dinner tonight? It would still leave you with enough money to donate and make a difference to the orphans."

Ebony admitted that didn't sound like a terrible idea, except that she hated going into places that didn't usually serve halflings. Even if they didn't outright discriminate, they still made her feel uncomfortable and awkward, like they didn't really think she would be able to pay the bill or that she was going to leave a stain behind from her dirty half soul. "Sounds like a hassle," she admitted.

"Everything worth having is a hassle," Taylor said, heaving the garbage out the door and down the hall.

Alone in the room, Ebony picked up the shiny dress and sighed, she would never have anything half as nice. But if she could figure out a way, her life would make a difference to someone, and she clung to that bit of hope to keep her going. It just wasn't going to be easy without Lark's help.

"Maybe I should try to find another searcher," she said to Taylor when she returned with the vacuum, "before giving up and donating to the orphanage."

"Another searcher? I can ask around, get another name for

you. But Lark is the best in the country, or so I hear, and definitely the best one in town."

"Well, he already turned me down," she snapped and threw her rag on the cart, pushing on to the next room.

"Pissy," Taylor shot back. "A nice meal would fix that attitude!"

"Or it would show me what I'm missing every day for the rest of my life," she grumbled too low for Taylor to hear.

"I got a job!" Peter said, running down the hall toward Ebony with a huge smile on his young face.

He'd been waiting for Ebony and Taylor promptly that morning with the hopes of finding employment with the hotel. Ebony had been doubtful that it would work out, but she was glad it had. The kid was eager and energetic, willing to do anything, or so he'd said. He was tall and lanky in the way of eighteen-year-old boys, with short, almost shaved, blond hair and dull, blue eyes large in his face. He had sunken cheeks and a sharp nose. He didn't look like he had lived well at the orphanage, and she wondered if he'd been giving his rations to the younger ones.

"Great. In maintenance?" Ebony asked.

"No, in the kitchen, but hey, it's work."

"That's great, Peter," Taylor said, coming out of the next room with an armload of dirty towels and sheets. "When do you start?"

"Tomorrow."

Ebony remembered that feeling of accomplishment at a first job and she didn't envy the downward spiral he was going to take when he realized the pay was crap, the work was hard, and their boss was a jackass. But at least it was something, he was lucky to have work, they all were.

"Hey, I'll see you guys later, I can't wait to tell Maralynn." He waved happily and hurried away.

"Poor kid is going to hate working in the kitchen. Steve is a jerk," Taylor said.

"You only think that because he wouldn't go on a date with you," Ebony teased. The head chef in the hotel kitchen was a halfling whose mother had come from a wealthy family on the east coast. They'd sent her away when she'd gotten pregnant, but they'd set her and the child up outside the halfling district in one of the neighborhoods where the poor fullsouls and the rich halfsouls mingled. It had given him certain advantages, like the ability to attend a trade school where he'd learned to cook. Taylor had gotten a major crush on the guy, but he'd told her he refused to date, took his suppressants regularly and threw himself into his work. It resulted in a bit of an asshole attitude if Ebony was being honest. Anyone fighting that hard to appear above their station in this society was bound to be wound tight and taking it out on those around them.

Taylor huffed and went back into the room. Ebony ate a potato off the plate before scraping it into the garbage.

She glanced at the clock that was hung on the side of the cart. It was time for their break and she needed some air. "Hey, I'm going to store the cart and walk down to Gimball's for a quick treat, want to join?"

Taylor appeared in the hall with a huge smile. "Yes! A girl needs something sweet every once in a while."

A few minutes later they were walking out of the hotel through the employee entrance and heading down the block. The fresh air was really nice, usually they didn't leave the hotel during the work day because their breaks were short and their boss was an asshole. But today it felt worth the risk of his dirty looks. Ebony breathed deep and listened to Taylor chatter on and on. Near the hotel were a few places she'd never enter. A clothing shop with items shipped in from across the country, a trinket shop that boasted the best souvenirs and local wine in all of LA, something she'd never been tempted to look at, and a place they were welcome into. Mrs. Gimball was a fullsoul who had a halfling child and so she had a special sort of love for the halflings who worked nearby. Her store was full of convenience items, food, snacks, toilet paper, all locally produced, nothing shipped in. It meant there were often empty shelves and no real options, but the prices were reasonable for a halfling with a little extra spending money.

"What are you girls doing in here in the middle of the day?" Mrs. Gimball asked as they stepped into the small shop. Today it held a lot of fresh fruit and vegetables, all in season.

"We needed a little fresh air and a treat to keep the depression away," Ebony admitted.

Mrs. Gimball nodded knowingly, the depression was real, a lot of halflings fell into it so deep they never were able to crawl back out.

Ebony didn't bother going up or down any of the aisles, she wasn't here for anything more than a little sugar boost. She grabbed two small pieces of chocolate wrapped in wax paper and set them on the counter.

"That's it?" Mrs. Gimball asked looking from her to Taylor.

"That's it," Ebony said.

"Rations?" Mrs. Gimball asked.

Ebony held out her right wrist and Mrs. Gimball scanned it then glanced at the screen on the device. She smiled up at Ebony.

"You're good to go, girl, but getting low, good thing payday is around the corner, right?" Mrs. Gimball said.

Ebony nodded and gritted her teeth. She hated the

information that she had to give away every time she bought something. That little device told the owner everything they needed to know about her. She was a halfling and she lived on government rations and her meager paycheck.

No one would guess that she had a stack of cash in her purse that she'd managed to save because she didn't treat herself to little bits of sugar often and she didn't splurge ever.

"Thank you," Taylor said as she took the candy Ebony handed her. "I don't think I've had chocolate in months!"

Ebony unwrapped the chocolate as she walked and slipped it into her mouth. She let it sit on her tongue, melting slowly as they walked in silence, both savoring the treat.

Taylor grabbed Ebony's arm and leaned her head on Ebony's shoulder. They took their time getting back to work knowing they would be catching a glare from their boss, Mr. Glick.

"I would bathe in chocolate if I was a fullsoul," Taylor said.

Ebony laughed and agreed. Chocolate was an amazing invention, right up there with wine. Something she'd only had the pleasure of trying once.

CHAPTER SIX

Six hours later, Ebony was exhausted and ready to go home where she could collapse with a good book, a familiar book. She punched out for the day, trying not to think about what the weird stain on her pant leg might be. This was why new clothes made no sense for her. It would be a waste of money to buy clothing, even if she wished she could slip into something that wouldn't immediately scream *halfling,* as she walked down the street. More than once, a young mother had pulled a child to the other side of the street to avoid her as she'd made her way to or from work. Having to pass through the nice neighborhood around the hotel was an exercise in humiliation most days.

Since new clothes were useless, giving the money to the orphanage would make her feel better than anything. If she couldn't find another searcher in the next couple of weeks, she was excited to do just that. She would give it a little time before giving up all hope though, she wouldn't give up after the first '*no*'.

. . .

At the end of her shift, Ebony was grabbing her purse out of her locker when she heard a voice in her boss' office that stopped her in her tracks.

It couldn't be, she was just hallucinating.

"She works here, right?" the familiar voice demanded sharply.

"Well, yeah, we have a halfling named Ebony Landry," her boss, Mr. Glick, was saying. "I'm sorry sir, did she not do what was necessary to clean your room? I can assure you that—"

"When does she work next?" the other man demanded.

Ebony gasped, it was definitely Lark, and he was definitely looking for her. Why the hell was he looking for her? Did she dare hope that he had changed his mind about helping her?

"Ebony!" Mr. Glick called. "Get in here!"

"What the hell is going on?" Taylor asked, coming up to her with a look of concern. No one got called in at the end of a shift unless they were about to be fired.

"I don't know, but don't wait around, I'll catch up or meet you later."

Taylor hesitated, looking unsure.

Mr. Glick stuck his bald head out the doorway and glared at them.

"What do you need? My shift is over," Ebony said, pretending she didn't know who else was in the office.

"Get in here, customer wants to see you," Mr. Glick said with annoyance.

Ebony bit her lip and entered the room with as much grace as she could manage. She shot a look back at Taylor from the doorway that she hoped showed calm, but she was pretty sure by Taylor's worried face that she didn't hit it.

"Isn't your shift over, too?" Mr. Glick snapped at Taylor, making her jump and hurry away. No use in both of them getting fired today.

Ebony entered the room with her head high. Whatever this was, she was not going to show how scared she was. She stopped just inside the doorway of the office, ready to bolt as soon as possible. If this conversation ended in tears, she didn't want either of these men to see them.

Mr. Glick hurried back behind his desk, his round body wobbling slightly as he took the corner too tight. Ebony almost laughed but turned it into a cough as Mr. Glick's glare turned on her, full force and accusing.

Lark was there, just watching the interaction with a cool, calculated look. He sat in a too-small chair in front of the desk. He'd turned it so he could eye both the door and Mr. Glick behind the desk at the same time. Ebony wondered if that was a purposeful move to keep himself safe, he had to find himself in dangerous situations often, and he'd gotten that scar somewhere.

Ebony's cheeks heated as she remembered following it with her eyes last night and how it had led to a very vivid imagining of his taut nipples.

Lark's green eyes narrowed on her, and his lips pressed into a thin line as if he knew what she was thinking and disapproved. His dark hair was slicked back today, she liked it better the way she'd seen it last night, a little shaggy and wild, like she imagined he was.

She quickly looked away from him, hating how her thoughts ran away where he was concerned. She turned to Mr. Glick who was now seated behind his desk.

"What is it? I don't want to miss the bus," Ebony said.

He just motioned to Lark as if it were an utter annoyance that this was happening, and she would undoubtedly be punished for it in some way later on. Mr. Glick was probably already deciding to give her all the worst shifts for the next month.

And it was all Lark's fault. Why was he here? She looked

back at him and met his glare with one of her own. "What?" She demanded, grabbing the strap of her old leather purse, and hating that he was seeing her at her worst; worn-out work clothes, hair in a messy ponytail, and zero makeup on. She probably smelled like cleaning solution, sweat, and whatever was on her pant leg.

He smelled woodsy and fresh of course, and all man; it wafted to her because of the air conditioning unit in the office and sent a tingle through her body.

Who the hell smelled that good?

"Leave us, Glick," Lark ordered.

Mr. Glick sputtered and slammed his hands on the top of his desk, but one glare from Lark was enough to send him rushing awkwardly from the room. He didn't leave without a final threatening look at Ebony though. Lark had probably just lost her job for her.

Shit. She would have to keep some of the money she had planned to hire a searcher with, or donate to the orphanage, to live on until she found something new.

When the door closed, Lark stood and towered over Ebony. Even though he didn't touch her, she felt the heat from his body so intensely he may as well have been pressed against her, skin-to-skin. She was alive with response to his presence, and she couldn't hold his gaze. She looked away, stepped back, and fiddled with her purse strap.

"What the hell do you want? I don't have eight, I'll never have eight, and I think you know that," she accused.

"I changed my mind. I'll take you on."

Ebony couldn't believe her luck. She smiled as she looked back up at him, he was still glaring, but she didn't care. He was going to help her. "Really? Why?" she asked cautiously. His quick changes of mind were definitely a red flag.

"Isn't it obvious?" Lark snapped.

Ebony tilted her head and raised an eyebrow, "I guess not." Why was he so angry with her if it was his decision to help her? This man made no sense.

He leaned down until his nose almost touched hers and his breath swept across her face like a soft caress. His gaze bored into her eyes, she felt it straight into her soul and he hissed. "You really don't have a full soul." His voice was tight, dripping with anger.

Ebony gulped. Fear filled her, replacing the sexual desire he had brought to life. She'd heard that disdain before, knew that kind of hate. But coming from him it didn't make sense; he helped halfsouls, didn't he?

"Obviously," she said with a shaky voice. She stepped back but came up against a cabinet and she was completely trapped in this small office with him.

Lark put his hands on the cabinet on either side of her head, blocking her in. She couldn't think straight, he was angry and strong, he could destroy her so easily. Her mind flashed to another time, another situation filled with hate and the blue-eyed man who smelled of alcohol and cigarettes who thought he could take his anger out on her body. That man had gotten a few good hits in before she'd managed to spray him with her pepper spray. His intentions had been to rape her, and she'd never known such fear in her life.

Ebony shoved her hand into her purse, knowing she'd never be able to take more than a single hit from such a large man as Lark. She grasped the pepper spray, ready to pull it out spraying, not caring if she got herself with it too. Surely someone would come in to investigate if they were both screaming with burning eyes.

"We're soulmates," he hissed angrily.

His words couldn't have shocked her more. Her head started

to spin, and she dropped the pepper spray on the ground between them.

The sound caught his attention, and he stepped back, grunting when he saw the small black thing roll. "Smart girl," he said with a half-smile that made her heart do a flip.

With the granted space she was able to stumble toward Mr. Glick's desk and take a seat on it so she wouldn't fall down. "S-soulmates," she stammered. "That's not possible, I'm not a fullsoul, I—"

Lark huffed and stood straight. "I know, that's why I had to make sure you actually weren't a fullsoul. You're not," he said with a hiss. "I can see it clear enough in your eyes. They may be a little brighter than usual for a halfling, but you are not a fullsoul, there's no spark there."

She bristled at his tone, his anger at her halfsoul state. How dare he? She hadn't asked to be his anything, didn't want to be anyone's anything. "Gee, what a smooth talker you are. It's impossible, we both know that, what gave you such a stupid idea?" she snapped.

"Don't tell me you didn't feel the spark when our hands touched last night," he said with exasperation.

Of course she had, she'd have to have been dead not to have felt it, it was amazing and unexpected and... fuck was that a soulmate spark?

"I did," she admitted carefully. "But soulmates? I just thought it was lust." She looked down at the hand in question and shook her head in denial.

"Lust?" he hissed. "That's what you feel between your thighs, woman. A soulmate spark is, well I guess it's what happened last night. It's not like I've felt it before, but I know lust." His mouth quirked up in a smile that told her he was no stranger to lust, and giving in to it too.

She hated the way that knowledge sent a shot of jealousy

through her. Her body already claiming this man as hers and hers alone. "I don't understand," she whispered. But what did it matter anyway? She wasn't a fullsoul and she had no interest in finding her soulmate, that's not what she'd been after when she went to meet with him.

It had been the farthest thing from her mind, actually. It ruined everything, it complicated her entire plan. It was... impossible.

"Me either, it shouldn't be able to happen, but it did."

She shook her head. "No."

"No?" he said with a quirked eyebrow and amusement in his voice.

"I don't believe you," she said with force.

Lark crossed the distance between them in one smooth step, pulling her to his body with a firm hand on her back. She gasped at the very real feeling of electricity that pumped over her body even though it wasn't skin-to-skin contact. She looked into his face, her eyes wide, her jaw hanging open and unable to speak as a near orgasmic experience was happening to her and no one had even touched her clit yet. His mouth quirked up as if he knew exactly what she was experiencing and his eyes became heavily-lidded, giving him a sexy look that only amped up the desire she was feeling. His hand on her back remained firm and hot while the other lifted to touch her chin. When he ran a finger over her lower lip, it quivered, wishing for him to kiss her. Ebony moaned, unable to stop herself.

With a very satisfied grunt Lark stepped back, dropping all contact abruptly. Ebony stumbled back against Mr. Glick's desk, her head spinning and her body on fire. It was intense and it was confusing but she refused to believe it was anything more than desire. He watched her carefully as her head cleared and she shook it in denial.

"It is nothing more than desire, and sorry, but I don't do

that." Her words weren't as firm as she would have liked, her voice alien to her ears with its soft breathy quality.

Lark crossed his arms over his chest. "Then where did you get the five?"

"Fuck you!" she yelled and threw the first thing her hand hit on Mr. Glick's desk, which happened to be a tray of papers. It wasn't going to do any damage, but it made her feel better, and distracted Lark while she fled out of the office and out the back door.

Her panties were wet but that didn't mean she had to believe a damn word out of that asshole's mouth. Lust and desire weren't reserved for your soulmate, otherwise the suppressants wouldn't be necessary. Any handsome man with a deep voice and chiseled features could have made her feel those same things. Even as Ebony told herself it was nothing more than simple human desire, she knew she was lying to herself. She knew that the electricity she'd felt when Lark touched her wasn't normal. If it was, it certainly would have been described, in great detail, to her by Taylor when regaling Ebony with one of her nights with a lover. Not even when Taylor had been in love had she mentioned anything like that spark.

Ebony might have gotten away from Lark if she had a car to jump into. Unfortunately, she had a three-block walk to the bus station and he caught up to her in half a block with his long legs and determined attitude.

She ignored him as he fell into step beside her. She half expected him to grab her and force her to stop but he didn't touch her, and she was grateful enough that she glanced up at him.

"You're not my type," she said.

He grunted an amused sound. "I thought you said you didn't do that."

"I don't."

"So how do you know what your type is?"

"If I had a type, it wouldn't be moody assholes," she assured him. Her mind went to some of her favorite books that would very clearly speak to the opposite of that statement, but fantasy and reality were two very different things, and she did not like his attitude.

"So let's find your soulsister."

"Why?" Ebony snapped even though she knew why. He wanted a soulwife with a full soul to give him little fullsoul babies. Well fuck that. Tears stung her eyes because it could never be and even though she didn't want it, it didn't mean she couldn't mourn the loss. She glared straight ahead so he couldn't see the glint of moisture in her eyes.

"Isn't that what you wanted?" Lark's voice was steady, but she could feel his exasperation under the surface. He wasn't used to people arguing with him, she would bet.

"Yes, but I'm not your soulmate and if you're doing this because you think you can live some kind of fullsoul fantasy family life with me, you're sorely mistaken."

He grabbed her arm then and forced her to stop and face him. His expression was unreadable, and she had to stop herself from reacting like he was threatening her.

Heat built where he touched her and a spark of something she didn't want to think about passed between them. She steeled herself against it and doubled down on her assertion. "If you want a fullsoul soulmate wife to have your little fullsoul babies and all that happy shit, then you're barking up the wrong tree. I can't spark with you, I don't have my whole soul and I am *not* interested in that crap, even if I did have it."

He narrowed his eyes at her. "Let's take it one step at a time. You want to hire me. I'm hired. We start now."

Ebony stuttered and shook her head, trying to grasp what was happening but it was hard to think when he was touching her. "Now? I don't know. How does it even really work? What do you do, what do you need from me?" Her mind swirled and she felt breathless.

This was it, she was going to find her soulsister.

"I buy you dinner," he said softly.

A group of people walked past them and snickered. Ebony caught more than one admonishing glance and she stepped back, forcing Lark to let go of her arm. She didn't want to make a scene, and hated when people were looking at her, judging her. Part of her regretted the loss of contact, but she needed a clear head and his touch messed with her. "What does dinner have to do with anything?"

"We have a lot to discuss before I can start the search," he shrugged. "I'm hungry and you look like you could use a good meal."

Ebony bit her lip, unsure and yet knowing she needed to take this leap. This is why she'd gone to him in the first place. "Okay, dinner." It wouldn't hurt to get a free meal as they discussed the details of the deal.

"I know a great place down the street." He grabbed her arm again and started walking.

"Woah! I can't go anywhere like this," she said, digging in her heels, a little frantic. There was nowhere in this neighborhood that would welcome her, but they might look the other way if she was at least dressed in clean, decent clothes.

"You look fine, and besides, who are you trying to impress?" He turned to her with a sharp angry look, pinning her in place with just those green eyes. "Let's get one thing straight, Ebony, you are mine. I don't know why, and I don't know how, but you are, and I expect you to act like a soulwife, starting *now*."

Fear and anger flared in her, but she knew he was her best chance at finding her soulsister, so she swallowed it and took a shaky breath. She hoped there was a reasonable man inside him somewhere. "I look like I worked hard all day, I look like a damn halfling," she snapped. "Is that really what kind of *soulwife* you want to walk into a restaurant with?" She gained a bit of pleasure from throwing it in his face. He wanted her to be a soulwife, but she would never be anything more than a halfling and he couldn't bully or demand her into anything else.

He froze and dropped her arm, assessing her more closely. "You're right, you look terrible. You can clean up at my place," he finally said, his voice a little gruff.

Her cheeks flushed with embarrassment, and she couldn't stop herself from hating that he was seeing her like this. She wanted him to see her clean and pretty, wanted him to be happy that she was his soulwife.

No, she chastised herself, she didn't care, she wasn't, wouldn't be, his soulwife for real so what he thought of her didn't matter.

She couldn't be his soulwife and that reality hurt more than she ever imagined it could. She suddenly wanted to go home more than anything, wanted to curl up in bed and hide from everything that he'd told her.

"I can't. I—"

"It's not up for debate," he snapped and led her back the way they'd come.

CHAPTER SEVEN

She was too confused by his back and forth attitude and her own unsettled feelings to fight back, so she hurried along beside him and kept her eyes down, hoping no one would notice the halfling being dragged down the street by the very angry looking fullsoul. When she did peek up, she noticed that anyone they passed took pains to look in the other direction, to not notice what was happening. No one wanted to get involved to help someone like her. This was how all those halfling girls ended up naked and strangled, tossed into the river with no witnesses to the crimes. Goddamn fullsouls too worried about their own asses to do anything to help anyone else. She wanted to scream at them, but it wouldn't matter, and she didn't relish the thought of making Lark angrier.

She shuddered and tried to keep the image of that blue-eyed man out of her mind. Lark wasn't him, Lark didn't smell like he'd bathed in alcohol and smoked a hundred cigarettes. She glanced at Lark, he smelled wonderful and his eyes were a brilliant green.

"Don't look at me like that," he demanded.

She jumped and a tremble ran through her. "Like what?" she asked.

"Like I'm going to hit you," he hissed.

"Then maybe you shouldn't look like you want to hit me," she whispered. "I've seen that look before, and it didn't end well for me."

Lark stopped so fast she almost fell as his arm yanked her. He looked at her with such leashed anger she wanted to shrink away and hide.

"What happened?" he demanded.

She shook her head, unable to speak in the face of such fury.

He pushed her back into a dark doorway, she was thankful to be away from prying eyes, but she didn't want to face his anger, directed at her or not it was intense.

"What happened?" he demanded again.

She couldn't look at him and answer, she stared at her scuffed tennis shoes and took a shaky breath. "It was a long time ago."

"It's why you carry pepper spray?" he asked.

"Not exactly, I mean, I already carried the pepper spray before the incident, the pepper spray is the only thing that kept him from finishing what he intended to do."

"Who?"

"It doesn't matter. It was a long time ago."

"It matters when my soulwife flinches away from anger not even directed at her."

"I'm not your soulwife," she said, bringing her eyes up to meet his gaze.

"You are, and you will tell me who hurt you."

"I don't know who he was," she admitted, annoyed that a nameless figure haunted her, that someone who she didn't know held a power over her still. It wasn't fair, but she knew very well that nothing in this life was fair.

"He didn't—" he looked suddenly uncomfortable. "You were able to keep him from—"

"Yes," she said, taking pity on him trying to ask if the bastard had raped her. She looked away as she continued. "He hit me a couple times and threw me on the ground, but I sprayed him and ran. Never saw him again." She shuddered. "But I will never forget the hate and anger in his bright blue eyes as he called me a lust baby and a whore for being on the street at night." She hated the way her voice trembled a bit at the memory. "I was just trying to walk home from work."

Lark grasped her chin gently and nudged her head up until she was meeting his gaze. "I wouldn't hesitate to painfully kill anyone who would dare to hurt you."

Ebony believed those words more than any she'd ever heard in her life and she wasn't sure what to do with this side of him.

Visions of everything that being his soulwife would entail sprang up in her mind and sparked a desire in her belly. She could almost feel his hands on her bare skin, his lips trailing down her neck, his—

She nearly groaned as she forced herself to not think of the undoubtedly impressive part of him that would soothe the ache between her thighs.

Lark's nostrils flared and a rumble rose from his chest as his eyes darkened. He grabbed her arm and they were once again hurrying down the street, gathering no less attention from passersby. The firm presence of his hand on her and the rushing down the street didn't seem like it was coming from a place of anger this time though. Ebony could practically feel the desire vibrating over his body in reflection of her own and sparking where his hand gripped her arm. She wasn't sure how much more she could take before she started panting or just burst into flames right there on the street. His touch filled her with so much unexperienced desire, so much spiraling tension she wasn't sure how to handle it. If others felt even a fraction of this with someone not their soulmate, she had to wonder how they could *not* be sleeping with everyone they encountered. No wonder the government pushed their suppressants so hard.

"Stop it," Lark hissed.

"I'm not doing anything," she whined, because she was far too busy feeling these new desires to be angry at his demands.

"I can practically smell your desire and your face is flushed, you're vibrating under my hand and the fucking sparks are sharp."

"Like I can control that!" Ebony ripped her arm out of his grasp. "If you stop dragging me around you won't feel it... and neither will I," she whispered the last as a shudder ran through her body mourning the loss of contact with him.

Lark grunted and grabbed her arm again. She almost smiled as he angrily continued on. He might hate that he wanted her, but he obviously craved contact between them, and she was starting to as well.

Lark stopped beside a large black truck parked a few blocks past the hotel and opened the passenger door for her. She hopped inside quickly and without argument, glad to break the contact and get off the street. He was parked in front of Mrs. Gimball's shop and Mrs. Gimball was standing at the entrance watching her with narrowed eyes. Shame threatened to overtake her as the lust Lark inspired receded at his absence. She'd never be able to face Mrs. Gimball again without knowing she thought Ebony was whoring herself out.

It smelled like him in the small space, woodsy and fresh. She couldn't help taking a deep breath and letting it roll around in her lungs like a drug. It made her body feel soft and happy. She wanted to close her eyes and soak it up as long as possible. It was a comforting smell as if she'd been waiting all her life for it.

Lark had his phone out when he slid into the driver's seat,

speaking to someone about appropriate clothing for her it sounded like. He turned to her as he started the truck. "What else do you need? Makeup? Tampons?"

She nearly choked on his casual mention of tampons. Dear lord, tampons were a commodity that halflings could rarely afford. She had lip gloss in her purse and mascara, that was enough makeup, she wasn't trying to pretend to be anyone she wasn't, and if he was trying to make her into someone else, he was going to be sorely disappointed.

"No, thank you, just something appropriate to wear and a shower would be great. Oh, maybe some deodorant," she added, embarrassed, but she wasn't about to walk into a fullsoul restaurant without a barrier against her stress sweat.

He relayed the message and flipped the phone closed, then pulled out into traffic. She stared at the shiny little phone he set in the cup holder and thought about how worried Taylor was going to be when she didn't show up back at the district soon.

He must have read her mind, or more likely noticed her obvious staring, because he handed her the phone. "Do you need to call someone? Or quit your job? You certainly won't be in for a while."

That surprised her. "How long do you think it will take to find her."

He shrugged. "Depends, sometimes I get lucky, other times it takes months."

Ebony touched her chest where the dull ache was a near-constant reminder that she didn't have months.

"I need to make a call." She dialed Taylor's number, knowing she'd just get her machine, no one in the halfling district could afford a cell but they all had landlines and answering machines. She told Taylor that Lark had changed his mind, that she would be gone for a week or more and she promised to check in again soon. She told Taylor to tell Mr. Glick that she quit. He didn't deserve a call.

"Thanks." She handed Lark the phone. "Oh, and I guess I need to give you this too." She pulled the money out of her purse.

He just looked at it with disgust. "No, you aren't paying me."

"Yes, I am. I need you to find her, and I don't expect any favors."

"I don't search for five, remember."

Ebony stuffed the cash back in her bag with anger. "Well then what the hell do you want?"

"Your soul," he said simply, and stepped on the gas, darting out into traffic.

Ebony didn't know what to say to that, so she stared out the passenger window as they drove through one nice neighborhood after another. The lack of contact and distraction of the passing sights was enough to calm her body from its heightened state of need. She absently rubbed at her chest and tried not to think of anything except the beauty of the world they were passing through. Clean streets, brightly colored buildings, trees, and flowers planted strategically to add a touch of greenery and color. Nothing overgrown, nothing out of place and the people, they were beautiful too, they reminded her of her mother.

She started to cry silently.

Lark ignored Ebony's silent tears while they drove because he didn't think he could ask her anything without anger being present in his tone. It wasn't anger at her; it was anger at his inability to take from her what he wanted, and despite the fact that he definitely didn't want a soulwife, he wanted to possess her. He was fighting his instincts to pull off onto a dark alley and drag her into the back seat right then. He'd never wanted anyone the way he wanted her. This tiny woman who looked like she was starved half to death and with hardly any makeup on made his dick stand at attention just being near her.

His hands gripped the wheel with murderous intent as he remembered what she said about her past experience, how she'd been hit and almost raped by an asshole who thought halfling women were his for the taking, his to abuse. Lark still wanted to lash out and kill every man he could find just in case they'd been the one. He couldn't explain the level of protectiveness he felt towards her.

He'd seen the effects of the horrible things men could do to women. He'd watched more than one halfling girl in the orphanage come home broken and bleeding. He and his boys used to go out and hunt down the bastards when they could, more often than not the girls' stories were the same as Ebony's though. No idea who the guy was, no name, a face they didn't recognize enough to find again. His heart ached remembering a few who hadn't been able to keep going after, who'd chosen to take their own lives rather than live in a world where that could happen to them with no consequence, no reassurance that it wouldn't happen again.

What kind of world didn't protect its weakest members? His grip tightened on the wheel. Knowing how weak Ebony was, could he protect her? He wanted to lock her away from anything that could possibly harm her and at the same time a part of him wanted to run from her and the obligation she presented, the possibilities she brought up that he had never wanted. The contradiction was infuriating.

The whole situation was unfair to both of them, and he was angry at himself for not handling it all better as Ebony wept beside him. No matter what the future might hold for them, he knew that he didn't want her tears or fear.

When they pulled up in front of his two-story brick house with its manicured lawn and attached garage, she was no longer crying. He was thankful for that, but his nerves were on edge, and he was wound tight, ready to explode. He had to keep a calm façade for her, he knew he might scare her with his intensity, and he wondered, not for the first time, if she were a virgin. He knew she didn't take suppressants, but the way she'd reacted to him, how she'd melted with desire against his touch felt so raw, so untouched. Was she? He didn't care either way, it wouldn't ruin her to know she'd been with another, but he found himself liking the thought that she'd be only for him, now and always. The thought made him want to get Stone and Granger out of the house. He didn't want her to be around those two horn dogs.

"You live here?" Ebony asked as she wiped at her eyes and cheeks. Her skin was still splotchy from her tears but somehow it only made him want her more, made him want to kiss those tear trails and keep her safe from anything that would ever make her cry again.

"Most of the time," he said in a clipped tone, uncomfortable with the direction of his thoughts.

She looked at him and raised an eyebrow in question.

"I travel a lot, comes with the job," he explained.

Ebony nodded and turned back to the house where Stone stood on the porch now, watching them curiously. Lark hadn't told them where he was going when he'd left that afternoon. After half a day trying to convince himself that he didn't need to find her, he'd given up and stormed out of the house without a word to anyone. He really wished he'd sent them away. Something about them being around her made his skin prickle.

He'd trust either man with his life, but with his soulmate, not a chance.

Lark jumped out of the truck feeling his anxious energy ramp up as he walked around the truck and opened her door. She was still looking at Stone with a touch of surprise.

"Oh, thanks," she mumbled and hopped out quickly. "Who's your friend?"

"Stone, he's head of security, you met him last night."

"Oh yeah. Security?" she asked worriedly.

"Yeah, more for you than me, I can take care of myself."

"Why would I be in danger?"

"The search for soulsiblings doesn't always take us into friendly territory, Ebony. I try not to let my clients die before we find their soulsibling."

Ebony gave a nervous laugh and turned back to Stone on the porch. He was watching them but hadn't moved or said anything and Lark wondered what he was thinking of this development.

"Stone, you remember Ebony Landry," Lark said as he led her to the porch, not daring to touch her this time.

"How could I forget?" Stone said with a wide grin that Lark recognized as the one he used at the bar with women he was hoping to bed.

"Asshole, you threw me out on the street and bruised my ass," she said with a frown.

"Kinky," Stone said with a laugh.

"What?" Lark gritted out; eyes locked onto Stone. All reason flew from his mind as the images those few words brought up in his mind overwhelmed him. He wanted to kill his friend and ask for clarification later.

"Woah, boss, I did nothing to her pretty little ass, but if she was offering…" he said with a wink.

Lark moved fast, he grabbed Stone's throat and pressed him

up against the door. In that moment he wanted to kill, wanted to relieve some of the tension in his body through violence.

"She is my soulmate. That puts her well beyond your filthy reach, brother. I don't want to see you even look at her."

Understanding flashed into Stone's eyes and his mouth quirked up into a smile. "Soulmate?" Stone said, unfazed by the hand around his neck.

Stone's gaze moved past Lark to Ebony behind him. "You lucky bastard, I thought she was a halfsoul, her eyes are dull enough. What the hell was she after, coming to your office?"

Lark dropped his hand and stepped back but kept his body between Ebony and Stone. "She's a halfsoul," he said darkly, not liking the interest Stone was showing in his soulmate.

"No way! She's a dominant?" Stone said excitedly, leaning around Lark to see Ebony.

"A what?" Ebony asked from behind him.

Lark turned to face Ebony. She was obviously confused, and he wondered how she didn't know. "It's a soul that is more than half, not full, but enough that, apparently, it recognizes its soulmate. I have heard about it in theory, but never seen an example. Honestly, I didn't think it was real, seems like a mistake of the gods and their delightful punishment." Lark let his hatred of their situation and the ones who'd cursed it drip from his voice.

"What does that mean for my soulsister?" Ebony whispered.

"It could mean that she's very nearly a nosoul," Lark said darkly.

Ebony gasped, "You believe in nosouls."

"Not just believe in them, I've dealt with them." Lark pulled up a sleeve and showed her bite mark scars all along his forearm. "But I lived. They aren't strong, they aren't smart, but they are dangerous, especially in a group."

Ebony bit her lip and reached out a hand, tracing the scars and sending a delightful tingle through Lark's body.

"I saw one born. Most people don't believe they're real," she said and looked up into his eyes. "What does this mean for our search?"

"I don't know yet," Lark said honestly.

Ebony stared up into his eyes with a confusing mix of hope and fear. Her hands gripped his forearm and a constant pulse flowed where there was skin-to-skin contact. He didn't want to lose it, it felt so good, he wanted more, wanted to know what that electricity would feel like all over. He nearly groaned as he saw desire in her eyes reflecting his own, a desire that he knew she was fighting. She pulled her hand off of him and stepped back, shifting her eyes to the ground. The loss of contact was stark, and his hand twitched to reach out and touch her.

"Ebony—" he breathed it like a question, wanting permission to grab her and drag her up to his bedroom.

"Shit, Lark," Stone said, breaking the moment.

Lark grabbed Ebony's arm, leading her into the house. "Warn Granger, no one touches her," Lark ordered.

His home was very modern with accents of dark wood and clean white floors and walls. It didn't look very lived in and he worried she wouldn't like it. He knew what she was used to in the district, knew it was homey and dark, lived in and messy in a way that came from small spaces filled with lifetimes of possessions. She slipped out of her old tennis shoes inside the door and gripped her purse like a lifeline. He hated that everything she had was old, used, and abused. He wanted to see her adorned in every luxury he knew he could offer. Even when she'd dressed her best, which he knew she had when she'd come to him last night—they all did—it was nothing special. Just a clean T-shirt and slightly ripped jeans. Her shoes had been the same as she wore now, and he wondered if they were her only pair.

Not that she needed anything more to be beautiful. Even before he'd known she was his soulmate he'd been attracted to her. He'd have to be dead not to see the beauty in her smooth skin, dark hair, and full lips. Yeah, she was too skinny, but it didn't detract from her beauty, just gave her an air of fragility that made him want to scoop her up and take care of her.

Her eyes were wide as they took in the space and her mouth pressed shut. She looked nervous and it frustrated him that she would feel anything other than happy to be in his home. He knew he was frowning as he led her up the stairs, but he couldn't help it. This wasn't how he wanted things to go. He hated that he wanted her to like his home. Hated that her look of unease made his belly ache. She followed, of course, silent as he led her down the hall to the room at the far end, closest to his.

He stopped at the door and pushed it open. "You can stay in here; it has its own bathroom there and clothes should be here soon." He knew his voice was gruff, his posture stiff, but he knew that if he didn't hold himself completely in control, he'd grab her and drag her to that bed. Downstairs he heard the voices of his men. Granger had returned with the clothes he'd requested for her. No doubt Stone was telling him everything about their arrival now.

Ebony looked around the brightly-decorated bedroom but didn't speak or move.

"You don't like it? You can always use my room." He spoke quietly, bent forward so he could whisper in her ear. His body tingled being this close to her and he knew by the little shiver that ran through her, she felt the same.

She stepped away and turned around, plastering a smile on her face that did little to hide her anxiety. "It's great, it's just so nice. I'm not used to such luxury."

Lark looked around the room with a frown. "You'll be comfortable here." This *would* seem like the greatest luxury to her, better even than the rooms she cleaned at that hotel and that hurt him to know how she'd suffered so long, that all the halflings did.

"Yeah, thank you." She gave him a genuine smile this time and it made his heart flip. He wanted to reach out and run a finger over those lips, he wanted to spend his life making sure she never stopped smiling like that.

It was difficult, but he nodded and left, closing the door behind him. He hurried down the stairs to his waiting men.

"Soulmate?" Granger questioned as soon as Lark was down the stairs. Granger was standing just inside the door with bags in his hands and Stone stood beside him smiling like an idiot.

"Oh yeah, you should have seen the way he attacked me over her. He's in deep already," Stone laughed.

"No one touches what's mine," Lark growled.

"You never were good at sharing your toys," Stone teased.

Lark glared at his friend, still very ready to punch that pretty face of his and make sure he wasn't attractive to Ebony any time soon.

Granger must have sensed the downward spiral of the situation; he shoved the bags at Lark. "Well then, why don't you deliver these yourself. I have no interest in the woman."

"That's because you haven't seen her," Stone said, then hurried from the room as Lark's chest rumbled.

"Relax," Granger hissed. "You know he just wants to bait you. Keep your shit together, man."

"Never in my life has my shit been more apart," Lark said. "She's not a fullsoul."

Lark met his friend's eyes and saw pity there, then

determination. "We'll find her soulsister, you'll have your soulmate one way or another."

Lark shook his head. "I don't want it if it isn't her." And the realization that she could possibly lose in a battle with her soulsister and leave him with another version of herself was devastating. There was no precedent for what was happening with them, no record of anyone sparking to a soulmate who wasn't a fullsoul. He had to assume that if she found her soulsister and Ebony was killed in the soulbattle, that he'd feel the soulmate spark with her soul still. Her piece of soul that would unite with the piece in her soulsister, the winner of the soulbattle. He couldn't imagine the torture of feeling a spark to a body that wasn't Ebony's, only because it housed this piece of her soul. It wasn't fair and it scared the shit out of him.

"You'll have her," Granger assured him.

Lark knew his friend would do everything in his power to make that happen, but there was no guarantee, not really.

CHAPTER EIGHT

Ebony stood staring at the closed bedroom door for a moment, trying to wrap her head around everything that had occurred in the last hour. Her entire life had been turned upside down and when Lark was near, she couldn't think clearly. Well she could think very clearly, but only about his naked body and his strong arms wrapped around her.

"Damn," she whispered and gave herself a shake. She needed to concentrate on what she was after with him. Needed to keep in mind what she'd gone to him for last night because nothing had changed, soulmate or not.

She hurried to the bathroom, ready to wash the stink of work off of herself and hopefully refocus her body. The bathroom was clean and well stocked with essentials. She shouldn't be surprised, they did this for a living, they probably brought halflings here all the time when they started a job. She stepped into the shower and soaked in the high-pressured hot water, hoping it would help ease her mind.

She'd always known she had two choices, live a short but good life with friends and die a young halfling like so many others, or find and kill her soulsibling. Well, it wasn't really a choice, Ebony knew she could never take someone's life just to benefit herself. She'd never wanted that kind of guilt hanging over her head, especially since she had no desire to get married and have babies. A full soul would be wasted on her, especially now. She grimaced as she looked down at the scar that marred her chest. Long, red, and angry. It went from above her left breast around to the middle of her ribcage. Underneath it she felt an ache most days and with an increasing frequency that reminded her of how short her time could be. She ran a bar of soap over the rough skin, hating the odd sensation of the numbed part of her body. She avoided touching the skin over the fake breast the doctors had convinced her she needed. It looked remarkably like the other one, but it was a cold mound with almost no feeling to it at all and she could never forget that it wasn't really a part of her. She shuddered to think what Lark would do if he saw her like this, he'd probably curse the Gods even more for giving him such a defective soulmate.

She didn't want to care, but she did.

Anger filled Ebony and she leaned forward, resting her head against the shower wall. When she first found out she had cancer, she thought that was it, she was going to die very young. Then they removed it and she thought she had a little hope, a little time. But at her first checkup she'd found out that there was no hope, the doctors had missed too much and it had already gone too far. When she'd heard the prognosis, she had come to a sudden epiphany. She knew that her choices had changed drastically and if she didn't want her life to be a waste, she could find her soulsister and give up her half of their shared soul to her. She could benefit someone else, or die knowing she was dooming her soulsibling to a half-life with no options.

And now there was a new part of the complicated decision swirling around in her mind. Was Ebony's soulsibling almost a nosoul? What was the woman's life even like right now? Ebony felt even more desperate to help her, whoever she was, and wherever she was. Ebony couldn't leave her in whatever horrible state she had to be living in.

It had been an easy choice from the beginning and she'd made peace with it. Ebony was going to give someone the chance to have all the choices and it felt right, it felt worthy of her death. She felt good about giving someone else a real chance to make something of their life and find their soulmate, if that was their dream, which was a done deal now. Lark would be the woman's soulmate.

The discovery of Lark as her soulmate changed nothing, she reminded herself fiercely. Standing up under the spray and angrily scrubbing at her body and hair as if she could wash away any desire to be with him. Ebony was still dying of the cancer inside her chest, and she still refused to take someone else's life to benefit herself.

In the end, Lark would still have a fullsoul soulmate, so what did he care anyway? He should be just as happy with her soulsister as he would be with her.

That thought hurt more than Ebony was willing to admit, but it was a good thing to keep close to mind. He wasn't in love with her, he didn't even know her. He was attracted to her soul and any body that held it would be just as good as another, better perhaps. Fuck, Ebony didn't even know if she was Lark's type; maybe he was really into redheads with freckles or blondes with big boobs.

Ebony rinsed with a new determination to ignore the sparks that passed between her and Lark and to keep the end goal in mind. She stepped out of the shower and looked at herself in the mirror. It was never meant to be her and Lark. Whatever the Gods or fate had in mind, it certainly couldn't have been Lark and a girl dying of cancer. He was too... much, too special, too big for a fate so sad. Maybe Ebony was the mistake, maybe her soulsister was just as special as Lark, just as amazing and beautiful.

She had to hope Lark and his fullsoul soulmate would find happiness together. Her heart squeezed and tears stung her eyes as she mourned the loss of something she'd never let herself want but was suddenly just out of her reach. She shook the feelings away, burying them under determination.

When she left the bathroom with her emotions tightly under control she was happy to find a pile of fresh new clothing on the bed, everything from underwear out. All of it brand new and perfectly her size.

"Wow, he's good." She picked a black skirt that hit just above the knee and a pink T-shirt, then brushed her hair straight to dry naturally, and applied a little makeup. She was feeling pretty good as she slipped on a pair of clean black sandals, then she grabbed a jean jacket and reached for her purse with a frown, it was definitely not clean and new. It would give her status away even if she kept her eyes down.

She looked at herself in the bedroom mirror and lifted her chin a notch, she was who she was and that was just going to have to be good enough for him and anyone else. When she opened the bedroom door, Lark was standing across from it, leaning against the wall, arms crossed over his chest.

"Oh, hey, thanks for the clothing, I'll pay you back."

"Not necessary. Let's go eat, I'm starving."

Ebony bit her lip, she'd hoped he would at least tell her she looked nice. Shit, she wasn't sure when the last time was that she'd worn anything this nice and she wasn't immune to the need for a little flattery. He was dressed in a pair of black slacks and black T-shirt. His hair was messy and damp, he must have showered too, and he looked effortlessly amazing.

"I like your hair like that," she said as she followed him down the stairs.

He just grunted, not taking the hint that she wanted the compliment reciprocated.

She sighed, giving up. He was not a man who complimented, fine. They weren't in a relationship. This was a business arrangement, sort of. She'd feel better about it all if he let her pay him though.

"So where are we going?"

"Steakhouse close by." Lark hesitated at the front door. "You aren't a vegetarian, are you?"

"Not by choice," she said with a nervous laugh. Most of the time halflings couldn't afford good meat to eat with their half rations and she rarely spent her money on something as unnecessary as meat, unless it was her birthday perhaps, or Christmas.

"Good thing I'm paying," he said, holding the front door for her.

"You don't have to—" she said but the look of anger on his face stopped her.

"Let's get one thing straight," he hissed. "I will be providing everything you need from here on out. I won't have you getting sick and dying from lack of nutrition or feel embarrassed because you don't have appropriate clothing to wear. Whatever you need, I'm going to handle it, got it?" As he spoke, he got closer to her until he was almost touching her, and his hot breath fanned her face.

She could only nod, afraid that if she argued he was going to get really mad. He seemed like the type who might rather fight than talk when angry and she had no desire to find out if that included with women or not.

"Smooth, Lark," Stone said behind her, startling her.

Ebony spun around to see Stone standing there with a sandwich in one hand and a beer in the other.

"Stay out of it," Lark growled and grabbed Ebony's arm,

pulling her out of the house.

She didn't speak as he led her roughly to the truck and opened the door for her. Once she was settled in the seat, he shut the door and stalked around to the driver's side.

She decided to let him stew in his anger as they drove the short distance to the restaurant. When they pulled up outside, she looked down at her hand and frowned. "If they scan me, they'll kick me out."

"They won't scan you; they'll scan me," he said as if it were obvious.

She supposed that was a normal date thing to assume though, she'd never been on a date before, so it hadn't even occurred to her. Apparently, it wasn't anything new for him and a little tingle of jealousy rose up unfamiliar and strong. "Do you bring halflings here often?"

"Yeah," he said and hopped out of the truck.

She ignored the hurt that his simple answer brought up. She didn't care who he'd been with in the past or would be with in the future, because it wasn't going to be her now or ever and that was the only sure thing about their situation. When he opened her door, she avoided his eyes and pretended to care deeply about smoothing imaginary wrinkles from her shirt.

He offered her his arm as they began to walk but she ignored it until the curious eyes of other patrons started to bore into her with disgust as they walked toward the entrance of the restaurant. The people they passed could tell she wasn't one of them and they didn't want her to sully their environment. She latched onto Lark's arm for comfort, stretching for a semblance of belonging. He was such a striking figure and she hoped that most eyes would gloss right past her and onto him when she was this close. Unfortunately, they just glared harder, seeing her as a halfling slut after a free meal.

"I'm not really hungry," she mumbled as a woman passing them made a particularly nasty remark.

Lark paused and looked down at her with a frown. "You're worried about what other people think?"

"I just don't want to make people uncomfortable," she said, avoiding his eyes.

"Then how do you expect to live a worthwhile life?" he asked with a raised eyebrow.

The simple gesture combined with the intensity of his gaze made her heart speed up a bit. "That's what I tried to hire you for," she said with a laugh. She was going to make her life worthwhile before she died, by sacrificing her half of their soul to her soulsister. That didn't necessarily include an uncomfortable dining experience.

He just grunted and opened the restaurant door, putting a guiding hand on her back as she stepped in. She gasped as her eyes adjusted to the low light and she saw the place he'd brought her to. It was by far the fanciest restaurant she'd ever been inside of and that included the one at the hotel. There was a bar off to the right that had a wall full of alcohol bottles and a glass bar top. The restaurant side, what she could see of it from the entryway, had tables with black cloths and candles, seats cushioned with red velvet and the smell. *Oh my!* It smelled like the most delicious concoction of meat and butter she'd ever encountered in her life.

Her stomach rumbled and she put her hands over it in embarrassment as the hostess rushed forward with a scan pad.

"How can I help you?" the hostess said to Lark, her gaze raking over his body. Her eyes were bright. She was a fullsoul, and judging by the way she was posturing her body toward Lark and pushing out her chest, Ebony would guess she wasn't into taking suppressants.

"Table for two," Lark said with a wide grin.

The woman's smile widened and then faltered as she looked at Ebony. "Oh, she's—"

"With me," Lark said, holding his hand over the scanner she still held. It lit up green and Ebony knew it was sending information into the woman's earpiece, giving her all kinds of information about Lark. Ebony would give anything to hear it all herself. What was this man worth? Had he ever used a ration credit in his life? Probably turned them in every year for the tax break.

"Oh!" she said, her eyes widening, "Right this way, Mr. Duport."

Lark motioned for Ebony to follow the hostess which she did reluctantly. Every table they passed eyed her and whispered. Once seated in a dark corner of the restaurant, Ebony felt more comfortable, though she wondered if the hostess put them there so that they'd be out of sight of most patrons, wouldn't want to sully the restaurant with the presence of a halfling. However, if no one could see her, then no one could judge her so she was also thankful for the somewhat private table.

Lark ordered for them both, food and drinks, when the waiter quickly appeared with waters, another thing that was kind of annoying but she also appreciated. She was so nervous she wasn't sure she could have coherently perused a menu and picked something to eat.

As they waited for the food to arrive, Lark started asking questions. "What do you know about your soulsister?"

"She's five years younger than me and she doesn't reside in the LA halfling district."

"Have you searched anywhere else?"

"I've never been out of the city."

"Did your mother ever meet her soulmate?"

"No."

Lark nodded, "That's too bad, if we had a name, we could check the database."

"The halfling database?" Ebony leaned across the table, her eyes wide. "You have access to the halfling database?"

Lark smiled and winked, "Of course I do, how do you think I've been so successful as a searcher?"

"Isn't that illegal?"

"Yes, sort of."

Ebony bit her lip. She knew she was getting herself involved with a dangerous business, but knowing it and being in the middle of it were two totally different things.

"If you're afraid of breaking the law, you should probably stay in the halfling district and wait for her to find you," Lark said dryly.

"I'm afraid of sitting in jail for the rest of my life," she grumbled, not that it would be very long.

"Don't worry, I'm very good at what I do," he said in a husky whisper that made her shiver. "And besides, the government looks the other way when people like me are digging around their system, they want halflings united."

Ebony nodded and sipped her wine that had been brought. Lark had ordered her a red wine and she loved it instantly. She'd only had wine once and it had not tasted this good. This was not too sweet, not sour and just amazing, she wanted to gulp it but didn't. Stopping at a small sip and smiling at him. "This is good," she said.

"Should be," he said with no more explanation.

"Did you look me up in the database?" she asked, suddenly worried he might know too much about her.

"No," he said a little too quickly. She had a feeling he wasn't telling the truth. She was his client, if he hadn't looked her up he wouldn't really be doing his job, would he?

The waiter came then with their plates and Ebony was

thankful for the distraction. Her eyes widened at the plate of steak, mashed potatoes, vegetables steamed and slathered in butter and garlic, and a roll. It was so much food, so much good food, she almost wanted to cry at the sight.

They ate in silence for a while and Ebony had to force herself to take it slow, the food was delicious, better even than it had smelled, she wanted to shove it all in her mouth at once. But at the same time, she wanted to savor every last bite.

"Do you like it?" Lark asked with amusement, and she was embarrassed to note he'd eaten half what she had in the short time.

"It's great," she said around a mouthful of buttery mashed potatoes.

Lark laughed, "Good."

She slowed down then, concentrating on the taste sensations and not making a fool of herself. It was hard when all she wanted to do was taste every bit of food on her plate all at the same time and feel her belly fill with the nutrient-rich morsels.

When he was done with his meal, he sighed heavily and sipped his beer. "With no idea of where to start looking, and you having only eliminated the city we are in, we'll start at the bottom."

"What does that mean?"

"We will go to Vegas."

"Las Vegas?" she gasped excitedly.

"Yep, we'll fly out in the morning."

"Fly!"

"Sweetie, you are in for quite a wild experience, not everywhere is like it is here."

"I know," she huffed, she'd *heard* about other places, she just never thought she'd *experience* other places.

"And once you're whole we can travel the world first class," he added with a sexy grin.

Whole, the word hurt more than a little. He saw her as missing something, as something less than him, less than all the others in this restaurant. There was something wrong with her in his eyes and it had nothing to do with her being sick. She excused herself to find the bathroom, her dinner suddenly not sitting right.

"Back there," Lark directed as she stood. His eyes were cautious when she glanced at his face.

Ebony kept her eyes downcast as she made her way through the crowded restaurant. Once safely tucked in a bathroom stall, she gave herself a moment to feel. He was offering her the world, literally. But only because he thought he had to. He'd feel the same way if he'd met her soulsister first, he *would* feel the same way when he met her soulsister and that cheapened it even more. What did feelings even mean when they were directed by such a ridiculous thing as your soul? A soul was just a small, cursed part of a person, it shouldn't be able to decide so much about your life against your will. She resented the apparently more than half a soul she had, resented the feelings Lark inspired because of it. She wanted to do one good thing with her life, and it didn't include being soulmated.

Ebony couldn't stop a few tears from falling and she hated the weakness. Why cry over things she couldn't change? Things that were a result of cursed fate.

She took a little comfort in the knowledge that she wasn't going to be leaving Lark without a soulmate if it was indeed what he really wanted. She was going to help two people have their best life, it was noble and it was sort of what she'd wanted to do anyway. She just hadn't intended on knowing the soulmate, hadn't thought about how that could feel to give up. She dried her eyes with toilet paper that was softer than she'd ever used in her life and had to hold back the temptation to take the roll off the holder and stuff it into her purse to share with Taylor. Would she ever even see Taylor again?

She bit her lip as new tears wanted to fall, heavy ones this time. She knew if she let herself cry for her friend, she'd never get them to stop, so she breathed deep and centered herself. She didn't want Lark to see her like this.

When she once again felt in control, she was about to leave the stall but the sound of the bathroom door opening, and voices, stopped her. She didn't want to face anyone she didn't know, so she hesitated.

"Did you see him! Oh my god, those green eyes, and that hair!" One of the women said.

"His body is magnificent. I would be all over that, suppressants or not," the other one giggled.

Ebony was pretty sure they were talking about Lark, and she bristled a bit at their casual talk of something that was hers. Well, should be hers, but she wasn't going to take it. She shook her head; it was all too confusing.

"Yeah, but did you see he's with some halfling slut, probably a prostitute. Why he's bothering to buy her dinner is a mystery. She can't be that good."

"It's gross, why do they come this far out of their district? Aren't there enough halfling men?"

"I heard halfling men can't get it up."

"Oh! That would make sense why they creep out here to find a good romp. And they're usually too dumb to make sure the guy wears protection, which is why so many of our men are willing to sleep with them."

Ebony's fists tightened on the handle, and she resisted the urge to open the door and tell those bitches that Lark was her soulmate. Whether she planned to claim him or not wasn't any of their business. They had it all wrong and she wanted to shove it in their faces, as if it mattered what a couple of fullsoul know-it-alls thought.

When she heard two stalls close, she rushed out.

Lark met her outside the bathroom door with her purse in hand, already having taken care of the bill apparently and ready to leave.

"Is everything alright?" he asked carefully, taking in her appearance.

"Fine, let's go," she hissed, grabbing her bag from him. She didn't want to see those women come out of the bathroom. It was bad enough she could guess what the people were thinking, but to actually hear it was so much worse. She had never felt the desire to be what those women thought she was. It paid well, she knew, but she refused to give any more ammunition to the prejudices and to explain to them the reality of her situation would be a waste of time and breath; they didn't matter. But that didn't mean that their words didn't sting.

CHAPTER NINE

Lark had heard what those women in the bathroom were saying and it had taken every ounce of control he could muster to not rush in there and tell them exactly what he thought of their self-righteous bitch attitudes. They had no idea what it was like for halflings because of people like them.

He rubbed at the small bump on the back of his hand where his implant was. There had been a time when he'd been afraid every time he'd had to scan the damn thing. Rejected more often than not and kicked out onto the street to try and find what he needed on his own. The life of a halfling orphan.

When Ebony came out of the bathroom looking upset, he wanted to pull her into his arms, tell her it was going to be alright, but he held back, knew she wasn't ready to accept that from him. The best he could do was walk with her back out of the restaurant and hope that his presence would keep all the comments restrained until they were out the door.

He'd brought other halflings here when on a job, but he'd never noticed the talk or the looks before. Had they always been there, but he hadn't cared? Because it hadn't been her, hadn't been affecting his soulmate. He hated that he might have put the others through such uncomfortable situations unknowingly. When had he become so blind to the daily plight of the halflings? He'd thought he was giving them a great meal, a great experience on their journey. Perhaps he'd been wrong.

"Have a good night, Mr. Duport," the hostess said as they passed, and he had a sudden idea.

He stopped and swung around to face the woman. "Excuse me, Miss."

Her eyes brightened and she leaned forward to show off her cleavage while she gripped the edge of the podium. He could feel Ebony stiffen beside him. This woman was new here, he had to admit if he'd met her before Ebony had walked into his office and disrupted his life he might have taken her up on the offer she was presenting, but now all it did was make him think about what he really wanted, Ebony. No other could hold a candle to the desire that burned through him when he looked at her.

"What can I do for you, handsome?" the hostess asked, obviously assuming he was about to hit on her, despite the presence of Ebony.

"My wife would like a piece of chocolate cake to go, sorry I forgot to order before I paid at the table," he said it loud enough for most of the restaurant to hear him.

Ebony went even stiffer beside him at the word *wife* and the woman gasped and pulled back, straightening. Her face went red, and she stuttered a few words of understanding before rushing off to do as he asked.

He turned to Ebony while they waited. She was staring at him with a red face and blue eyes wide and still a little watery from the bathroom incident. Damn she was sexy. Even when she was embarrassed, and a little pissed, he was sure. There was a glint in her eyes that spoke of held back anger that was pushing the sadness away and that made him happy. Her bottom lip was trembling as if she wanted to spew all kinds of words but wouldn't in such a public place. She would never make a bigger scene, but he could see how much she wanted to tell him and anyone else listening that she most definitely wasn't his wife. His eyes locked onto her bottom lip, and he wanted nothing more in that moment than to taste it.

And why shouldn't he? She was his soulmate.

He still couldn't believe he'd actually found her. It had taken a day to get used to the idea, but he couldn't get her out of his head after kicking her out of his office. She'd invaded his every thought, his dreams too and when he'd woken rock hard and wanting nothing more than to drive into her waiting body, he'd known what everyone else talked about. Once you met your soulmate you were ruined for anyone else. He couldn't help but assume that she didn't feel it as hard as him only because she had half of her soul, but he was going to fix that. He wanted her to want him just as much, wanted their passions to match and wanted to give in to that ultimate experience of fucking his soulmate.

Damn, he was getting hard again and hoped no one noticed, luckily the restaurant was dimly lit, and the sun had set outside already.

He heard more than one whisper around them and decided to give them a show and treat himself to a little dessert too. He leaned forward and captured her bottom lip between his teeth. The reaction was more intense than he was expecting. Instant heat filled him, and a spark of electricity passed between their lips, making him want to take things all the way, right there. His hands grasped her shoulders, and he pecked her lips lightly, then pulled away. He turned and put her at his side, one arm around her back, holding her against him as if he'd done it a thousand times.

The way she allowed it made him think she was as affected

as him from the kiss, pliant and curious. He wondered how long it would be until she trusted him enough to reveal the diagnosis that was in her file. It had to be what was behind her decision to find her soulsister, but why didn't she just say that? It wouldn't be the first time a dying halfling hired him for one last chance at saving their life by acquiring the strength of a full soul. Did she think she was being selfish, that she wasn't deserving of going after her full soul because of her condition?

The hostess came back still looking embarrassed and handed him the box of chocolate cake. "Have a great evening, Mr. and Mrs. Dupont," she said, and it made Lark smile.

He led Ebony out of the restaurant feeling like he had just won an argument for her. She didn't pull away from the hand he kept on her lower back all the way to the truck and when he opened the door for her, she climbed in without a word. He handed her the cake and walked around the truck hoping she realized now that he would do anything to protect her from the prejudices that surrounded them.

"I hope you like chocolate, but if not, I'm sure Stone will eat it. He's a bottomless pit," Lark said as he climbed into the driver's seat.

"I do like chocolate," she said quietly and stared out the passenger window. After a few minutes of heavy silence she spoke again. "Why did you do that? Why did you kiss me and call me your wife?" she asked, still not looking at him.

"Because I felt like it," he said with a shrug. And because he wanted to make her feel special and important in that moment, but he wasn't going to say that out loud.

She turned to him then, her eyes flashing in anger. "And you do whatever the hell you want? Because you think you are better than us lowly halflings? Well fuck you, Lark, I am not yours to use, I am not your *wife,* and you may *not* kiss me whenever the hell you feel like it."

Lark's hands gripped the wheel and he stared ahead, not wanting to lash out at her. "You have no idea what I think," he said and sped down the road to his house.

When he parked in the driveway, she jumped out without waiting for Lark to open her door. He hurried out of the truck with gritted teeth, ready to chase her down but Stone opened the front door to let her in and she rushed past him and presumably up the stairs to her room. Lark watched her from the driveway, glaring. This wasn't his fault; she was assuming things about him and she showed zero interest in getting to know him despite the fact that they were destined for each other. She wasn't behaving at all like he'd expect, like he wanted, and it pissed him off. He thought of himself as a very good predictor of people's behavior but she wasn't like anyone he had ever met.

Lark stalked forward to the door. Stone still held it open, a beer in one hand and no shirt on. He had a dumb grin on his face that made Lark want to punch him.

"Well done, boss," Stone said with a mocking shake of his head.

Lark glared at his oldest friend. He trusted Stone with his life, but he didn't always like the way Stone butted into his business. "Stay out of it."

"Lark, you have to woo her," Stone said dramatically.

"No, I have to find her soulsister." And make sure Ebony lived long enough to be wooed.

"Oh! Threesome!" Stone said with a laugh.

"Watch it, Stone, that's my wife you're talking about," Lark snarled, not sure what to do with the angry jealousy that was welling up inside of him when Stone talked about Ebony. It wasn't that he really thought Stone was going to pursue her, they never went after the same ladies, it was the brotherly code, and she hadn't looked at Stone twice since they'd met. Lark didn't think Ebony was attracted to the goof, but all these new feelings needed an outlet, and better to be angry at Stone than at sweet, frustrating, Ebony.

"Oh come on, you can't tell me you haven't thought about it. I mean, Ebony is something sweet to look at but, damn, what if her sister is even hotter? Remember that chick we searched with, the short brunette with a bad attitude? What was her name?"

Lark knew exactly where his friend was going with this. "Janett."

"Yeah! Janett, well she was alright to look at, nothing special. I slept with her," he said the last with a huge grin. "But her soulsister, when we found her in Vegas, damn! That woman was like a goddess, all legs and short blonde hair, big blue eyes. Wow, she'd been even better in the sack. Her name was Bri, I think, or was it Lea..."

Lark rolled his eyes at his friend. "No."

"No?" Stone asked, already having forgotten the point of his little trip down memory lane probably.

Lark turned to his friend and met his gaze. "No, I know what I feel with Ebony, its intense and trust me, I *want* to deny it." Fuck did he want to, had tried all night last night and had hardly slept. "But it's there and I don't think there is any possibility that the other half of her soul holds even a fraction of the draw. She may only have part of a soul, but it's all mine," he growled and looked up the stairs. He wanted to rush up there and rip open the thin door that closed her off from him. He wanted to demand she give him all of herself, her passion and her pain, her entire being with nothing held back.

"I'm not sure if you're lucky or fucked," Stone said with a frown.

"Both," Lark said.

"Granger has been doing some recon, can't find any old boyfriends, no living relatives. Not on suppressants."

That didn't surprise Lark, she was pretty insistent that she did not do that sort of thing and she reacted to him with too much honesty to be jaded by past experiences.

"Her mother died of breast cancer when Ebony was seventeen, couldn't get good medical because she was living in the halfling district working at the hotel restaurant. Ebony worked there since she was fifteen cleaning rooms, I have no idea how she saved up all that cash, could be she was doing something illegal." Stone shrugged, none of them cared about illegal for the most part.

Lark gave him a disparaging look. Ebony was *not* capable of illegal even if it was pretty normal for people in her situation. More than likely she'd just gone without any luxuries or extras her entire life to save it up. Barely enough food, no new clothes or comforts. It made him want to shower her with everything and anything her little heart could desire.

Stone rolled his eyes. "Okay, maybe she's just a saver, who knows. But one thing really interesting I found." Stone pulled a piece of paper out of his pocket and handed it to Lark.

Lark stared at the letter. It was addressed to Ebony at the hotel where she worked. He looked up at Stone with a raised eyebrow.

"Found it in her employee file at the hotel, opened. I'm guessing boss man didn't want to lose a good employee and never showed her. Check the date, it would have reached her right after her mother's death. Why he kept it, I have no idea. Maybe he would have given it to her eventually, maybe he just forgot about it?"

"Looks like we need to pay Mr. Glick a visit." Lark frowned down at the letter.

Stone's face lit up; he was never upset about the chance to put a little pressure on someone for information.

"Did Granger go to the orphanage?" Lark asked.

"Yep, withdrew everyone's rations and made the monthly deposit there and the halfling retirement community as well."

"Good, we will be out of town for a bit, I hope going early didn't mess with their routine."

"Granger didn't say they minded."

Lark nodded and started up the stairs. "Make sure the plane is ready early tomorrow, I'll want to arrive in Vegas before noon. We'll go see Glick in an hour."

"Sure thing, boss. Say goodnight to Ebony for me," Stone called after him, voice heavy with innuendo.

Lark ignored his friend's attempt at goading him. He stopped outside Ebony's door and knocked lightly.

He listened to her feet pad across the room and when she opened the door she didn't say anything, just looked at him, clearly still irritated by his actions in the restaurant. There was a smear of chocolate on her lip and the knowledge that she had immediately indulged in the cake made him extremely happy. He couldn't stop himself from reaching up and wiping the frosting from her lip and sticking it into his own mouth.

The shocked expression on her face was everything he could have asked for in response. "Are you going to share, or do I have to kiss you fully so I can get a taste of dessert?"

"I—uh—I—yeah, come on in," she stumbled over the words then moved to let him enter.

He was glad to see that his question had made her forget her earlier irritation. The cake was sitting on the bed in its open box, and it looked like she'd only taken a bite or two. He doubted she was saving it for him and that meant she was savoring it. His heart ached to think of how she had been living. He knew all about life without enough, without any extras or indulgences. He wanted to give her everything, anything. Until they were both old and grey. His eyes flicked back to her, searching for signs of illness. There was a slight darkness around her eyes, but that was likely just emotion, she was skinny, but most halflings were. Her hair was thick and shiny, her eyes a little bright for a halfling despite their pale color and he had to hope her diagnosis wasn't as bad as it seemed.

"Why are you staring at me? You can have some cake. I didn't think you wanted any, sorry." She looked uncomfortable and she wrapped her arms around herself.

He felt bad instantly, it hadn't been his intention to make another awkward situation for them. "I wanted to apologize," he said with a sigh. Apologizing wasn't his strong suit, but he had a feeling it would go a long way to easing things between them. "I shouldn't have taken liberties with your mouth in public," he said, his lip twitching with a held back smirk.

"Oh," her face flamed at the mention of their small kiss. "Thank you."

He crossed the distance that separated them and grabbed her chin. "We aren't in public now though," he said, a breath before his mouth descended to capture hers in a deep kiss.

This wasn't the playful tease he'd given in the restaurant; this one was everything a kiss should be. His mouth devoured hers and his tongue played against hers. She went stiff, unmoving, not responding but accepting. He kept it up, putting his hands on her lower back and gently massaging with his fingers, trying to coax a reaction. It was as if she had no idea how to respond, and that pleased the deeply possessive side of him.

He pulled away and gave her a thoughtful look. "Be ready early tomorrow."

She nodded silently, and he left the room, closing the door behind him.

"Well, that answers that," he said to himself, not expecting Stone to be nearby.

"What's that?" Stone asked.

"She's definitely never been with a man, probably never even had a boyfriend."

"You'll have to be careful with her then."

"Indeed." Lark retreated to his office and thought about the situation. He wanted to be sure she was interested in him, but the fact that she didn't push him away wasn't enough. He was going to have to up his charm to get her where he wanted her and that wasn't something he was good at.

CHAPTER TEN

Lark sat behind his desk and pulled the letter out of his pocket, reading it again.

"What does Senator Buchanan want with a halfling from across the country?" Lark had a natural distrust of government officials, but something about the senator had always given him an extra bad vibe. If he was somehow involved in Ebony's life, that could be a very bad thing.

He clicked the television on and turned it to the news. As usual, Senator Buchanan was filling the screen with his agenda. Tonight he stood in front of a room full of likeminded individuals who would hang on his every word. His daughter wasn't there this time. That surprised Lark; Buchanan liked to let her talk. She was a well-spoken, twenty-year-old going to school to be a geneticist, hoping to solve all the world's problems. Meanwhile Buchanan was asking for more money to be invested in the wars across the seas, keeping the peace, keeping the borders closed, and not allowing the U.S. citizens to find out how true the rumors of nosouls were. The message was always the same and as always, Lark didn't trust it.

"What do you have to do with my soulmate?" Lark whispered at the screen.

A knock at the door had him turning the TV off and shoving the letter in a drawer. "Enter," he called, and his pulse jumped, hoping it would be Ebony standing there.

"We're ready to roll on Glick whenever you are."

"I don't want her left alone. Tell Nelsen to stand guard at the front door. If she leaves the room or needs anything, he can assist." Nelsen was a halfling, but he'd aged well, strong and sure of himself. Years ago, he'd assisted Lark and the others when they'd left the orphanage at eighteen, and later had become a sort of father figure even though they hadn't known they needed it. When they all became fullsouled and started this business they'd hired him on as an assistant. Nelsen ran the house, kept things secure when they were out traveling on a job, that sort of thing. It was the least they could do for the man who'd taken them in and given them a home where they were able to live while fighting for a full life. Nelson hadn't ever had the opportunity to have a fullsoul life, his soulsibling had never been born but that hadn't stopped him from being happy. He'd found his calling in helping orphans who aged out of the orphanage.

"And he's old enough to be her father so she won't be attracted to him," Stone said with a wink. "Good thinking, boss."

Lark grunted. It had crossed his mind that he didn't want to leave anyone young and dumb in charge while they were out, but Stone seeing through it was more than a little annoying. "Everyone knows I'll cut off their dick and feed it to them if they so much as think about touching what's mine, so it really doesn't matter if she is attracted to the old man, he wouldn't cross that line."

Stone held his hands over his crotch mockingly and backed out of the room, "Got it, I'll tell him."

Lark ran a hand through his hair as Stone shut the door. He had no idea how to have a soulwife. He couldn't deal with the feelings of possession he felt toward her even though he barely knew her, it was frightening. Which really pissed him off.

He stood and strode from the room, ready to take his anger out on Glick; he hoped the guy gave them trouble. He hesitated outside Ebony's door, debating whether or not he should tell her he was leaving. He could hear her moving around in there, probably getting ready for bed, and once his thoughts went there, he couldn't stop the freefall into dangerous territory. Did she sleep nude? He doubted Granger had picked up pajamas for her.

He forced himself away from her door, hands clenched and jaw tight.

The last thing he wanted was to come on too strong. She wasn't ready to accept him, and he didn't blame her. He just hoped he could wait long enough that she wouldn't run screaming when he finally took her to bed.

They found Glick at home and Lark had no qualms about interrogating the man in his small living space. Lark knew the man had no family, a fullsoul destined to a sad lonely life because he had never been able to find his soulmate; maybe his soulmate had never even been born. Lark had seen it a million times. They came to him and paid big money to find their soulmates with no guarantee of success. They would deny themselves pleasure of others, deny the thrill of dating and close relationships of any kind, all with the hope that one day they would find the one. Then, once their soulmate was found, they would desperately produce babies and perpetuate the cycle. Or, as with Glick, they would wither away alone and die unsatisfied, a life worthless and dull. Glick obviously took his frustrations out on his staff, controlling and angry from what he'd witnessed today.

It was something Lark had thought he might come up against someday, no hope to find his soulmate but he thought he'd probably be okay with that conclusion to his life. He had found many willing beds, though, and lived a dangerous life in order to feel the thrill of being alive. Who needs a soulwife when you have that? Men like Glick just accepted their fate, and it pissed Lark off because he knew it gave all the power to the government. Halflings would always be treated like shit if the born fullsouls didn't stop acting like they had to sit back and take it up the ass from fate and the men in charge.

Lark walked into Glick's house uninvited, with Stone and Granger at his back. The man was looking haggard on his couch and jumped at the sound of intrusion, spitting out crumbs of his microwave dinner, now spilled on the carpet. His shirt was unbuttoned, and his hair was a mess. Lark knew this guy was a fullsoul because he could see it in the glint of his brown eyes. Glick's fat body told Lark he'd been born that way. No one with a repaired soul was unfit, they had to be strong to take their soul from their soulsibling and they valued the second chance at life they were given. This man was a lump, a waste of a soul, in Lark's opinion.

"Mr. Duport!" Glick squeaked in surprise. "If this is about that halfling girl, I have no idea where she is, probably the halfling district."

"I know where she is, she's currently sleeping in my bed," Lark growled darkly.

Glick's mouth dropped open in shock then quickly a look of disgust passed over his face. "If she's been sleeping around, I'm going to have to report her. She's a worthless halfling and I can't have her tainting my respectable business." Glick tried to stand straight, grasping at the upper hand futilely.

Lark reacted fast, reaching out and landing a punch to Glick's cheek.

Glick fell to the floor. "What the hell!" he yelled as he scrambled to his feet. "I'm going to call the police," he snapped, hand to his already swelling cheek.

"We won't be here that long," Lark said calmly. "Tell me why you never gave Ebony this letter from Senator Buchanan." Lark pulled the envelope from his pocket and watched Glick's face closely.

Anger filled Glick's face. "You broke into my office."

"We'll break more than that if you don't start talking." Stone and Granger stepped forward and by the look on Glick's face, Lark knew he wasn't going to give them a hard time.

Glick sputtered and tears were visible in his eyes as he spilled the whole story.

Glick had received the letter and, not wanting to lose a good employee, he'd waited to give it to her. After doing a little research on the senator, it had seemed he took a particular interest in young halfling women, employing them in large numbers in his homes and offices, all outside of DC of course. So, assuming the senator was only interested in her because she was attractive and poor, possibly wanting to add her to his own staff to seduce her, Glick had done what he felt was right and kept the letter from her. He told the senator that she was dead, and he never contacted Glick again.

"Had he been in your hotel? Had he seen her?" Lark pressed, glad that this idiot had done something decent to protect Ebony, even if it had been a bit selfish.

"No, the man has never been in this city that I know of. But maybe one of his staff members had been? Why they picked Ebony I don't know. She's nothing special," Glick shrugged, and

Lark hit him again, delighting in the way his fat ass bounced through his mashed potatoes on the floor.

"She is never coming back to your hotel, forget she exists. I suggest you burn hers and her mother's files." Lark tucked the letter back in his pocket and turned.

"What do you care about one stupid halfling whore or her whore mother? She can't be that good a lay," Glick mumbled.

Before Lark could react and likely kill the man, Stone lashed out and landed a punch hard enough to knock the man unconscious.

Lark was slightly disappointed, but it was probably better not to leave any dead bodies. Granger slapped Lark on the back and urged him toward the door.

As they drove back to the house, Lark's mind was spinning. What if there was something more to the senator's interest? It didn't sit well with him that the man had requested Ebony without ever seeing her.

"Find out where the senator is going to be the next few days, I think we need to arrange a meeting," he told Granger.

"On it," Granger said and pulled out his phone. Granger was a whiz with finding information of all kinds on the internet and used those skills often in their searching.

"Stone, I want you to find out all you can about the halfling women the senator employs; what they might have in common with Ebony."

"Will do, even if I have to personally meet them all," he said with a smile and wink.

Lark gave him a sharp look. "Keep your head out of your pants. This isn't our usual mission, this is my soulmate," he snapped.

The rest of the drive was silent, and he didn't relax until he was through the front door and saw Nelsen there with a smile on his face. "Your lady has not left her room," he said.

"Thank you, Nelsen, go to bed."

Nelsen didn't move but his face broke into a huge grin. "You are on a path most have only dreamed of my boy, don't fuck it up." Nelsen patted Lark's shoulder then waltzed away.

Stone snickered as he came in behind Lark, and Granger just grunted as he headed toward their home gym. No doubt he would be working out half the night.

"Are you really going to let her sleep alone all night?" Stone asked as Lark stared up at the stairs debating that thing exactly.

"I think she isn't ready to accept all I have to offer," Lark admitted.

"Nelsen's right about not fucking it up. You wait too long, and you could miss your chance. There's no guarantee about the soulfight, and I saw her file," Stone said gently. "The diagnosis is not good."

"Yeah, I think that's why she's doing this now," Lark said, and his feet started to move. He hurried up the steps and stopped at her door. Just a peek, then he would go to his own bed. He listened to the silence on the other side of the door for a moment, then pushed it open slowly. The moonlight filtered in through the window and showed Ebony's small form curled up in the center of the large bed. He crept close, thankful for the well-built house and floors that didn't creak. How would he explain his presence if she woke up?

He got to the side of her bed and stood staring down at her. She looked so serene in sleep, and it took all he had to simply whisper a goodnight and creep back out, closing the door between them. He wanted so badly to scoop her up and carry her to his room, a place he'd never brought a woman before, where she belonged.

In time, he told himself. He just hoped they had time.

Instead of going to bed he walked to his office and pulled up her file on his computer then he sent off an email that included her medical records. He would leave nothing to chance where his soulmate was concerned.

When that was done, he went to bed and lay awake staring at the wall that separated him from her.

Was she dreaming of him?

When sleep finally came, he dreamed of her.

CHAPTER ELEVEN

Ebony woke to the smell of bacon and coffee. She was sure she was still dreaming; she'd never had bacon in her home in her life. She rolled over and felt unfamiliar soft sheets, a bed that was practically enveloping her, and a pillow overstuffed and delightful. She had a moment of panic thinking she'd fallen asleep at work, tucked into someone's hotel bed.

Glick was going to kill her!

She sat up in bed with a gasp, and when her eyes darted around the room she remembered where she was and why.

"Fuck," it hadn't been a dream. She was actually in Lark's guest room, he thought she was his soulwife, and she was going to be flying to Vegas today to try and find her soulsister.

"Fuck," she said again and this time she smiled. She was on an adventure, her first and last.

Her hand went to her chest where she knew the cancer ticked like a bomb, just waiting to take her out of this life. Maybe she'd have a better go of it next time around. She liked to think reincarnation was real and all those who lived a decent life, even as a halfsoul, would be lucky enough to be reborn next time as a fullsoul. It made the sacrifice she was journeying toward all the more acceptable.

She'd dreamed of him last night. Dreams of erotic passion she'd never experienced, but apparently her imagination had no problem coming up with scenarios to make her fill with desire. It probably came from the spicier books she read over and over. Even now her body felt sensitive, and she thought a cold shower might be needed before facing Lark or anyone else.

The thought of bacon was too tempting however, so she threw on a pair of jeans and a sweatshirt she'd found in the bag and left the room to follow that amazing scent.

She knew the smell well but had never actually eaten bacon. No guests left bacon on their plates, sausage links sometimes, but never bacon. Her mouth watered as she entered a small dining room set with beautiful dishes and trays of eggs, bacon, toast, and fruit. Coffee was in a pot alongside a pitcher of orange juice and ice water.

It was almost distracting enough for her to ignore the three gorgeous men sitting around the table with plates full of food they were devouring.

"Good morning," she said quietly from the doorway.

All three men froze and looked at her. Her face turned red, and she wished she had showered first, but then her stomach growled, and she felt her face get redder.

"Ebony, did you sleep well?" Lark asked, standing, and motioning to a chair at the table. "Come eat, we will have a long day."

"I slept fine," she said as she hurried to take the seat, hoping the other two would stop staring soon. Stone she recognized from yesterday, but the other man was new. He had long black hair and brilliant brown eyes, definitely a fullsoul. He was enormous, muscles bulged everywhere, he was by far the biggest and most intimidating of the three men. Every inch of him that she could see was covered in tattoos, even his neck and hands. His face was clean of ink and freshly shaved, it was a bit of a paradox in her mind and only made looking at him more uncomfortable.

He noticed her staring and winked at her, the action sent a little thrill through her, and she hurried to look away. Unfortunately she turned to Lark who was glaring daggers at the man and gripped his knife like he was about to use it.

"Bacon?" Stone asked, breaking the tense silence, and holding a platter out for her.

Ebony took it gratefully and put a few pieces on her plate. "Thank you," she whispered, afraid to look at the other two men at the table.

"Eggs?" the new man offered, holding out a serving bowl of scrambled eggs.

"Um," she hesitated, not sure what to do. She flicked her gaze to Lark, then chastised herself, he didn't own her. She met the man's eyes and took the bowl. "Thanks, I'm Ebony."

"I know, and I'm Granger," he said gruffly.

"Nice to meet you, Granger," she said as she spooned eggs onto her plate.

She grabbed a piece of toast from a nearby stack and started eating, hating the intense silence in the room. At least everyone had started eating again. She picked up a piece of bacon and took a tentative bite. Flavors of salt, fat, and meat exploded on her tongue and she moaned before she could stop herself.

Lark choked on his food, Granger winked at her again as she darted her eyes around the table, embarrassed by the sound that had come out of her mouth, and Stone laughed.

"If you think that's good, wait till you try the strawberries, fresher than anything the halflings are ever able to get," Stone said and offered her the fruit plate.

She took one large berry, redder than any she'd ever eaten,

already anticipating the taste. A halfling maid hurried in then with a big smile. She was carrying a fresh pot of coffee and set it down in the middle of the table, taking the other one, apparently empty. Her gaze flicked curiously to Ebony, but she didn't say anything, just hurried back out to a round of thanks from the men.

"Coffee?" Lark asked after slapping Stone's hand away from the pot.

"Sure, thanks," she said, uncomfortable with the service as he poured some in her cup, then his own and set the pot back to the table for Stone and Granger to fight over. Stone won, grabbing it half a second before Granger could. Everyone settled back into eating silently after that.

"When are we leaving?" she finally asked when she could stand it no longer.

"As soon as you're ready," Lark said.

"What's the weather like in Vegas this time of year?"

"Hot," Lark said.

Okay, so conversation was a no go apparently. She scarfed down the food and burnt her mouth gulping the coffee then stood. All three men were watching her, and her face flamed. "I'll just go get ready then. No time to waste." She fled the room, but not before she heard Granger comment on her appreciatively and then there was a crash, something had been thrown across the room. Stone's laughter followed her as she hurried up the stairs.

Ebony didn't really need a shower, but she decided to indulge anyway. All the guaranteed hot water was a luxury she didn't usually have, and it settled her nerves. That was the most uncomfortable breakfast she'd ever sat through, and it really ruined the delicious food and coffee. Her stomach was currently doing flips and she felt like her nerves were raw from the constant waves of desire that just being around Lark sent through her body. Her eyes drifted up to the removable massaging showerhead knowing that she could do something about one of those things.

Lark didn't bother knocking, he walked right into the bedroom expecting to see her ready to go. She'd been dressed when she came downstairs, so hearing the shower running was unexpected. She hadn't shut the bathroom door and he couldn't stop himself from taking a few steps in that direction, catching the scent of the shampoo coming out on a wave of steam.

He had thought to see how long she needed to be ready to leave but it seemed the answer was probably at least twenty minutes. He turned, ready to go downstairs and tell his men to hold off for another half hour, but then he heard her moan. She'd moaned like that when she had taken a bite of bacon and he'd instantly hardened at the breakfast table. Hearing it now, knowing what she must be doing in the shower, he thought he was going to explode.

His entire body stiffened, and his cock went rock solid, straining against his jeans. Every fiber of his body was screaming at him to go in there, to do all the dirty things that would make them both scream in satisfaction. He wanted to be the one causing those moans to slip from her lips, not some goddamn bacon or a fucking showerhead. He wanted to press his mouth to hers and swallow those sounds, claim them for himself.

He knew he couldn't, not yet. He also knew he should leave and let her have this private moment. She'd probably be pissed if she found out he had heard that one little moan. The way her face had pinked when she'd let one slip at the breakfast table had been one of the most adorable things he'd ever seen. He hated that he'd shared that moment with his men.

Lark knew he should go, but he didn't leave, he stood there and listened to the sounds she made and the water splashing. He shoved a hand down his waistband and gripped himself, stroking to the rhythm of the splashes he heard and when she gasped out a sound that had to be his name, he exploded in his hand and bit his lip to keep back his own moan of pleasure.

The sound of the water turning off had him rushing from her bedroom and to his own. He felt like a teenager hiding his shame and despite his release he couldn't stop his erection from reappearing when he thought of her stepping out of the shower covered in water and flushed with her own release.

"Lark we ready or what?" Granger said through the closed bedroom door.

"Thirty minutes," Lark shouted back as he shoved his pants and underwear down and headed for the shower. He needed the cold water before he could sit in a small space with her.

CHAPTER TWELVE

Ebony dressed in jeans and a purple tank top with matching sandals, feeling like a princess in her very own fairy tale. Too bad it was going to have a Grimm Brothers' ending and not a Disney one.

She pulled her hair into a ponytail high on her head and applied a bare minimum of makeup. She was feeling pretty damn good about herself when she left the room, purse, and the clothes she'd come here in were bundled in her arms. She decided to leave the clothes she hadn't worn, not wanting to be greedy, but she did stick the deodorant in her purse since it couldn't be returned. She was going to ask Lark to take her to her place first so she could grab some things for the trip, she didn't want to keep relying on him for everything. She had money but she couldn't get over the instilled fear of spending anything she didn't have to. If Lark really didn't want it in the end, she would tell him to donate it to the orphanage when she was gone, or maybe her soulsister would need it to start her new life. Ebony shook her head, no that wouldn't be necessary, the woman would be showered with wealth as Lark's wife.

Ebony's throat stung, her eyes watered and she had to take a few deep breaths to keep those thoughts from surfacing further. She needed to keep her mind on the end goal, the end goal hadn't changed. She took one last glance in the mirror to make sure she didn't look upset, then left the room.

Lark was standing outside her door freshly showered and dressed waiting for her. "Are you ready?" he asked sharply.

She nodded, unsure at the anger in his tone.

"Leave that," he said, motioning to the bundle.

"They're my things," she'd said feeling dumb in the moment as she looked up at him. "Actually I was hoping we could swing by my place so I could grab what else I might need."

He frowned at her and glanced at the pile she was now hugging to her chest. "Are they important to you?"

"Well, no, these aren't," she admitted. "I do need my purse, but the clothes are just clothes."

"Dirty clothes, leave them here, we'll get what we need in Vegas."

"Oh, okay," she whispered and turned to dump the clothes on the bed. "You don't have to," she whispered, knowing he had followed right behind her. "I have clothes to take, clean clothes at home." Was he embarrassed by her dirty things? He probably didn't want to walk around Vegas with a halfling who looked like she did most of the time. "I have a few nicer things I can grab to fit in better." That was a bit of a stretch to the truth, but she was trying to be reasonable.

He grunted. "I don't care what you wear, Ebony, but we already had this discussion," he whispered back and put his hands on her shoulders. "I'm taking care of you, because you're my soulmate. You deserve to have everything you want; do you really want that?" he motioned to the pile on the bed.

Ebony shivered. "Because I'm your soulwife?" she asked quietly.

Lark leaned forward; his lips brushed over her ear sending a lightning shock of desire to her core. "Is that what you want, to be my wife before you let me take you to bed and show you all the things our bodies can do together? You want to get the government even more involved in our lives? Track your cycle, report how many times I come inside you so they can decide if we are truly trying to procreate? Do your civic duty?"

Ebony bit back a groan and somehow managed to pull away and turn to face him. His words were a mix of the most ridiculous crap she had ever heard, and the filthiest. Why did it turn her on? "No, I want to find my soulsister," she said, voice shaking slightly, and walked past him out of the room on wobbly legs clutching only her purse to her chest.

How easy it would be to fall into bed with him, to give in to all that her body was screaming at her to do. But then what? She could die at the hands of her soulsister. She could die of cancer before she even finds her soulsister. She could kill her soulsister and become a fullsoul just in time to die of the cancer creeping through her body.

They could both know what love and lust and fulfillment feels like, and then she could leave him alone for the rest of his life.

Tears stung her eyes. The kindest thing for her to do was keep a distance, to give her piece of soul to her soulsister and let the woman and Lark have a real full life together.

So why did she want to risk everything and make a different choice?

"Looks like the lady is ready to go!" Stone said cheerily as she reached the bottom of the steps. She appreciated that he didn't mention her teary eyes.

"I am," she agreed and gave him a shaky smile.

"And the boss?" Stone glanced up the stairs behind her.

Ebony turned to look as well but there was no sign of Lark. "Oh, I think he's coming."

Stone's lips quivered with a held back smile. "You're really giving him a run for it, little Ebony. I've never seen him so off his game."

"Off his game?" she asked in a moment of confusion she could only blame on the haze of desire and confusion Lark had coated her brain with.

Stone just winked and she got it. Lark obviously wasn't used to women denying him. They probably fell over each other to get a chance with a man like him, she'd seen a bit of that at the restaurant. Ebony felt suddenly cold, and she wrapped her arms around herself and rubbed her arms. A man like that, with all that experience would never be happy with what she would reveal under her clothes, or her lack of experience in bed. Just another reason to keep her distance. Seeing disappointment on his face would probably break her.

"Here comes Casanova now," Stone said loudly, and Ebony turned to see Lark descend the stairs with a calm look of annoyance. It seemed to be his resting face and didn't give away what he was really thinking under it.

"Is the truck ready?" Lark demanded of Stone as his eyes roamed over her.

Ebony dropped her arms and tried to relax her face into a neutral position, but she doubted he missed the redness of her eyes or the way she clasped her hands nervously in front of her.

"Yep, Granger's out there already. He was on the phone with the airport."

"Great, let's go," Lark said and put a guiding hand on Ebony, pushing her out the door and toward the waiting truck. He opened the passenger door, and she hopped in. Stone and Granger sat in the back and Lark was driving. No one talked for a while as they wound their way through parts of the city she'd never dreamed she'd see. The sparks of sexual tension between her and Lark tingled through her but the distance kept it at a low hum that she could actually enjoy, and as she stared out the window, she relaxed with a contented sigh.

Lark sucked in a breath at the sound and she swung her gaze to him. He was sitting stiff, hands gripping the wheel tightly and his lips pressed together in a thin line.

"Have you ever been on a plane before?" Stone asked, distracting her from Lark's discomfort.

"No," she admitted. "I'm a little nervous."

"Lark only travels in style, I think you'll like it," Stone said with a laugh.

"Well then, hopefully I don't puke all over," she said with a grimace She'd hate to embarrass herself and she'd especially hate to mess up something nice. If the plane was anything like the house, it was far cleaner than anything she'd ever been in.

"Don't worry, there's a private bathroom and puke bags too. But the day is clear and hopefully our flight will be smooth," Lark reassured her, then reached over and patted her leg.

It was a gentle touch, meant to be reassuring, but it sent a thrill through her body that only added to her nerves. She looked over at him, but his eyes were forward again as if the touch had meant nothing, though his body was once again stiff and focused.

"Lucky me," she said quietly and stared out her window again, no longer feeling relaxed. She wondered what Taylor was up to. Probably already at work and getting yelled at by Glick because they were short a girl today. Ebony felt bad for her workmates, she wouldn't have chosen to leave them in a lurch if it hadn't been so important to go right away. Glick would have her replaced by tomorrow though, she had no doubt, it was easy to find halflings who wanted a semi-decent job.

"So you two going to get hot and heavy in Vegas? It's not illegal you know, you *are* soulmates," Stone said, breaking the silence.

Ebony wanted to curl up and die, she crushed herself as close to the door as she could, as far from Lark as possible.

"Nice," Granger chastised.

"What?" Stone said with a laugh.

"You've embarrassed her," Granger said. "Lark, aren't you going to defend your lady?"

"There's nothing to be embarrassed about. She's my soulmate and I have every intention of doing every goddamn dirty thing to her that she'll consent to, and making her scream my name over and over again. In Vegas or not," he said simply.

Granger and Stone laughed. Ebony stared at Lark with mouth gaping, unable to respond. She'd never heard such a horrifying thing in her life. Horrifying and titillating and damn if she didn't love it even as her entire body flamed with embarrassment, and desire.

Lark finally glanced her way when the boys in the back stopped laughing and the silence settled. "What did you expect darling? You may be able to ignore the pull of our souls but fuck if I can or will. The only legal sex in my life will be with you and I actually look forward to spending the rest of my life between your sweet thighs."

"Oh my god!" she screeched, gaining laughs from the boys in the back again. "You can't be serious! You don't even know me."

"Doesn't matter," he said simply.

"Doesn't matter? Are you fucking kidding me? It sure as hell matters. I've resisted going to bed with anyone for this long, I'm not about to jump into yours just because we're soulmates. That shit was made up for us as a punishment, did you know that? This is hell! Hell on earth, brought about by the gods who are supposed to love us? Fuck that shit. I will *not reproduce, ever.*"

"Who said anything about reproducing, babe? I'm just talking a lifetime of great sex." Lark flashed her a devilish smile.

"You're not the only one who grew up in this fucked up world," he said darkly. "I've spent my entire life trying to find a touch of good in this shithole. You just might be it."

Stone and Granger grunted agreement in the back.

Thankful that silence sat in the truck the rest of the drive, Ebony didn't know what to think or how to respond, so she didn't. He wanted to sleep with her, that was no surprise, but him being a fullsoul and still not wanting to have kids, that *did* surprise her.

It didn't change the fact that she was on her way to sacrifice her soul though.

She wouldn't enter into any kind of a relationship with him, knowing that. She flicked a glance at him and along the scar that ran from his ear and disappeared into his shirt. For the first time she wondered if he had grown up a halfling. Was that a soulbattle wound? Did she dare to think he might actually understand something of what she was going through? Or was he just saying what he thought would get him laid?

When Lark parked outside a small airport, she took a few deep breaths to gather her nerve as he walked around to open her door. She appreciated the gallant act but refused his help in stepping down. She didn't want to touch him, didn't want to feel that spark that meant they were legally allowed and morally obligated to fuck and reproduce.

Stone and Granger were already heading toward a small plane with its engine roaring. She moved to follow them, but Lark grabbed her arm. "We aren't going with them."

"What? Why not?"

"Different leads, we're heading to Vegas, they're heading to DC."

"There aren't any halflings in DC," she said with confusion.

"I'm certain you're right," he said dismissively and led her to a tiny plane.

She'd thought the others were heading toward a small one, but this looked like it wouldn't hold more than herself and Lark. "Um, where's the pilot?" she asked as they got close. The engines weren't running and although the staircase was down, there didn't seem to be any movement anywhere.

"Don't need one."

Ebony blinked up at him, her stomach clenching in fear, "You?"

"Ouch, such doubt. You don't know the half of what I'm capable of, Ebony," he said huskily, his tone and intense green gaze filled her mind with what some of those things might be, sending a thrill throughout her body. He leaned close enough that she could feel his breath soft against her cheek. "But I'm looking forward to showing you a few things."

"I—I can't," she stuttered. "Lark, I—" she almost told him everything right then, but she couldn't. What if he refused to help her, knowing the truth? She wasn't paying him. He was doing this because he thought he was going to have a life with her. She wanted to tell him, but she couldn't, she had to make sure he kept helping her. And selfishly, she didn't want to hear him say that he was fine helping her go to her death, because he'd have a fullsoul soulmate waiting for him in the end anyway.

Lark straightened and gave her a mocking smile. "Ebony, love, how long do you think you can deny us something we both so desperately want?" He ran a finger along her chin sending sparks of recognition straight to her brain, her eyelids fluttered, and her heart threatened to melt. He leaned close and brushed his lips against hers softly. "I have never been very good at denying myself something I desire, and I have never desired anything as much as I desire you. I will take you to my place on the coast, we can spend weeks doing every filthy thing that comes to mind once the soulbattle is done and you're safe."

That snapped her out of the melting state he'd so quickly

brought her to, back to reality. She didn't have a future past the battle and any involvement with him before then would just make things harder. She pulled away from his touch and turned around. "Let's keep this strictly business," she said shakily.

"You *are* my business Ebony," he said and gripped her shoulders tightly. He leaned down and pressed a kiss to her neck, making her shudder.

"Lark, I—"

"I'm not a patient man, Ebony. I do take no for an answer, just don't expect me to stop asking."

He moved slightly, put a hand to her lower back and pushed her on toward the plane. She didn't know what to say and she was glad he didn't seem to expect a real answer.

Once they entered the plane, he was all business. He helped her get strapped into the copilot seat, told her to not touch *anything*, then went about turning on engines, closing the door and pushing all kinds of buttons and switches.

"How did you learn this?" she asked, hoping to distract herself as they started to move. She gripped the arms of the seat and stared straight ahead, as if she could warn him if they were about to crash.

"A couple years ago I helped someone find their soulmate, they paid me with this plane and so I got lessons," he said, flipping a switch and telling someone, somewhere, that they were about to take off.

"All clear," came a female voice through the speaker. "Have a wonderful time in Vegas, Mr. Duport. Win big."

He glanced at Ebony with a wink, "I always win."

The female on the other end laughed and he hit a switch, cutting off whatever else she may have been about to say.

Ebony closed her eyes and braced herself as they took off. She was sure this was it; this was how she was going to die. Her stomach flipped and jolted; the tiny plane dipped as it climbed.

"I'm going to be sick," she gasped, two hands covered her mouth and she looked at him helplessly. She was going to lose all that delicious bacon.

"Oh shit," he said and handed her a small paper bag. "We'll level out soon, try to breathe through it."

"Fuck you," she snapped and grabbed the bag seconds before everything she'd eaten flew out of her mouth.

"Aw, sweetie," he said with a little too much mirth for her liking, but at least it helped with the mortification of having just thrown up in front of him. She groaned and turned away.

She was startled by the feel of his hand rubbing her back. "Don't worry, it happens to Stone every time; he hates flying."

That did make her feel a little better.

CHAPTER THIRTEEN

Lark wanted to wrap her in his arms and comfort her as she shivered and puked beside him. The downside of being the pilot meant the best he could do was offer a soothing word and back rub.

He hated when Stone puked, saw it as a weakness that needed to be dominated, squelched, and overcome. But seeing Ebony do it made him feel all kinds of different things. He could imagine a life taking care of her when she was ill.

His thoughts went dark as he pictured the email response he'd gotten from the doctor he'd sent her records to. The best in the country and someone he trusted implicitly.

Get her to me as soon as possible. She'll never survive without the rest of her soul and even then, things don't look good.

He'd nearly thrown his laptop across his office this morning. He was more determined than ever to get her soul to her so she could have a better chance. With that and the best doctor and medicine that money could buy, he'd help her, he'd stay by her side, and he'd see her better.

Lark glanced her way. She was looking pale but improving and staring straight ahead. The way was smooth from here so she should be alright. "You can lay down in the back, the seat reclines back there but watching the horizon is usually the best cure."

The small plane had a space for two in the rear with seats that reclined into beds and a bathroom. It wasn't as nice as the plane Stone and Granger were on right now, but for such a short flight, it was all they needed.

"I'm afraid to move," she said with a bitter laugh.

"Trust me to get us there safe, Ebony, and I promise it'll be a worthy trip."

"An experience like no other," she agreed.

They settled into companionable silence and the sparks of desire that flowed through him from just being near her didn't irritate him like they had in the truck. Probably because he didn't have two idiots in the back seat, worrying him with what they were thinking about his soulmate. Simple possessiveness didn't even come close to what he felt about her.

He relaxed with the feelings, letting it become a low hum of desire as he went through the familiar routine of flight.

The rest of the flight went smoothly. Ebony watched the sky pass and as they got closer to Vegas, her nerves about what they were here to do started to resurface. She puked again as they descended to land, and she practically jumped out of the plane as soon as he opened the door. She was breathing deeply, trying to calm herself when an airport worker hurried up to scan her hand. She nearly panicked but Lark stepped in front of her and stuck out his hand.

"My wife," he said as the woman scanned him.

The woman didn't argue, and Ebony was surprised by the ease of it. She'd expected travel as a halfling to be full of questions and hassle, maybe Vegas was just more accepting than other places. The woman enthusiastically greeted Lark.

"I'll have your plane stored until you're in need of it again, Mr. Duport," she said as Lark slyly passed her a folded bill.

It wasn't until then that Ebony realized the woman was a halfling. The woman's eyes widened at the money she clutched desperately. Ebony could see the dullness in her eyes, and yet she looked healthy and happy, and had—in Ebony's opinion—a pretty good job. No halfling she'd ever met looked that good.

"Thank you, Jamie," Lark said, obviously reading the woman's nametag. Lark moved to Ebony's side and grasped her arm lightly, guiding her away from the plane. "You look surprised," he said quietly.

"I am. I guess I expected travel into a new city would be more difficult. Don't they care that a new halfling is here to plague their city resources?"

"Is that why you never left the city?"

"No, I never left because I couldn't afford to," she said with a shrug. It was normal to her; it was what every halfling she knew dealt with.

"Where would you have gone, if it were possible?" Lark asked as he led her to a waiting car.

"Somewhere tropical," she said with a sigh. "I've always wanted to be on a tropical island without many people."

"Sounds heavenly," Lark agreed. He held the passenger door open for her, then walked to the driver's seat. "I'll put tropical island into the travel plans first," Lark said when he got in.

Ebony only grunted in response and looked out the window. She stared like a kid in a toy shop at everything they passed. She knew she probably looked like a total dork as she oohed and aahed at the buildings, the lights, and the people; but she didn't care, she'd never seen anything like it.

The main strip of Vegas was open to halflings and fullsouls without discrimination. It was one of the last cities in the U.S. where there was almost as much normal interaction as there had been before the curse. Her mother had talked about it like a sinful place to never want to visit. Ebony was fairly certain it was where her mother had met her father and that was one of the reasons she'd felt so negatively about it. Ebony's father had seduced her mother and left, never even knowing that a baby had been conceived. Her mother's story had been that promises of all sorts had been whispered between the drinks he'd plied her with and the bed he'd brought her to. But that in the harsh morning none of it had mattered. She'd been left, and when she knew she was pregnant, had decided that she was going to make the best of it, halfsoul child or not.

She loved her mother for her strength. Ebony wasn't sure she could make the same decision if she'd been in that situation. Of course that was probably because she knew the reality of what a halfsoul grew up with. Her mother had been under the impression, because of the lies perpetuated by the government, that the halfsouls lived a decent life; separate, but decent. That their parents could survive nicely, provide well for their children, and go on maybe to meet their soulmate and have more children, fullsoul children, even after having a halfling child.

It wasn't true for anyone Ebony knew.

Looking around at the unfamiliar city, Ebony could almost understand her mother's belief in that lie. Growing up in Vegas would have given her mother a very different view of what a halfsoul went through on a daily basis. Maybe if her mother had stayed here, she would have been able to afford better healthcare for herself, maybe Ebony wouldn't be counting down her own last days. She rubbed at her chest but dropped her hand quickly when she noticed Lark's angry glance. If her mother had stayed, maybe she never would have met Lark. That would have made this situation less complicated.

Her mother's choice to move to LA when she found out she was pregnant was because she didn't want to make trouble for the father. Apparently, he found his soulmate soon after their one-night stand and it would have been very scandalous and unpleasant to be faced with a halfsoul child when you were busy making fullsoul babies with your soulwife. He probably would have demanded her mother have an abortion, which was easy enough to get if a woman wanted one. But her mother had decided she wanted the child, never knowing if she'd have a chance with a soulmate to make another. She'd wanted a child no matter what.

That was a viewpoint that Ebony could only imagine came from a fullsoul who'd grown up with two happy fullsoul parents. She didn't blame her mother; her mother didn't know how hard it was going to be.

Ebony held no hard feelings toward the man that had fathered her, either, but she did wonder what it would have been like to know him—what it would have been like to meet her fullsoul half siblings.

Probably devastating.

Her mother had likely done the best thing, keeping her existence a secret.

Ebony looked out at the city and tried to let go of the past and what ifs. The energy here was definitely different than LA With all the flashing lights and smiling faces, she felt like anything was possible. And what a dangerous feeling that could be, she thought as she dared a look at Lark and his enticing body so close to her.

Lark was silent as they drove but she couldn't forget he was there. Her body sparked, even at this distance, with awareness of him. It was as if her cells were reaching out and trying to make a connection to his, as if they wouldn't be whole until they were pressed against him. Would that awareness ease if she gave in to her desire? Would one good romp around the bed with him satisfy the aching need that had settled over her? Would her skin quit lighting up at the mere thought of him naked and looming over her?

Ebony took a shaky breath, she had to calm herself down. She pressed her thighs together to try and stop the pulsing ache, but it only seemed to amplify it and she squirmed in her seat until Lark made a strangled sound beside her that told her that he was aware of what her body was doing. She glared out at the street and willed her body to relax. She couldn't wait to get out of this small space and get some air.

When he pulled into the parking garage of a hotel, she finally turned to look at him again. "What's the plan?"

"We'll get settled in a room and then I want you to meditate."

"Meditate?" she said with doubt.

"Yes, I want you to reach out for the connection to your soulsister, see if you can tell whether or not she's in the city."

"And if I don't feel anything?" She already had her doubts about her soulsister being here. As soon as they'd landed she had decided that she felt no different and that could only mean they weren't about to get lucky.

"Doesn't necessarily mean she isn't here. We'll walk around and you can assess as we go. Some soulsiblings have strong connections and seem to feel each other over hundreds of miles, others don't. You may have to be in the same room to feel her."

This was feeling more and more like a wild goose chase to her and she didn't hide the frustration in her voice. "Is that your usual method for finding soulsiblings? Seems a little farfetched."

"It's just a shot. Stone and Granger are investigating another lead and yes, it is a usual place to start when there is so little information to go on. Most of the time a soulsibling can sense another within a reasonable distance. Like how you knew for certain she wasn't in LA. Generally you can count on a sense when you're within a hundred miles of each other."

"True, she felt so... far away, so small," she shook her head feeling like her words were ridiculous.

"Does she still?" Lark asked.

Ebony frowned. "Yes, I think so."

"It certainly won't hurt to give meditation a shot, and then we'll walk, just in case. You also might need to give your senses the time to adjust to the surroundings. If you're too amped up with travel and getting sick on the plane and... other things going on in your body that are new."

He didn't have to say it, she knew what he meant. She was overrun with desire and that was not something she was used to feeling at all.

"So we will take a walk. We may get lucky. At the very least you'll get to enjoy the city, see something new."

"And the guys might find something in DC?" she asked, though she wasn't sure what they could possibly think they'd find in a city that didn't allow any halflings in it. What leads could they be following? Where was Lark getting his information?

"Yes, they might."

She eyed him skeptically but didn't comment. He was good at what he did, it was why she'd sought him out in the first place. Her hand rubbed absently at an ache high on her chest, she just hoped he was as fast as they said.

"Where do we go if she isn't here? What is the next place you usually search?"

"Chicago," he said with a frown, and she gasped.

Chicago was a terrible place, or so she was told. Mostly halflings lived there now which meant there was a large underground nosoul population. It was dangerous, she had never in her life wanted to go there.

"Don't worry, I'll protect you no matter where we are," Lark said.

Ebony nodded and looked up at the tall building they were parked outside. One new experience at a time she told herself.

"This is a nice place, they're going to scan me," she whispered mostly to herself.

"No, they are going to scan me."

"And assume I'm just your halfling whore?" she asked with a resigned sigh. It was what she had to do she supposed. It would be common here, even in a place as open to halflings as Vegas, one of the main occupations for them was prostitution; highly illegal prostitution now that sex between non soulmates was illegal. Places like this probably turned a blind eye to a lot of things like that.

"You care a lot about what other people think," he said with a cock of his head.

"You would too if you were constantly judged by other people," she snapped.

He laughed and she glared. How dare he make fun of what her life had been like.

"You think I'm not judged? You think that anyone who knows what I do thinks I'm a great guy to be around? I'm not welcome in fullsoul society because they all think I'm tainted by the halflings I help; all are afraid I'm going to dig into their little secrets," he spat. "The women come to my bed looking for a trip out of their daily boring lives knowing that they won't have to see me at daddy's dinner party. You think you're judged because you're not a fullsoul. Try being one and still seeing the judgment in their eyes because you refuse to conform to their ideal of what we should all be; how we should all work to appease the whim of the gods who cursed us." He turned and stared out the front window. "I grew up a halfling, Ebony. In an orphanage. I thought getting my full soul would fix my entire life but it's just a new set of problems. A new set of rules they want me to conform to. It isn't the freedom everyone thinks it is."

"Oh." She didn't know what to say.

"So yeah, let them talk, let them assume because you know what, it'll give them a little thrill to gossip about their guests, and their dull lives deserve a little titillating if you ask me."

Ebony couldn't help laughing. "It's true. We gossiped about the guests constantly, best part of the job some days."

"Well then, soulwife, what do you say we give them something to tell their friends about?"

"Not your wife," she insisted as he got out and came around the car to open her door.

"Details," he said with a sly smile, and offered her his arm.

She wasn't sure what to do with this change in attitude of his. It was disconcerting to see him smile and tease. She almost preferred he went back to angry and annoyed. She took his offered arm and the thrill of connection zinged through her as they walked. He handed his keys to a valet and gave instructions for the bags in the back, then they walked into a gorgeous lobby.

Everything was gold and white and shining brilliantly under the many lights and there was a fountain in the middle of the lobby that made the most delightful sound to cover the murmur of voices. There were a lot of voices, the lobby was packed.

"Why are there so many people?"

Lark frowned. "I don't know for sure, but I'm glad I called ahead for a room."

A room, singular. Ebony's mind tripped on those words and she didn't hear anything else he was saying as they went through the crowd to the front desk. He had made reservations for just one room here. She knew she shouldn't be surprised, especially after what he'd said in the truck on the way to the airport, but still. It filled her with unease and anticipation, and she wasn't sure which was going to win.

The distraction was enough to keep her from noticing anyone staring at her as they crossed the lobby and once they were at the desk in front of a pretty girl in a white uniform, she knew it was too late to beg Lark for her own room.

"How can I help you, sir?" The woman said with a wide smile, her eyes glossing quickly over Ebony and dismissing her.

Lark held out his hand to be scanned. "We have a reservation."

She looked down at the screen in front of her. "Oh yes, welcome to the Garden Palace Mr. and Mrs. Duport."

Ebony made a sound of disagreement in her throat but Lark gripped her arm tight in warning, so she didn't correct the woman who was clacking away at the keys as if she had to write a novel in order to check them in.

"Your keys," she said finally, handing Lark a packet with the key cards and a map of the hotel.

"And the room for my associates, I expect them tonight, late probably."

This was news to Ebony, and she stared up at Lark in question, but he was smiling at the woman across the desk.

"You know we can't check someone in who isn't here, no matter who's paying, sir."

"If you give away their room to one of these suited buffoons, there will be a problem," he hissed and the woman took a step back.

"No, of course I wouldn't, Mr. Duport. You're a very good client, we will honor the reservation."

"Great then," Lark said and pulled Ebony away from the desk.

"Did you just threaten that poor woman?"

"Did it sound like a threat?"

"Yes!" Ebony hissed.

Lark just chuckled darkly and led her to a waiting elevator. "I have no intention of being forced into sharing a room with Stone and Granger tonight."

"Just me," she said under her breath, but by his grunt of mirth she knew he'd caught it.

"Besides, we stay here often enough we really should always have a room on standby."

When the elevator doors closed them in, she wasn't sure if she was relieved to be away from the busy lobby and so many questioning eyes, or nervous about the close space with Lark. He was still holding onto her arm and it was sending waves of tingles from her arm to the rest of her body. She couldn't hold back a slight shiver.

"That wasn't so bad," he said, dropping her arm and hitting the button for their floor. "They may have all looked because you're a very attractive woman, but they didn't think anything of it. They weren't judging."

"Just another halfling whore."

"Maybe to them, but they don't matter," he said with a smile and touched her chin gently.

"Right," Ebony said. "The only thing that matters is what *you* want."

He smiled wickedly and let his finger trail along her jawline then down her neck and stopping at her shoulder. "Just me?" he asked as she shivered from that single touch.

Ebony was thankful that the doors opened then, keeping her from having to answer. They stepped off onto their floor, and a few doors down, Lark was swiping the keycard. He held the door open gallantly and she stepped inside, not expecting it to be anything more than she'd cleaned a hundred times.

She was wrong.

CHAPTER FOURTEEN

Ebony was speechless when she entered. There was a large sitting area set up around a fireplace and television. A balcony that looked out high over the city strip, and up on a landing, as if set apart, but not quite private, was a large bed. Only one.

Ebony stared at it and bit her lip. Lark tipped the bellhop who'd arrived right behind them to deliver Lark's bags. She was frozen, thinking about that bed.

"Ebony?" Lark said gruffly after he'd shut the door behind the grateful young man.

"Lark, I—there's only one bed," she blurted.

He rubbed her arms from behind and bent close to whisper in her ear. "I decided to push you into my way of thinking." He kissed her neck, sending a shockwave of desire through her body.

"Please," she whispered but she wasn't sure if she was asking him to stop or keep going. Her knees were weak, her breath coming in pants and when his body pressed against her from behind, a groan escaped her lips.

"I never wanted a soulmate, Ebony, never sought you out,

but since you're here. I find I can't stop thinking about what it will be like to have you beneath me."

"Lark," she pleaded, her mind racing around all the reasons this was a bad idea. Why she needed to tell him no, to keep him at a distance. But when it came right to it, none of those reasons held a candle to her desire and underneath it all she was afraid. "I don't know how to do this." She finally admitted, afraid of disappointing him as much as anything.

He pulled back and turned her to face him, a satisfied look on his face. "You're a virgin?"

Her face flamed and she stepped back. "As are most halflings," she snapped.

He stepped toward her like a predator after its next meal. His eyes bright with desire. "No, most halflings are searching for a way to feel alive any way they can, and sex is the cheapest way to get it."

"Not me," she whispered. "I never wanted anyone, even without suppressants."

"What about now?" he asked, closing the distance between them and hooking a finger into the waistband of her pants, pulling her forward until their lower bodies touched and his face was a breath from hers.

Her breathing was erratic, her body on fire and she couldn't resist reaching out and touching his arms to steady herself. She looked into his green gaze and felt her heart flip, and everything she'd put in place to prevent this very thing from happening was suddenly gone. "Now I want you," she admitted with a whisper.

As soon as the words were out of her mouth, he was smashing his lips to hers. His tongue was hot and sweet as it pressed between her lips, demanding she open to him. She did, with hesitation and fear of not being enough, not being able to give him what he was asking for. She tried to ignore the doubts and worries as his hands ran up and down her back, finally settling at her ass and squeezing it as he pressed her closer. She could feel his erection, pressed hard into her belly and it sent another rush through her.

Giving her no time to think, he moved them to the bed and gently guided her down onto it. He hovered over her, lips still clasped to hers. Then he moved them to her neck, licking and nipping, tasting her flesh as his hands worked at her clothing. His fingers moved under her shirt, leaving a hot trail where he touched her and stopping when he hit her bra. He sat up so he could pull her shirt up and off. He froze then, staring down at her.

She wanted to cry, she knew what he was seeing, and it tore her apart. She moved to cover herself, but he reached down and ran a finger over the red, angry scar that went from above her left breast, around and down to the middle of her ribcage where it ended in a deep purple mark.

"I'm so sorry I didn't try to find you sooner," he whispered and the emotion she heard in those words broke her.

Tears flooded her eyes and when he bent to kiss along the scar, leaving not a single inch unloved, she let the tears flow unchecked down her face. His hand caressed over the fake mound and he didn't frown, didn't retract from the coolness that was ever present there, just gave it a loving touch and that act made her accept herself in a way she never thought she would.

"I could have given you better, I could have bought the best doctor in all the world," he whispered as he laid his face against the scar.

Ebony reached out and ran a hand through his hair. "It wouldn't have mattered," she whispered. "I'm dying."

His grip on her tightened and she could feel him shudder; this big, strong, beautiful man trembled with emotion. When he moved, it was with a new determination. He kissed her deeply and tore at the rest of her clothing, then his own. Soon she was lost to sensation as he played on the mate spark they shared. His hands ran over her body and a trail of fire ran behind them. He kissed her belly, his hands gripping her thighs as his thumbs rubbed so close to her apex that she was sure he must feel the wetness that was already seeping from her.

"Ebony," he growled and laid a chaste kiss to her mound then moved until his face was even with hers once again. "I want you so many ways but knowing this is your first time we'll take it slow."

She could only nod, she wanted him every way possible and she wouldn't have cared if he demanded her get up on her knees and shove her face against the pillow, all she wanted was him inside of her and this deep ache to go away.

He hovered over her with passion in his eyes as she was trembling with need, ready to accept him, no matter what the future held. Then a tingle of a thought flashed through her mind and she put a hand to his chest, stopping him as he parted her thighs with a knee.

"You're stopping me now?" he growled, but he didn't move and the knowledge that he would indeed stop if that was what she wanted was further proof that he was the perfect kind of man.

"I can't get pregnant," she said, embarrassment making her cheeks red. "I won't do that."

He smiled wickedly and leaned down to kiss the tip of her nose, her chin and finally her lips. "I had a vasectomy years ago, love. I won't add to the world's problems either."

She couldn't believe how sexy those words were, and illegal for a fullsoul. She wrapped her legs around his hips and urged him forward like a hussy and delighted in the groan he let out as he slid into her. He took it slow as promised, pausing and relishing the moment with her. It was an interesting feeling; a fullness, a tightness but it wasn't uncomfortable and she wanted more. She lifted her hips, telling him to proceed.

"You're sure? I don't want to hurt you," he asked, holding himself still above her as her heels dug into his ass.

"I'm sure, Lark. I want all that you can give me."

His eyes half closed and he groaned. "Oh baby, you have no idea what you're asking for," he said then finally he entered her fully and his eyes locked to hers. She never imagined such an intimate moment and the gasp of pain was so short lived it wasn't even worth mentioning. It was nothing in comparison to the absolute completeness she felt with him buried inside of her. And when he started to move it was as if the world didn't exist, the future didn't matter, and everything she'd been through in her short life was worth it to be right here, right now experiencing this with him.

It was the most perfect moment, and she was sure no one had ever experienced anything like it. She was sure that no heaven could compare and if she died and spent an eternity in hell, she'd remember this moment with a smile because she was his, and he was hers, and their souls were singing to each other.

Lark held her close as she dozed, listening to her heartbeat slow and her breathing relax. Her eyes were closed and he thought she might actually fall asleep despite the fact that it was still daylight outside. Good sex did that, and fuck, that had been good. He'd never believed in the stories of soulmate sex being exquisite, but now he couldn't imagine settling for less.

In his mind he saw her scar, the very real reminder that they didn't have time to waste. She needed her full soul to fight the cancer. Even his money and the best doctors might not be enough without it, but he definitely planned to get her at least that. He would take her to the doctor he knew in Texas as soon as she was whole. Now more than ever, he knew he didn't want to live without her. No substitute would do, not even another body housing her soul would be enough for him. He'd rather die beside her body than accept a substitute for Ebony.

Her breathing became steady and her body relaxed in sleep. He couldn't remember the last time he'd had a woman asleep next to him. Usually he was sending them on their way as soon as their good time was over, or going on his. Anxious to move on to something else, work usually, with no interest in ever seeing their face again. Right now, with Ebony, he felt like he could stay in this position happily for the rest of his life.

How was he going to make that a reality? He'd had high hopes about stepping off the plane and having her feel her soulsibling nearby. It wouldn't have been the first time it had been that easy, though that wasn't the usual route his jobs took. No, a case like hers really was worth eight because it could likely take six months to find the soulsibling with no leads to go on.

She didn't have six months.

He thought about the letter from Senator Buchanan. It meant something, it hinted at a knowing and Lark was determined to find out why. He slipped out of the bed, immediately mourning the loss of her body against his, and headed for the shower, grabbing his cell on the way.

A message from Stone said they'd made it to DC and were requesting an audience with Shine Buchanan under the guise of discussing the halfling orphans. She wouldn't deny a request like that, it was her biggest talking point when vying for support for her father's reelection. It also said that Senator Buchanan was holding a campaign fundraiser in Vegas tomorrow night.

Perhaps the fates were going to work in his favor after all.

Another message had come, this one confirming two tickets to the Senator Buchanan campaign fundraiser tomorrow night in Las Vegas. Granger was a damn good man; he was almost always a step ahead with stuff like that. Lark set the phone down and started the shower. If Senator Buchanan knew something, Lark was going to convince him to reveal it. By any means necessary.

His phone rang with an unknown number before he could step under the spray. Lark debated for just a moment before picking it up and answering. It wasn't unusual for an unknown halfling to get his number, though it wasn't his official business line, he liked to field those calls through Stone and Granger.

"Yes."

"Oh, um, I'm not sure I have the right number... is this Lark the, uh, the searcher?" The voice was quiet and feminine, hesitating at the end like she might be struck down for saying the word out loud.

"What do you want?" he asked, knowing better than to reveal too much. If she needed a searcher, he was going to send her to his competition, he wasn't taking anything else on any time soon.

"I'm looking for Ebony," the woman said with a little more confidence.

Fear spiked through Lark as if this voice could reach through the phone and take her from him. "Who is this?" he demanded.

"Her best friend. Who the hell is this?" she snapped back.

"Lark."

"I need to talk to Ebony."

"She's sleeping."

"In the middle of the day?" she asked, clearly disbelieving.

"Yes, what do you want?"

"I want to talk to Ebony."

"No."

There was a sound of annoyance on the other end of the

phone and Lark debated hanging up but figured if this really was a friend of Ebony's, he didn't want to piss her off too much.

"Tell her to call Taylor. Something happened and I think she needs to know."

"What happened?"

"Glick was killed."

Lark's mind spun around the way they'd left the man, clearly still alive at the time, hadn't they? Lark had been so angry, so filled with hate for the man. He'd wanted to kill him, but had he?

"How and when?" Lark demanded.

"Well he never showed up to work this morning and so the police went to check out his place and they found him dead on his living room floor, shot in the back of the head."

Lark let out a relieved breath. It hadn't been him, they hadn't taken guns, there was no need when fists did just fine for a guy like him.

"I'll let Ebony know."

"There's more," Taylor said quickly before he could hang up.

"What?" Lark let his annoyance seep through, Ebony wouldn't care about Glick's death, the man was an idiot. Did this Taylor think Ebony would want to attend the coming funeral or some shit? If so, she obviously wasn't that close of a friend.

"The police want to question her. They know she's the only employee who just didn't show up to work today. It makes her look suspicious."

Fuck, that wasn't good.

"Don't tell me where you guys are, but tell her to call me. I want to know she's safe, and let her know that she needs to avoid scanning. I'm at work now, borrowed a moment on the phone but I'll be home later and I hope she calls me."

"Fine," Lark snapped.

"Hey!" she called before he could hang up.

"More?" he demanded, annoyed and staring at the warm, waiting shower.

"Be good to her. She's special."

"I know," he said and hung up the phone.

This was a complication they didn't need. Who would want Glick dead, besides him?

CHAPTER FIFTEEN

Shine Buchanan hated everything about her life. Every morning she was forced to go about a routine that would hide what she was because of the embarrassment and political destruction it would cause her father if revealed. She was taught to be ashamed of herself, and she had grown up determined to make him proud. So she accepted the shots that the nurse gave her, though she'd had no idea what was in them until recently, and she wore uncomfortable contact lenses that made her eyes a bright blue. She stood in front of groups of people on a regular basis wearing expensive suits with her hair perfectly styled and proclaimed the need to keep the populations safe, and separate. Most importantly, separate.

All the while she knew everything about herself was a lie. A lie that could destroy what her father had built for them. At least that's what he wanted her to believe; that everything he did was for her as much as him. She had come to doubt that more and more lately. She had begun to rethink the narrative he'd fed her, the narrative that she had been regurgitating in interviews since she was sixteen. Talking of things she had no experience with. She was a fool, and she was certain that ninety percent of the world saw her as such.

She'd never even met a halfling, let alone spent time with orphans. No halflings were allowed in DC and *she* wasn't allowed out. She looked down at her hand, she had no implant which meant she didn't even technically exist, and yet, she was one of the most well-known faces in the States, perhaps the world. She couldn't walk out of her house without security and a female companion. She was never alone in her home, and she didn't leave her room until Nurse Reagan told her she was ready.

"Good evening, love, ready for your vitamins?" Nurse Reagan walked in with a tray right on time. On it was a needle full of a red liquid and a glass of orange juice, always the same.

"Yes," Shine said with a sigh and turned from her desk where she'd been reading letters from supporters. All of them had been prescreened of course. Her father and his advisors saw everything before she did.

It kept her safe. Or so he had always said.

She lived in a perfectly curated life, the only thing her father couldn't control was her thoughts, and lately they'd begun to wander into dangerous territory.

Shine closed her eyes as the nurse jabbed the needle into her upper arm. The red liquid flowed into her, and she felt a deep relief.

"It's still sunny out there, so make sure you stay in the shade if you go out to the gardens this evening," Nurse Reagan said as she pulled the needle back and handed Shine her orange juice.

"Yes, Nurse," Shine said with a sigh, gazing down at her pale skin. She'd been blessed with a complexion that hated the sun, just another thing she kept to herself. It made other people uncomfortable to know her differences, at least that's what her father had always told her. She needed to represent the kind of woman that everyone else should strive to be. A fullsoul with a long life ahead of her, hopefully with her soulmate and lots of little fullsoul children.

There was a knock at the door, and she turned to see one of the maids standing with red cheeks and a smile. "Ma'am, your meeting is early."

"Meeting?" Nurse Reagan said with surprise and irritation. "I wasn't aware of a meeting."

"Oh, yes, some activists from the west coast wanted a quick interview about the orphanage efforts that Daddy put me in charge of over there," Shine said dismissively. It was the usual stuff she dealt with on a daily basis, no reason for Nurse Reagan to think anything of it.

"You really shouldn't be around anyone for the next hour, let the vitamins do their job," Nurse Reagan insisted. She gave a sharp look to the maid who was still standing in the doorway. "If I had known, I could have given it earlier."

She'd been dealing with the same thing all of her life, twenty years of three-times-a-day shots of vitamins followed by an hour of relaxation. All watched over and administered by Nurse Reagan. She had been born with a condition they said, and these shots kept her from going into seizures. She'd never experienced one, so she supposed it worked. The defect had been discovered as soon as she was born apparently, only once had she had the seizure and since then she'd been healthy and her father took great care of her. But if anyone knew that a fullsoul could have such a severe health issue, they would revolt against all the good that was being done in the country to keep people safe and healthy. Her mother had died at Shine's birth, perhaps she'd had the same condition? Her father would never say. The pictures of Shine's mother had showed a beautiful woman full of life and committed to the same political path as her father. Her mother wasn't pale and there'd been pictures of her on beaches so Shine knew her mother hadn't had the same condition. Her mother had been perfect, or so it would seem.

Shine had wanted to be just like her mother and had taken up the reins of the orphan plight as soon as she'd been old enough to stand in front of a camera and speak intelligently. She'd never thought to question anything her father or Nurse Reagan told her, until recently.

Nurse Reagan had been there at her birth, had witnessed the seizure and been by her side ever since, injecting her. Shine trusted the woman with her health, but she was a bit bossy about her personal life and Shine knew the woman was loyal to her father, not to her. No one was loyal to Shine.

"Tell them I'll be there shortly, Anne, and offer them some tea while they wait. I'll be fine in a minute, I'm sure. Always am," she muttered to herself.

"Yes, Ma'am," the maid said and turned quickly to do as she was bid.

"I don't think—" Nurse Reagan started.

"I'm twenty years old. Let me take a little responsibility for myself," Shine snapped and stood to change out of the casual clothes she'd been in.

Nurse Reagan pursed her lips but didn't argue, just watched with narrowed eyes as Shine moved about the room and got ready for the meeting. Shine knew that if she gave any indication that she wasn't fine, she'd find herself strapped down to her bed for the next few hours and probably getting an extra shot too. Her head was a little light, she had to admit, but she wasn't going to back down. She kept a stiff back and chin up as she dressed in slacks and a sweater, then pulled her blonde hair up into a ponytail. She added pearl earrings and decided she looked perfectly pristine and proper. No one would guess at the trouble with her health.

"Be careful," Nurse Reagan griped at her as she left the bedroom and headed down the stairs.

Shine didn't answer, she was always careful, because if she wasn't, she was contained for her own good. Her irritation was high as she walked into the room where the men were waiting, but she forgot all of it when she saw what was waiting for her.

The men sitting in front of her mother's antique tea service made her gasp. They were huge, and dangerous looking despite their suits and polished shoes. She knew now why Anne had been blushing when she'd announced their arrival. Shine's own cheeks heated as her eyes perused the two. They didn't get men like this in the house, her father would never allow it.

She eyed them with suspicion. She knew they weren't here just to talk about orphanages. She wasn't an idiot. She never met with new people without a quick background check, and they had to scan in to even get an appointment with her. She'd seen it all immediately but of course she hadn't alerted her security; too curious to meet them in person and see what they might really be here for. It was no secret that Lark Duport, the man who's plane they arrived in, supported the orphanages in LA, but it certainly wasn't his main focus. Which meant these men were searchers as well and they worked with the best in the country. What they wanted with her, she wasn't sure, but she was willing to bet it didn't have anything to do with the orphanages.

"Good evening, gentlemen," Shine said, gaining their attention.

They both stood, setting their teacups down gently.

"Ms. Buchanan," the blond one said, reaching out a hand. "I'm Stone and this is my colleague, Granger."

Stone was blond and beautiful, reminding her of a surfer. His skin was dark from the sun, and she was jealous of his ability to enjoy it. Granger had long dark hair and his looks made her think he must have Native American heritage. Tattoos showed on his neck and hands, and she wondered what was hiding under his suit. Her mouth watered a bit at the thought. Both men had bright eyes indicating their fullsoul status and by their muscular builds, she would guess they had fought for that. Definitely not the usual type of guest she saw here. They were likely orphans themselves; it could explain why they had an interest in them. Though she didn't believe for a second that was why they were really here.

"A pleasure," she said, shaking each man's hand then retreating to a chair. Once she was sitting, they both retook their seats. Perfect gentlemen. "You wanted to discuss orphanages?" she said with a raised eyebrow. She wouldn't call them liars, at least not yet.

"Yes, we hear that the ones on the east coast are run smoothly, and we hoped to gain some insight to take back to the west," Stone said, apparently the spokesman while Granger eyed her with a curious intensity.

Shine picked up a cup of tea and took a sip as she tried to decide how to approach this. After a moment she decided direct would get her more with these men. They weren't politicians, they'd value honesty and forthright conversation over verbal theatrics and trickery. "No," she said with a sigh.

"No?" Stone said with a laugh.

"That's not what you're here for," she said.

Stone sat back and smiled at her, it was a dazzling smile and almost distracted her from her determination. "No?"

"You arrived on a plane owned by Lark Duport."

Granger grunted and stiffened slightly. She kept him in her periphery but kept talking to Stone, he was obviously the one in charge here. He only raised an eyebrow in silent question, unperturbed by the revelation of her knowledge.

"What are two orphaned and fullsouled searchers doing asking for a meeting with me?" she pressed. "Does Lark Duport want political influence? I thought he did quite well, working below the surface to find his marks. No politician would interfere with that; they all want the same thing." She enjoyed the surprised looks on both men's faces as she rattled off her knowledge.

"You know a lot about us, but there's not anything in the system about you," Stone challenged, taking a sip from his cup of tea. It looked ridiculously small and delicate in his meaty hands. But he held it gently and set it down with barely a tink against the plate.

She laughed and bent her head, pulling out one contact lens. She sat up straight and was more than a little satisfied by the gasps from both men.

"Daddy's little secret," she said.

"Fuck," Granger hissed.

"I don't know why you're here, but I want to hire you," she said, putting the bright blue contact lens back in with practiced ease. If she let this opportunity slip by, she may never come across one again. Ready or not, she had to jump in with both feet here.

"We're currently on a case," Stone said.

"I can't get out; I have no chip and I have people watching me constantly. I want you to get me out, I want you to take me somewhere I can disappear."

Stone didn't give anything away with his expression, sitting calmly and sipping his tea. Granger was glaring at her, but he still didn't speak so she ignored him.

"Your father would be quite upset with us and there's record of our visit, we'd be first on his list of suspects."

"Not if he's in jail," she whispered into her cup as she took a sip.

"We're listening," Granger spoke for the first time, leaning forward.

She smiled. She had them. "He's been *testing* halflings," she whispered. "He brings them in from all over the world, has them breeding and he's taking the babies, seeing how much, if any, soul is in them and then killing them when he's done. I don't know what he's looking for, but whatever it is, he can't be right in how he's going about it and he needs to be stopped."

"Jesus," Stone hissed. "Where is he doing this?"

"He has a facility in Vegas."

"And you knew about it, spouting your drivel on television weekly and you knew this is what he was doing?" Granger hissed.

She stiffened, hating that it was exactly what everyone would think if she didn't do this. She met the dark and intimidating man's stare. "No, I swear I didn't. I just found out recently and I had no way of doing anything about it. I'm a prisoner here, don't you see. I can't leave without a chip. I'm never alone and... I have some medical needs. I couldn't do it on my own, but you're here. I know you two can help me. I know you guys care about the halfling community. Help me take one of its biggest predators down."

Shine could hardly breathe after the words were out but she kept her gaze locked on Granger's, watching as his eyes narrowed and he considered her words. She couldn't keep living this lie, didn't want to. If that meant her life was short because of lack of medicine, lack of *care* from Nurse Reagan well then fuck it. She couldn't go on letting horrible things happen to people under her nose.

She had always wanted her life to mean something, and until she knew better, she'd thought it did. Now she realized she was making meaning for the wrong side.

Granger finally shifted his gaze from her and met Stone's. They shared a look that Shine didn't understand, then Stone turned to her and nodded. "What is your plan?"

"I want to confront him, publicly, and then disappear. If I can reveal what he's been doing, there will have to be an investigation. While he's distracted, I can just, go away." She rubbed at her arm where she got three shots a day, uncomfortable with the decision even if it was right. "I don't want to be a pawn in his game any longer. It can't be what my life is meant for." Shine knew her voice was high and desperate but she didn't care, she *was* desperate. If these men walked out without her, she might never get another chance like this.

"He's got a campaign event scheduled for tomorrow night in Vegas," Granger said. "We can take you there, probably even get you in and then find you somewhere to hide when it's over."

"I can pay you," she assured them. "Just get me out of this city, get me there."

"We will get you to Vegas," Stone said.

She smiled and grabbed a cookie off the plate, excitement and nerves filling her body. She was really going to do this.

CHAPTER SIXTEEN

Ebony stretched in the unfamiliar bed and let the memories settle. She'd done it, she'd had sex, and it wasn't even illegal because Lark was her soulmate. She could hear the shower running so she knew she had a few moments alone and she was thankful. She flexed her body and realized there was a bit of soreness but that was expected after her first time. She waited for shame or regret, but it didn't come. She only felt satisfied, deeply satisfied and happy like she hadn't felt since her diagnosis.

She knew she shouldn't let it happen again, knew that getting any closer to him would just make things more difficult. But even as she told herself that, images of him embracing her as he ran his tongue over her scar and apologized, filled her head. As if he could have done a damn thing about it if he'd found her sooner.

She shook her head and hopped out of bed, threw on a robe, then made the bed to get rid of some of her anxious energy. Her cancer was no one's fault, it *just was*, and what she had to do before she died, *just was* as well.

Nothing had changed so she needed to get back to the plan.

She sat on top of the covers and closed her eyes. She didn't know how to meditate but figured it was just concentrating, so she searched in herself for the spark that told her she had a soulsister. She concentrated on it, coaxing it to reach out into the nearby universe in search of its other half.

A noise had her eyes popping open and she saw Lark emerge from the bathroom with only a towel around his waist, his chest glistening with water and his hair towel-dried and messy in the most delicious way. Her eyes followed a rivulet drip off a lock and make its way down his chest and dip into his bellybutton. She envied that drop of water and her tongue flicked at the roof of her mouth, wanting to dip in and sip it from him.

"Hey," she said quietly, feeling a bit of the awkwardness she was congratulating herself on not having earlier.

He smiled at her and winked, making a thrill of pleasure ripple through her body.

She gulped, willing her body under control. "I'm meditating, but I don't feel anything."

He shrugged as if it didn't matter in the least. "That's fine, it was worth a shot. Your soulsister probably doesn't have a huge pull, since you have more than half of the soul yourself. I imagine you'll have to get close to feel anything so it's worth a city search in person before we move on to another location."

"Oh," she frowned. How likely was it that they'd find her, she wondered with frustration. This seemed like the most ridiculous method for searching. She didn't know why she'd assumed the guy would have some kind of magical way of finding soulsiblings. He was so apparently successful at it; she'd just assumed it would be easy

"You look worried. Are you doubting my methods?" he asked with amusement.

"Well, actually yeah," she said with a sigh. "What about Stone and Granger, are they having any luck with their lead?"

"I don't know, but we still have something to follow here anyway. Don't worry, this isn't my first time."

Ebony rolled her eyes. "Are you asking me to just trust the process?"

"Mostly to trust me. Also you can't scan your hand, anywhere. You need to stay hidden for the time being."

This didn't sit well with Ebony. She narrowed her eyes at him and rubbed her hand where the small chip lay under her skin. "Why?"

"Glick is dead."

Ebony could have guessed a hundred things and that wouldn't have been one. She struggled a moment to understand. "What?" she whispered.

"Taylor called while you were sleeping to warn you. You disappeared and he was found murdered, so you obviously are a prime suspect."

"Why?" she whispered, even though he'd just explained it exactly. A halfling didn't willingly disappear unless they were on the run from the law. There was no easy life for a halfling living off the grid, they were almost a hundred percent reliant on the government to keep them alive. You couldn't work, buy food, travel, nothing, without scanning your chip in most places. Death awaited those who tried to hide.

"Oh no, they'll know I'm here. They'll know I'm with you and they'll come for me." Panic overwhelmed her, she started to pant, she couldn't get enough air as thoughts of prison filled her head.

"How? You haven't scanned since I met you at work yesterday. They have no idea where you are or who you're with," Lark said calmly.

She looked at him wide-eyed and barely comprehending.

He knelt on the bed in front of her and put his hands on her shoulders. He stared into her eyes and demanded she breathe with him. Deep calming breaths, one after another until she once again was able to think.

"I haven't scanned, but there are cameras everywhere and if anyone saw you at the hotel that day, heard you ask for me." She shook her head, willing the panic to stay down. "They'll be looking for you to find me."

Lark nodded. "You didn't kill him; you were with me all night. They have nothing but circumstantial evidence and that may be enough to convict a halfling under normal circumstances, but you are not a poor halfling without the ability to hire a good lawyer, or post bail. If, and it's a big *if*, love, they were to find you and arrest you, I would have you out and safe and the case dismissed so fast your head would spin. You are my soulwife, my mate for life, and I intend to take care of you in every way until forever," he vowed.

Ebony melted at his words even as the fear of being accused of Glick's murder cycled through her mind. "Taylor called you? She must be so worried."

"She wants you to call her tonight when she'll be home," he said, though he looked reluctant.

"You don't think I should?"

"I think that any contact is risky, if they are looking for you they might tap her line, or, if they took her in for questioning it would be easier for her if she didn't know where you are, if she hadn't spoken with you in a while."

Ebony frowned, she wanted to talk to her friend but what he said made sense. The last thing she wanted to do was make trouble for Taylor.

"Why don't you get ready to go out, we can walk the streets and get an early dinner since we skipped lunch," he suggested. "I promise you're safe with me."

She wanted to hide under the bed, but she realized that this new development only made her search more urgent. If she were arrested, she may never prove her innocence in time to find her soulsister. She hurried off the bed to comply. Lark caught the belt of her robe as she tried to pass and as soon as it opened, his hands were on her body, grasping her bare ass and pulling her to him. He captured her lips in a deep kiss that left her breathless and wanting.

When he pulled away, she was staring up into his green eyes without a thought in her head aside from the feelings he could bring to life in her. "Now that I have you, there isn't a power on earth that can take you from me." He traced her scar. "Nothing," he said firmly and kissed her again. "Now you better move before I take you back to that bed," he said with a smirk. "Your body responds to me so sweetly, but I imagine you're a little sore."

Her face heated and she pushed him away. "I'll just go shower."

She hurried to the bathroom, closing the door between them and heard him laugh as she did.

She gripped the counter and looked at herself in the mirror. How was she going to resist him when every time he touched her, she was filled with electric need?

Especially now that she knew what the ending of that need felt like.

Her body shivered at the memory of the best orgasm of her life. Granted, she'd only ever given them to herself, before today, but she still never imagined it could be that much better with someone else. No wonder people didn't take the suppressants and risked pregnancy and legal action to sleep with each other.

She figured a cold shower was what she needed to get her mind back on track but she wasn't going to waste a good opportunity for unlimited hot water. She stood under the spray and soaked in the sensation until she was beet red and slightly faint. She turned it down a touch and scrubbed her body before stepping out and towel drying. Then she realized she didn't have anything to put on.

A knock at the bathroom door made her jump and wrap a towel around her body before stammering, "Yeah?"

"I had something sent up for you to wear. We can pick up whatever else is needed while we're out, but I thought you might like something fresh now."

Damn he was thoughtful. Ebony opened the door and accepted the bag he held out as his eyes ravaged her. "Thank you," she whispered and shut the door, her body already returning to the heated state it had been in when she'd entered the bathroom. And all with just a look from the man.

She was doomed. Maybe she should stop trying to resist and just take what she could while she could. She wasn't afraid of judgment, only of hurting him or changing her own mind and dooming her soulsister.

When she emerged from the bathroom dressed and ready in a black miniskirt and a flashy gold tank top, he was sitting on the balcony in black slacks and a black button up. He was sipping a glass of amber liquid and looking like a fucking sex god.

"I'm doomed," she whispered as she walked to the open door. "I'm ready to search," she said cheerfully.

He looked her up and down, leaving her feeling as though he could see underneath her clothing and into her soul.

"You look amazing, love," he said with a smile.

"You're not so bad yourself." She gave him a playful wink.

He finished off his drink and pulled her down into his lap, kissing her deeply. He tasted like sweet alcohol, and she couldn't stop herself from running her hands up into his hair. The kiss was full of all the passion she had been telling herself she could ignore, and he matched her with his own. He adjusted her body without breaking the kiss so that she was straddling him. She was glad she'd made the naughty decision to go without underwear as his fingers slid up her thigh and touched her naked flesh. He groaned and she quivered.

"Fuck, Ebony, I was just going to tease you a little, but you're already ready for me."

"Lark, I'm scared."

He grabbed her chin with one hand while the other played against her exposed body. His bright green eyes bored into hers with such intensity she couldn't even think to try and look away. "I am going to fucking fix this," he growled as his fingers entered her. Her hips bucked against him, and she gasped. "I am going to give you your soul, your health, and every goddamn thing you've ever wanted, and you are going to give me this, every day for the rest of your long life. Do you trust me?" He punctuated each word with a thrust of his fingers that sent a spiral of heat through her until she wasn't sure she could take much more.

"Yes," she groaned. And she did trust him, and it hurt that she did, because with that trust came an awful realization. She didn't want to die, and not wanting to die made everything a hell of a lot harder to deal with.

"Good girl," he said and pulled on her chin with his free hand. When her mouth opened he pulled his fingers from her and slipped them inside so she could taste herself. It was the most erotic thing she had ever experienced.

Lark meant every word of that vow and as her tongue slid around his fingers that had just been inside of her, he knew that he'd kill anyone who thought to stand in their way.

He pulled his clean fingers from her mouth and kissed her, his tongue lapping up the taste of her pleasure from her mouth. His hands worked as they kissed, releasing his erection. He had wanted to give her time to heal from her first time, but she was so wet and ready for him he couldn't resist her now. He entered her with one smooth stroke, delighting in the groan of satisfaction that came from her mouth. She gripped his shoulders, and he grasped her hips, guiding her as she rode him. He didn't care who might see, who might hear, as he took her on the balcony. She was his soulmate, and he would fuck her anywhere, anyway she'd allow.

"Look at me," he demanded and she obeyed quickly, dipping her chin to meet his gaze with hers and the way her eyes darkened with pleasure only amped up his own enjoyment. She slid her hands into his hair, gripping it tightly. He could see the moment before she came and he moved faster, slammed her down harder, taking her over the edge with force and as she trembled and cried out his name, he exploded inside of her.

Trembling and gasping, she laid her head on his shoulder as his hands ran up and down her back. "You are my soul now, Ebony. Trust that I will fix everything."

"I trust you, Lark."

Those words had never meant more to him.

CHAPTER SEVENTEEN

By the time they made it out of the hotel room it was definitely dinner time, and Ebony was starving. She was also terrified of being scanned and immediately arrested. She wondered what was happening back in LA, and desperately wanted to call Taylor to demand all the details but knew it was a bad idea, so she just gripped Lark's arm and tried to breathe.

"What if they ask to scan me?" she asked as they stepped into the elevator.

"Why would they, if you're with me?"

Ebony wanted to roll her eyes at his male chauvinistic attitude, but she also really hoped he was right. And with that thought in mind she was ready to stay glued to his side to avoid any potential conflict.

"If anyone asks, you just say no, that you're with your husband and he does all the scanning. It's not unusual for married couples to keep all their resources together, no one will think it odd."

She supposed that made sense in a relationship where the husband worked and the wife stayed home. So she tried to stand a little straighter, look a little more wifey, whatever the hell that meant, and held his arm without gripping it like a lifeline.

"They'll know we're lying," she said as she looked at her own reflection in the door. Her eyes gave it away, even if she was dressed in nice clothes and had left her old purse behind.

"This is the city of sin, love. No one is going to blink at your little lie, especially when they scan me and realize I have more than enough to take care of any bills that might come up."

"I hope you're right," she whispered as the elevator doors opened and they stepped out into a bustling lobby. She was prepared to ignore curious and hateful looks as usual when she was somewhere outside of the halfling district, but none came. She walked next to Lark, hand on his arm, obviously a couple and him a fullsoul and her a halfling, yet no one was judging them. They got a few raised eyebrows but nothing more than curiosity. It was such a relief. "Why don't they care?" she finally asked.

"Why don't who care about what?"

"The people, no one's giving us dirty looks or whispering about us."

Lark gave a short laugh, "This isn't like other cities, Ebony. People come here to get away from all of that restriction. It's likely why Senator Buchanan is campaigning so hard here. He doesn't have much of a following in a city that really is built for sin," he gave her a wink and she blushed.

"Technically not a sin," she said as casually as she could. "Seeing as we're soulmates."

"Mmm, and that makes it all the more delicious," he agreed. "It doesn't mean they don't notice and there will always be people against it, it just means there is less of it. This city is an experiment that the people in charge like Buchanan would like to see shut down."

"And who is fighting against him?" she wondered aloud.

"There are people, full and halfsouls that feel people are generally smarter than the government gives them credit for; people who think that a city without all the regulations and separations can survive well and not result in massive numbers of nosouls threatening the population."

"What do you think?" Ebony asked as they stepped out onto the warm street, bathed in fading sunlight and neon.

"I think people as a whole are dumb, but part of that is because of all the things the government keeps from them. If they all knew the whole truth, I think they'd make smarter decisions."

"My mother must have agreed that this life wasn't the best way, or she never would have run to LA when she got pregnant."

Lark shrugged. "Perhaps, or maybe she was just too scared of what her daughter would grow up to be if she were surrounded by all this choice."

Choice, what a bullshit idea. She hadn't had much growing up and the cancer took away even more, and here she was, with her soulmate, on the path to finding her soulsister and the choice she'd made about how she was going to leave this world was suddenly something she didn't want... but still she didn't have a choice, not really.

"What does my lady want to eat? The options around here are nearly endless."

"Oh, well I don't know, I'm just starving honestly. Whatever you know is good should be fine."

"Well since we had steak last night, I think we should do seafood. You're not allergic to anything are you?"

She shrugged. "Not yet. I'm willing to risk it though," she said with a laugh.

Lark hated that she had experienced so little while at the same time, he loved to see the joy in her face over something as simple as eating seafood. He led her to a quiet restaurant that he knew served the best oysters and would give them space to talk; he wanted to know more about her mother.

The host was friendly and led them to a table after a quick scan of Lark. Once settled with food and wine ordered, Lark asked about Ebony's mother.

"I don't know a lot," she admitted. "She never liked to talk much about her life before she had me. I guess she just didn't want to compare what she had, or could have had, to what she was forced into with me. Our life was good," she said quickly. "Don't get me wrong. We had what we needed, nothing extra, but we were happy, and I was loved. I grew up with Taylor next door and so with my mother and my best friend I feel like I was pretty lucky." Tears glistened in her eyes but she was smiling so he knew they were at least partially happy tears.

"You were," Lark agreed. Having grown up in an orphanage he knew the alternative very well, and it wasn't pleasant. "She came from here you said, did she grow up here? Did she have any family?"

"No living family. I don't know if she was born here, but I know that I was conceived here and before you ask, I have no idea who my father was, or is, or whatever."

Lark nodded. He knew that much from her file and although he hadn't pulled up her mother's file yet, he was anxious to do just that as soon as he could. He had a funny feeling about it all and his instincts were almost always right on. It was something he should have already done, something he would have done in a normal searching situation but this one was anything but normal.

The oysters and wine arrived then, and Lark concentrated on the looks of pure pleasure and erotic sounds of enjoyment that Ebony made as she tasted everything. He'd ordered for her again, and she giggled with delight when she was presented with a full lobster on a bed of rice and asparagus.

"I've never seen so much food on one plate," she whispered when the waitress had left.

"Well, let's see how much you can eat," he said with a wink, then instructed her on how to go about doing just that. Her early efforts to break the shell and find the meat were a bit comical but she quickly got the hang of it, and soon she'd eaten more than he expected, and it made him feel so good to know he was taking care of his wife properly, that she was not going to go to bed with an empty belly ever again. Not under his watch.

"There's a doctor I want to take you to in Texas," he blurted, not having intended to bring it up before they'd gotten the soul, but he wanted her to know that he was actively trying to get things in order to take care of her. Wanted to give her hope.

Ebony picked up her napkin and wiped her mouth, not meeting his gaze. "Oh, yeah sure."

Lark reached across the table and grabbed her hands, squeezing gently until she looked up and met his gaze. "Ebony, I won't let you give up."

"I know," she whispered and pulled her hands away. "I need to go to the ladies, no dessert tonight, okay? I'm stuffed beyond chocolate cake," she said with a weak smile, then walked away from the table.

Lark watched her go with a frown; he shouldn't have brought it up. He'd ruined the mood, and now he was pissed at himself. His glare was enough to make the waitress hesitate as she brought the check. She hurried away as soon as she'd gotten his payment.

Lark pulled out his cell and opened a message from a familiar number.

Greg was a searcher based in LA, one of the ones he'd

warned not to take Ebony's case if she'd shown up on his doorstep.

People are looking for that chick you warned me off of. Not just the locals.

"Fuck," Lark hissed and slammed the phone back in his pocket. This was a complication they couldn't afford. And what others are searching for his woman? Why?

His mood was not improved when Ebony rejoined him, but he did his best to keep his worry from her. He could tell she was doing her best to keep hers back as well.

"Where to now?" she asked as they left the restaurant.

"I say we do a little sightseeing, a bit of people-watching and all the while I want you to keep your awareness primed, ready to catch even the smallest hint of your soulsister."

Ebony nodded and her face took on a serious set as they moved through crowded streets. They walked the city, in and out of casinos and shops, anywhere that large crowds were gathered, but Ebony continued to shake her head when he asked if she felt anything.

"Not even a hint, but my feet are starting to hurt," she admitted after the fifth large casino had been thoroughly walked through.

"Well then, let's head back to the hotel and in the morning, we'll figure out our next move." He had a feeling it wasn't going to be the move she thought it was going to be. Something told him they were in the right city for the information they needed, but it might not be her soulsister they were going to uncover.

They were stepping out onto a busy street when a shout brought his head up and he grabbed Ebony, pulling her behind him. His head swiveled and he felt her hands on his back, gripping his shirt.

"You!" a voice shouted and a large man barreled through the crowd. It took Lark a moment to realize the man wasn't after him or Ebony, but after the small man beside them with glasses and khaki shorts, a T-shirt that said *I heart Las Vegas* and a bucket of casino coins. The smaller man was obviously here on vacation and if Lark was reading the situation correctly, he was about to die at the hands of his soulbrother.

"We need to get out of here," Lark said as the large man reached the smaller man and grabbed him by the front of his shirt.

"What is it?" Ebony said, still gripping him.

"Soulbattle," Lark said as the big man pulled a knife.

The crowd had all backed off, some were standing around to watch, others moved on as if it were no big deal. No one was trying to stop it, no one was calling the police. Nothing illegal was happening. When it was over the victor would register the death and reap the benefits of fullsoul status. It was a sickening reality of this world.

The small man closed his eyes and went limp in the bigger man's hold, not bothering to fight, he was scrawny, and the big man had a knife, there was no doubt about who the victor would be here. Lark's gaze drifted to the crowd and saw a woman in a matching tshirt and clutching a bucket of casino chips, tears streaming down her face. That was the trouble with dating outside of your soulmate, and one reason that Lark had avoided entering into any relationship that wasn't purely based on sex. He felt for the woman who was about to lose someone she obviously cared for. But there was nothing Lark could do about it, this was the fucked up world they all lived in.

Ebony buried her face against Lark's back. "I don't want to see," she said. "Please, Lark get me out of here," she pleaded.

Lark scooped her up and pushed through the crowd. Ebony pushed her face into his neck and gripped his shirt as he moved, and the crowd whooped over the lethal end of the very quick battle.

Battle, it was no battle. Lark was thankful that his own soulbrother had put up a fight and there'd been a moment or two he had thought he might actually lose. It hadn't felt like murder, not like what he'd just witnessed.

But just because your soulsibling wasn't prepared to fight did that make it wrong? Any more wrong than if your soulsibling was in good health and prepared to fight back or sought you out first?

They were questions he'd asked himself a million times and he had no answer. Somehow this was what the gods wanted from them, this horrible, brutal existence.

Lark didn't put Ebony down on her feet until a block later. He stepped onto a side street and set her down gently, putting his hands on her face and meeting her eyes.

"Are you okay?"

She nodded but her eyes were wet, and she was shaking.

"Ebony, love, was that the first soulbattle you've seen?"

She nodded and bit her lip, looking like the most innocent of souls. He couldn't imagine her in battle, and he wanted to scream at the injustice of it all. How was he going to make sure he didn't lose her?

He pulled her into a hug and held her until her shivers turned from fear to something else, sparks flowing between their bodies.

He couldn't wait to get his hands on her in private, to feel her alive and beneath him. To reassure himself that she was real and here and all his.

He pulled back, kissed her sweetly then offered her his arm and led her back to the street and toward their hotel.

Neither of them spoke, but the reality of what they were doing hung heavy between them, the sirens of cops and an ambulance heading to clean up the scene were an all-too-loud reminder.

As soon as they were alone in the elevator he pushed her against the wall and slammed his mouth to hers. She answered enthusiastically, her body melding to his, her lips just as hungry for him as his were for her. He wanted to rip her clothes off, wanted to take her immediately, but the ding of the door opening and shocked apology from whoever stood there had Ebony pushing on his chest for space. The man didn't get on the elevator to join their ride up, but it was enough to cool things for her at least.

"I need privacy for that," Ebony said, her cheeks turning a delightful shade of red.

"So you'll have it," Lark agreed and when the doors opened on their floor he swung her up into his arms and carried her like a new bride to the door. He didn't let her down, just shuffled her slightly as he grabbed out the keycard and swiped them in. He walked to the bed and set her down.

She looked up at him with such desire he nearly exploded in his pants. He stripped as quickly as he could, then shoved her skirt up and pushed inside of her. She was ready and willing and arched her hips to meet him as a cry of pleasure tore from her lips.

"Mine," he growled in her ear as he slid over her body.

"Oh, Lark," she moaned, clutching him to her tightly. She was just as desperate as he was, and their bodies continued the fast pace until they were both gasping, clinging to each other while their bodies spun, their minds fuzzed, and for one perfect moment, all was right with the world. All other thoughts were pushed away while they rolled around in bliss.

Lark kissed her when he could once again move his satisfied body, then undressed her properly and tucked her into the bed. He held her close and stroked her hair as she drifted to sleep.

"Thank you for everything," she whispered. "This has been the best day of my life."

"I'll give you so many more," he promised, kissing the top of her head.

She didn't answer, just sighed heavily and soon she was asleep.

When she was snoring in deep sleep, Lark moved away from her and pulled his phone out. Stone had messaged to say they were on their way to Vegas with a surprise, that worried him. Lark didn't bother responding, they'd be in the air by now with phones off.

He couldn't sleep so he decided he didn't care that it was the middle of the night, he slipped out onto the balcony and called the doctor in Texas.

"Mr. Duport," came the doctor's sleepy voice.

"I'm sorry to wake you," he said in answer, not really sorry at all.

"No worries, I'm used to it. What can I do for you? Did you get my email?"

Lark gritted his teeth. "Yes."

"Then you know there's not much that can be hoped for." There was regret in the doctor's voice and it only made Lark's heart ache.

"I know, but you're the best."

"That might be true, but the best chance is if you can get her full soul. I know you're the best at that."

"I am," he agreed, but the best wasn't always fast enough.

"She's got a month, two tops, if you don't. I might be able to extend it to a year, but that would be a rough year, Lark. She's pretty far gone and her quality of life would be severely depleted within three months to the point she would probably just be begging for you to let her go." The doctor took a breath. "I've seen it before, it's not a pretty ending."

Lark gulped back the lump that had formed in his throat. In his mind he watched her wither away and die in his arms. He wasn't sure he'd want to go on if that happened. "Her mother died of cancer as well, not sure what kind. I'll get the files and send them your way, maybe it will help."

"Sure, it won't hurt to have the information to compare," the doctor said in a placating tone that made Lark grit his teeth.

Lark hung up and stared out at the city. Her mother had hidden something, Buchanan knew something, and Stone was coming with a surprise. He hoped that whatever it was helped because he was about to burn down the whole goddamn country if that's what it would take to keep her safe.

He walked back in to stare at his soulmate while she slept. His heart ached with the need to protect her, to save her.

He'd grown up in an orphanage, Stone and Granger had been his best friends and become like family. None of them had been adopted, no halfling orphans ever were. But they knew what they had to do when they were old enough. They planned and plotted and one by one found their soulsiblings, killed them in battle, as was done, and came out the winner three times. All with fullsouls, they embarked on a journey of helping others like themselves, both the orphans and those halflings seeking their chance at a full soul.

He'd thought that was enough, he had women to bed, and he had money to burn, power and notoriety, it was an orphan's dream.

But this, this was better, she was everything he'd still been missing and not even known he needed. But the universe didn't give without taking.

He touched the scar that ran over his own body, proof of the battle he'd endured to get his soul whole. He'd had to take a life and it hadn't been easy. He bore the scar on his body and mind. He'd watched the light leave his soulsibling's eyes and had felt the man's half soul join with his own as he'd taken one last breath. It wasn't something done easy, and so many people he'd helped didn't realize the toll it would take on them to know what they had done in order to live a little longer, live with a little more freedom, and have a little bigger ration.

It wasn't talked about how memories came with the soul. Memories and feelings that were so foreign and yet felt like they were a part of you. It was as if he'd lived two lives before the soul became whole. It added to the guilt of the killing for many. For most it was difficult to align the taking of a life with the praise that society doled out when they were finally whole.

The obituaries were littered with suicides of recent fullsouls who couldn't handle the guilt and realized that their soulmate wasn't waiting around the next corner, that there was no happy house waiting for them to fill with children. The reality of the dream the government propagated was riddled with falsity. Those like him were the ones who survived, those who took having children out of the equation, those who accepted the darkness and learned to use it, finding comfort where they could, and seeing that the dream was just a nightmare in disguise.

So what was she? He wondered as he looked down at her. No nightmare, she was a light in the darkness. Together they could navigate the rest of the hell they would endure in this life. Together they could continue to help others.

He couldn't stop himself from reaching down and touching a lock of her hair as she slept. He had to give her a reason to fight. He knew she'd accepted death, knew she'd never planned to survive this journey. Any doubt that her plan was one of sacrifice was lifted by her reaction to the fight they'd stumbled upon. No halfling ready to kill for the other half of their soul was that squeamish. She was selfless beyond compare, ready to sacrifice herself so that her soulsibling could have a real chance at happiness. He saw it in her eyes when they first met and now recognized it for what it was, a determination born of no hope.

There was hope though, there had to be.

Lark took his laptop to the couch and began a search. Whatever information was out there about Ebony's mother, he was determined to find it; a piece of the puzzle just waiting to slide into place.

CHAPTER EIGHTEEN

Shine sat on an airplane bound for Vegas. She couldn't believe it had actually worked. They'd left the house under the guise of a dinner meeting and Nurse Reagan, although obviously disapproving, hadn't tried to stop her. Giving her security the slip was a little more difficult, but thankfully Granger hadn't minded knocking them out with a punch and laying them in the back of their car to sleep it off.

Shine wondered if her father had been alerted to her absence yet. It didn't really matter. He wouldn't be able to predict that she was on her way to take him down. She'd never done anything but what he explicitly wanted her to do. This was so far out of character he'd never see it coming, and that was probably the only reason it might work.

She fingered the glove they'd given her. It had a chip sewn into the lining that scanned her as a fullsoul nobody that wouldn't trip any alarms anywhere. The security was too tight in DC to avoid scanning altogether, so they'd had to do the bit of trickery. Luckily it was something they were apparently prepared for.

The real problem had been her face. She was far too

recognizable and that was an issue. The scan didn't include pictures, only data sent to an earpiece so she could go with any face she wanted, or no face at all as they'd decided. She'd taken off all her makeup and used the lace from her camisole to fashion a veil. She was playing the part of a widow in mourning. No one would question it, especially since she'd put on a business dinner-appropriate pant suit in black, she knew she looked the part perfectly.

She'd left her cell with the knocked-out guards so she couldn't be tracked on it and unfortunately she couldn't pack anything because it would have been suspicious. So she was a runaway, though her father would probably assume she had been kidnapped. She only had the clothes on her back and the creeping fear of what was going to happen in the morning after missing her bedtime shot and not getting her morning one. Maybe she wouldn't wake up at all. She glanced at the two very dangerous men she was with and wondered what the chances were that they were in fact just here to kill her. She never did get the purpose of their visit from them before she steamrolled them into helping her.

She took the gloves off and slipped her contacts out as well, setting them gently into their case she'd stuck in her purse. They weren't comfortable, though she was used to wearing them, she relished the feeling of taking them out and looking at Granger with her natural black eyes that she'd had to hide from nearly everyone she'd ever met. Only her father and Nurse Reagan saw them now and they both cringed at the sight. Not Granger. He stared at her, seemingly fascinated and though it warmed her, she darted her gaze away.

"Nervous?" Granger asked quietly, his deep voice jolting her out of her thoughts.

"No, just wondering how long before my father knows I've left DC"

"Do you think he'll leave Vegas to search for you?"

She laughed sadly, "And miss his big campaign appearance? No way. He'll send lackeys, but he won't want to let anyone know anything is wrong with his perfect family."

"Seemed pretty good to me," Granger challenged. "The whole world has watched you grow up. The only child of the infamous Senator Buchanan and his lovely soulmate wife who died in childbirth." He paused a moment, looking contrite. "I'm sorry about your mother. Growing up without her must have been hard."

"As you know, I suppose. You grew up an orphan, that had to be difficult."

"Yes, much different than your situation for sure. You were in luxury from the moment you emerged from the womb, surrounded by people to feed you, love you, and care for your every need," he scoffed. "You talk about how important it is to keep the separation of halflings and fullsouls, yet you yourself are a halfsoul entrenched in the world of fullsouls. How is that?"

She laughed. "You haven't figured that one out yet?" she teased.

"Enlighten me," Granger encouraged.

"How about a little trade? Tell me what you were really doing in DC, why did you come to meet with me?"

"We were following a lead, looking for information."

"From me?"

"From your father."

"But he wasn't even there. You had to know that."

"We did, but we also knew that searching the files in his home office was a chance worth taking."

Shine was surprised by that. "When?"

"Do you really think we sat and drank tea while you went up to change?"

"But cameras, and security, the house is full of staff!"

Granger rolled his eyes. "We are professionals, Shine."

"Apparently, Did you find what you'd hoped?"

"Could be," he said, obviously not about to give anything away he didn't have to. "Your turn, halfling."

"My father is impotent," she said with satisfaction.

Granger sat back, surprised.

"I do believe my mother was his soulmate. She didn't come from a powerful family so there's no way it was a match made for political gain. Unfortunately, they couldn't conceive and, not wanting to appear as if they weren't following the dictated order to breed, and not wanting to admit that he was anything but perfect," she sneered, "they found a donor who looked a lot like my father. He impregnated my mother knowing that I would be a halfling, but they were sure they could hide it from the world, that they could find my soulsister quickly and make me whole before anyone could find out what they'd done. They never could have predicted that I would be the soulsister of a dominant," she said bitterly. "That I would be less than a halfling and even though he was able to hide it from me for years, I know what's in those shots they give me three times a day now." She lifted her gaze, unhidden by contacts she knew they were black and soulless, she met Granger's dark eyes, bright with his fullsoul. "I can't survive without blood. I can't go out in the direct sunlight and I don't *need* to eat food."

"Fuck," Granger whispered on a breath.

"Yeah, I think if he'd known, he would have killed me but she was already gone. The birth was hard on her and she bled out before anyone could do anything about it. I think Nurse Reagan convinced him to keep me. She'd been at my birth attending to my mother. I think he agreed because a politician raising a daughter alone would win him votes, sympathy from the women especially. He never loved me, but I think my mother would have," she whispered and bit her cheek to hold back the tears. The familiar feelings of betrayal and disappointment welled up inside her.

"No wonder you hate him," Granger said comfortingly and reached across to lay a hand on her knee. "It's not your fault you know. You didn't ask for this."

She looked up angrily. "I know," she snapped, and he pulled his hand away, the sympathy erasing from his face. "I was a baby and they were idiots and until I figured it all out, I was an idiot, too."

"How did you find out?"

"I was always skeptical about my life, but I never wanted to push any boundaries. I really did think I had it good. When I started asking questions, I got shut down immediately which only made my curiosity grow, and then one night I found myself standing in my father's office waiting while he escorted some reporter out. I looked around and realized this was the only room in the house that wasn't wired, wasn't videotaped and I was free for just a moment. I rushed to his desk and rummaged. I found his journal from the years around my birth, just sitting on the shelf as if it were no more important than his copy of Moby Dick. It told me everything I was afraid to know. And now that I know, I'm doing what I can to expose him and reveal the truth behind this godawful curse."

"Which is?"

"We're a mere generation away from full vampiric overrun. There is no way to save us. This is our slow descent into hell. The curse wasn't just about changing our ways. Other countries already surpassed their threshold to stave off the takeover. It's what the war is about. If they breach our borders, we'll go even faster. Every full and halfsoul will be food for the monsters that have been created. It was a slow Armageddon curse—not a punishment; an execution."

"You're quite the angel of doom," Granger said with a half-smile that made her stomach flutter.

"I'm not sure you'd be smiling if you'd found your soulmate and thought the perfect life was at your fingertips, only to realize it was all going to make the end that much more terrifying," she said, leaning forward and licking her lips in a gesture she knew would draw him in. "People will panic when they find out."

"Not interested in soulmates, but I never turn down a good time," he whispered, his eyes locked onto her lips.

Shine looked over to where Stone was asleep and snoring. "You think he'll be asleep for a while?"

"I think I don't care," he practically growled.

He was up and pulling her to the bathroom at the back of the plane so fast she didn't have a chance to rethink her decision. As soon as the door closed them into the small space she started ripping at her clothes. He stripped fast as well and she ran her fingers over his muscled chest and arms, all covered in intricate tattoos that fascinated her. She thought she could spend hours touching them, discovering what was there. A scar ran from his right shoulder across his chest, a sign that he'd fought hard for the other half of his soul. She kissed it where it crossed over his heart then ran her lips lower. He groaned as she embraced his erect cock and ran her tongue around it.

He gripped her hair, encouraging her to take him fully into her mouth.

She obliged, swallowing him down and glorying in the sounds of pleasure he made. Soon she felt his body stiffen, his hands fisting tighter in her hair. She stood then and hopped up on the small counter, legs splayed and welcoming. She ran a hand over her thigh and smiled at him. "I won't bite," she said when he hesitated, watching her.

"I'm not afraid of a little bite," he said gruffly and pulled her in for a kiss, then lifted her ass and settled her over his cock.

As he pushed into her, she arched her back and broke the kiss, gasping and reaching out to hold on as the ride took her. She fisted her hands into his long hair, and he bent to capture a nipple in his mouth, rolling his tongue around it and making her scream again.

"Granger," she gasped, so close to reaching her peak already.

He grunted and flipped her around, pressing her stomach into the counter, he entered her from behind, one hand gripping her chin and forcing her to meet his eyes in the mirror.

"Fuck me," she groaned as the pressure built and she felt the spiral start to take over.

"With pleasure," he hissed and pounded in at a faster pace, driving them both to the edge and finally over it with a growl.

They collapsed together, both panting and sweaty. Granger kissed her cheek and turned her around. She gazed up into his eyes and smiled, feeling a warmth she'd never experienced before.

"You have really beautiful eyes," she said quietly.

"So do you," he whispered, kissing her nose. "Now, how about I help you clean up before we land."

Cheeks red, she let him wash her thighs with a warm washcloth. Then she dressed as he quickly washed himself. She reached for the door handle, but he pulled her in for a deep kiss and his hands cupped her cheeks.

"You're not less than anyone else, Shine," he whispered against her lips. "None of us were, and being forced to kill in order to feel whole is a kind of hell no one deserves."

Tears stung her eyes at his words. No one had ever truly seen her and told her she was enough. Her heart clenched and she bit her lip. "I know, and I never had any intent to find or kill my soulsister, even though I know I'm one of the lucky ones. She's out there somewhere and if she ever comes for me, I'll probably let her have the slice I've got in me."

"What if there's another way?"

"I think my father has been after that for years."

Granger pulled back from her and she left the bathroom, thankful to find Stone still snoring in his seat. "How long until we land?" she asked Granger as he strapped in next to her this time.

"Another hour, I think. We'll get a hotel room when we land." He grabbed her hand and squeezed, meeting her gaze. "Tell me what you are going to need."

"Need? I brought nothing with me," she said with a laugh. "I'll be happy with a toothbrush for tonight."

"I mean, blood wise."

She just shook her head. She hated the thought of what she might need. "I don't know," she answered honestly and turned to stare out the window. "I've always had the shots," she whispered.

Granger didn't say anything, just squeezed her hand again. The silent support broke her, and tears flowed down her cheeks.

Granger wanted to wrap her in his arms as she cried but didn't think she would accept the comfort. He barely knew her, but he knew enough to ignore it. She was a tough woman and prided herself on keeping her emotions in check, no doubt learned from years as the daughter of a politician.

He looked over to where Stone was no longer pretending to sleep.

Stone looked at him with an eyebrow raised in question. Granger gave a slight shake of his head to indicate he should leave it alone. Stone nodded and then went on to make a very suggestive gesture that Granger was glad Shine couldn't see but made him smirk.

He'd told Stone while they'd waited for Shine to join them in the car outside her home that he had every intention of seducing the woman. Stone gave no argument, they'd learned long ago not to go after the same women and since Granger had spoken his intentions first, Stone would make no play for her. Granger hadn't expected it to be such an easy conquest, he also hadn't expected to feel so strongly connected to her. A fierce need to protect her had risen as she'd told her story and now, he thought he might do anything to save her, even offer his open vein. He just hoped he wasn't going to have to choose between her and his best friend's soulmate, because he had a very serious suspicion that this was the small piece of soul that Ebony was missing. And the fact that Buchanan had at one time sought Ebony out made those suspicions even deeper.

When the lights of Vegas came into view, Granger was delighted by the obvious joy it brought to Shine. Her face lit up and she covered her mouth with a hand as she took in the sights. There was an innocence in the way she was enjoying it all that filled him with pleasure. Given the chance, he would take her everywhere possible so she could see and experience everything.

He wouldn't tell her what he was thinking, didn't want to scare her off. So he settled for reminding her to buckle up for landing after she had her contacts back in.

"Do you think it'll work again?" she asked as she slipped the gloves on. They looked like leather driving gloves, nothing unusual except that it was far too warm to be wearing them.

"I have no doubt, but still; if we can avoid them scanning you, we will. It's late so they may not bother to meet us, we fly in and out of here regularly and they know our plane. The security here is far looser than DC but I would still wear the veil, your beautiful face is far too recognizable."

She rolled her eyes at his compliment, and he chuckled, satisfied that she was no longer saddened by their earlier conversation.

The plane landed smoothly, and Stone's phone started dinging with messages as soon as he turned it back on.

"Lark has a place for us to stay lined up at their hotel. He wants to meet us in the lobby when we get there," Stone explained.

"Great," Granger hissed, not sure he wanted to introduce Shine to Lark just yet. He pushed her forward gently and caught Stone's eye, willing him to hold back. Stone got the hint and pretended to be busy as they passed him. Shine continued on to the stairs and Granger whispered harshly to Stone. "Text him back. Make sure he arranged two rooms. I'll watch her, and you can sleep by your damn self."

"Ouch, brother. How will I masturbate to your sex life if I can't hear her sweet moans coming from the bathroom?"

Granger reacted before he could think, he reached out and grabbed Stone by the neck, surprising the man. "Watch yourself," he hissed.

Stone narrowed his eyes but didn't struggle, there was too much trust between the men for him to be concerned that they might enter into any real fight. "She's not your soulmate," Stone snapped.

"She doesn't need to be my soulmate for me to want to keep her away from you," Granger hissed back and let go of Stone's throat. He hurried on, meeting Shine at the top of the stairs where she was thanking the pilots for the safe trip.

"Is everything okay?" she asked, looking past him to where Stone was following.

"Fine, let's get out of here. You must be exhausted."

"I'm doing okay."

"What if I said I want to get you alone so I can fuck you again, slow this time and taste you while you scream my name," he whispered in her ear.

Her cheeks flamed and she hurried down the stairs.

Stone chuckled behind him, obviously having overheard. "That's one way to get a girl moving," Stone said lightly. "There should be a car waiting for us out front."

They managed to dodge the one worker who was too lazy this time of night to come out and scan them, he waved through a window, and they went directly to where the car was waiting. Stone drove while Granger sat in back with Shine.

"Are you nervous?" he asked her quietly.

"Very," she admitted, and he reached out and grabbed her hand.

"Don't worry, I won't let anything happen to you."

She gave him a curious look. "You my bodyguard now?"

"Something like that," he said.

She smiled. "Just so long as you don't start telling me what to do, I won't mind you keeping me alive long enough to take down my father," she paused and frowned. "Not my father I guess, not really," she sighed.

"He's just an asshole," Granger agreed. "And we will take him down for what he's doing in those orphanages." Granger met Stone's eyes in the rearview and they held as much hatred and anger as he felt.

"What can you tell us about it all? What kind of evidence do you have other than your word?" Stone said it apologetically. "Not that we don't believe you, Buchanan is definitely scum. The files we found in the office are all private though, not related to the orphanages at all."

Granger didn't need any proof, they'd grown up in an orphanage, they'd woken up plenty of mornings to find someone just gone with no explanation, never to return. There was an underworld working against halflings like them and proof would go a long way to stopping it and he really hoped she had some.

"I have some files that detail some of his experiments. I took them from his downtown office one day when I was there waiting for him. After I found out the truth about myself, I wanted to know what else he was hiding. There's no denying his experiments."

"Where are they?"

"I sent them to a lawyer, one that I know hates my father and will do the right thing with them."

"So why not just wait for that to come out, why go through all this?" Stone pressed.

"That was the plan, until you two showed up, I didn't have a way out before. This opportunity presenting itself will only make my takedown of him all the sweeter. The lawyer should be getting the file in the next couple days, but I plan to ruin things tomorrow night," she said with a wicked grin.

Granger was satisfied with that, and he patted her leg as they drove on toward the hotel.

They pulled up in front of the hotel lobby and Stone handed the keys off to the valet. Granger grabbed his own bags out of the back and so did Stone, they'd have to get a few things for Shine, but Granger didn't mind taking care of her needs, it actually filled him with a bit of pride to know he could.

The hotel Lark had picked was familiar, a nice place they'd stayed often when in town and thankfully this time of night the lobby was mostly empty. Shine kept her veil on and walked close to Granger with her head down as if she were in fact mourning and sad. No one would give her more than a cursory glance, he was sure. Certainly no one would guess that it was the famous Shine Buchanan.

They let Lark know they had arrived as they checked in.

Shine didn't make a peep of protest when Granger told the lady that him and his wife would be taking the room Lark had reserved and that Stone would be in a separate one. It was an easy process, no need to scan his *wife* and they had keys in hand by the time Lark walked out of the elevator. Shine stayed close to him as they walked across the lobby to meet Lark, and Granger liked that very much. He had to fight his instinct to shove her behind him when Lark's eyes landed on her with curiosity.

Lark greeted them and then turned to Shine. "And this is the surprise?"

"Shine Buchanan," Shine said, lifting her veil briefly to show her face to prove it.

Lark made a sound of surprise and reached out to shake her hand. "Welcome to Vegas," he said.

Granger was about to stop her from reaching out, but he noticed her gloves still on so didn't. He couldn't stop the fear that slid up his spine as Lark gazed at her though. Could Lark tell anything? Did he see something in her that pulled on him? Was this Ebony's soulsister, was this technically Lark's soulmate? Could Shine tell?

"Nice to meet you, Mr. Duport. I've heard about your skills as a searcher."

"And I've heard about you," Lark said. "But you're more than what your father has wanted you to be, aren't you?" His gaze dropped down to her gloved hands now clutched at her middle.

"Not just a political princess looking to rally support for Daddy," she said dryly.

Lark raised an eyebrow and Granger could tell he was about to dig in with questions. When Lark was on track with something, he was like a bulldog with a bone. Normally Granger wouldn't care if he never got to bed, but tonight, he had plans and though they didn't involve sleep. They did involve fewer people and more privacy.

"We can talk in the morning," Granger said, grabbing Shine's arm and pulling her toward the waiting elevator. "See you all at breakfast."

"I'm certain it will be enlightening," Stone called after them, standing with Lark.

Granger met Lark's gaze as the doors shut. Stone was whispering to Lark, and Granger could see the connections being made in Lark's mind. Granger gave a slight nod, there was no use denying or hiding what Shine most likely was. If Shine had held more than a sliver of soul herself, she likely would have sparked to Lark despite the gloves she wore. It was something that they all would have to face in the morning.

"Rumors are that Lark's some kind of sex god," Shine said casually as the elevator music filtered in.

"Really?" Granger said darkly, jealousy welling up inside of him. Had Shine lusted after the image Lark portrayed? Had she hoped to someday meet the dangerous stranger and spend a night with him? If Lark recognized her as his soulmate too, would she get the chance? Granger would never allow it.

Shine turned and looked up at him with her fake blue eyes and a genuine smile. "Yeah, really. But I don't think he's half as hunky as you," she teased, reaching up and grabbing his face. She pulled him down for a deep kiss that ended with him throwing her over his shoulder as he hurried down the hall to their room as soon as the elevator doors opened on their floor.

He dropped her on the bed and undressed her quickly before settling himself, still fully clothed, between her thighs. He lapped up her pleasure until she was screaming out his name and pulling his hair like she was about to come apart at the seams.

Then he stood up with a grin on his face and undressed as

she stretched and shivered and looked at him with a satisfied grin of her own. And that's when he felt his heart overflow and he knew for certain in that moment that no soul picked by any god could be a better match for him than this woman, this perfect being with only a sliver of soul. She was inexplicably his everything and he would die to protect her.

Words wouldn't come, and they would have scared her anyway, so he showed her with his body all that he felt for her. He made certain that she came again before he did and when he finally exploded in her for the second time that day, he wondered what the before would have been like. To meet a woman like this and think about putting a baby in her as if it were no big deal. A piece of her and a piece of him. A perfect mix. It could never be. He had a vasectomy in a dirty basement clinic, highly illegal, but he didn't want to bring any other souls into this hellscape.

But if the gods had seen fit to let the world play out its own way, he could have coaxed her into his life with flowers and chocolate. He could have promised to take care of her and love her forever. He could have raised a family and grown old at her side.

It wasn't to be though; he had no idea what to expect for a halfling with so little soul. Would she even live to be old with the best of care? Of all the nosouls he'd ever interacted with, none had appeared to be more than mid to late forties, and that was a worrisome thought.

He held her tight as she drifted to sleep, trying not to let the panic of losing her overwhelm him.

CHAPTER NINETEEN

Lark sat in Stone's hotel room, passing papers back and forth as they studied the files Stone and Granger had stolen from Senator Buchanan's home office. Lark was interested in what they held, but he was having a hard time focusing. He couldn't stop thinking about Shine and what her presence might mean for Ebony. Not having touched the woman, he couldn't be certain, but the coincidence was just too much. Stone told him about her black soulless eyes and the shots she'd been taking three times a day all her life. Was Ebony's soulsister sitting in this very hotel, with Granger? Lark hadn't missed the possessive way his friend had treated Shine. It wasn't unusual for Granger to seduce a woman but never had he seemed so taken with one. Granger was usually the one night stand type, the once and out of his system type. But Stone said the two had gotten it on in the airplane bathroom and he had been possessive of her after that, insistent on sharing a room with her and for Stone to keep a distance. It was a massive change in his friend, one that Lark would have celebrated, if it had been any other woman. Someone was going to lose here, and as much as he loved Granger like a brother, Lark didn't intend it to be himself.

"Do you think that Ebony even knows this much about her mother?" Stone asked, pointing to the file Lark was holding marked *Henrietta*. "I doubt it," Lark said, focusing back on the file in his hands.

"What does Buchannan have to do with Ebony and her mother?" Stone asked.

Lark met Stone's eyes. "I think there's a reason we all assume Shine has the missing piece of Ebony's soul, Stone. I don't think all of this can be a coincidence."

"He searched for Ebony when her mother died but not before. Henrietta's death would have been registered. Do you think she somehow managed to not scan herself until then? Maybe Henrietta was able to live off an inheritance?"

"If Henrietta had some kind of inheritance, maybe, but even then it's doubtful she'd never have scanned herself, and the one person who might have been able to shed light on it is dead as of this morning."

"Dead? Who?" Stone asked in astonishment.

"Glick."

"Oh shit, did you go back there last night?"

"No, and it's worse than that. With no leads, the police are after Ebony for questioning because she disappeared the same night. Who else would they suspect?"

"Damn."

"Yeah, and since we know it wasn't her and it wasn't us. What are the chances that its unrelated to our little mission and that letter we found in Ebony's file?"

"I'd say not good, but why now? Why would Buchanan come after Glick after all this time if he took his word for it that Ebony was dead before? And if all Buchanan was after was another pretty young thing to work for him? It doesn't make sense," Stone said.

"Unless Buchanan wasn't after Ebony just because she's an

easy halfling to corrupt. He knew of her mother, maybe he was tracking Henrietta and her daughter specifically. It may have been random women he was looking at hoping to find the one he was really after. And he gave up on the lead of Glick after he was told she was dead." Lark hated to admit out loud what he'd started to think, he'd been the one to put Ebony back on Buchanan's radar. Something about his online searching had triggered Buchanan to go back and look for her and question Glick again.

"Okay, so then we assume he knew Henrietta and he knew she was pregnant when she left Las Vegas, but not where she went. For some unknown reason he specifically wanted her or the baby and all that was before his wife gave birth to what could very well be Ebony's soulsister. Why?"

"Let's assume that, yes. But not only why he was trying to find Henrietta and Ebony, how did Henrietta manage to not be scanned all that time? She couldn't have been working alone, not even if she had money from something. Ebony wasn't even registered until she was five, I saw that in her file and thought it odd. I didn't double check who she was registered to. I wonder if Henrietta used a fake name to keep her hidden."

Stone shrugged. "Maybe Henrietta was working the streets?"

Lark doubted that. "I think there's something more. I think we need to follow that money trail and we'll find something useful."

"Family? Friends? What about Ebony's father?"

Lark stood, "Well, it sounds like you have your hands full with research tonight." He wanted this solved sooner rather than later, but he also wanted to be with Ebony and he had been away from her long enough already.

"What?"

"Hey, you're the only one without a lady in your bed," Lark said with a wink and walked to the door. He stopped there and turned to look at Stone. "Do you think it's really her?"

Stone shrugged. "With all this evidence, I think it's likely, yeah, but I don't understand it. Shine made it sound like they just picked a random who looked like the senator to be the sperm donor and they had no idea she'd end up with such a small sliver of soul. There's no way they would have wanted her to end up like that, all the trouble they've had to go through to hide what she is and keep her alive."

Lark nodded and walked out. There was something they were missing. Some piece they didn't see yet.

He made his way back to his room where Ebony slept. He let himself in quietly and stripped down as he walked to the bed. She was laying so peacefully there. He just stood and stared at her for a moment before sliding in next to her and pulling her into his arms.

Never in his life would he have imagined wanting the feel of a body next to him in sleep, but he was sure he'd never get a wink of rest if she wasn't there. If he couldn't smell her sweet scent and hear her quiet breathing, he would lay awake missing her until the sun rose.

She was his everything now, she may as well hold his entire soul because he didn't want to exist without her.

Granger stared down at Shine as she slept. The sun was up and soon they would have to go down to breakfast and introduce her to someone who quite possibly wanted to kill her.

It would kill him to know that she was Lark's soulmate.

Of course, there was a possibility that Shine could win the

battle, but then she would belong to Lark. The two women were probably equally matched for a hand-to-hand fight, neither particularly strong or muscled. Granger wondered if either woman would have what it took to kill the other in soulbattle.

Granger didn't care that she would never be *his* soulmate, that they would never have a life together recognized by the government. It didn't matter that they didn't have some stupid electrical input that told their bodies this was the one best suited to make babies with.

Fucking ridiculous curse of the gods anyway.

He wanted to spend the rest of his life worshiping her body. He wanted to take away the pain of growing up with an asshole father and no freedom. He wanted to show her how to really live, outside of the bubble she'd been kept in her whole life and without the restraints her father had put on her.

He gazed at her mouth. He would have to solve one very big problem though.

A sensation filled him that was unexpected and erotic as he envisioned one way he could take care of that need of hers. He imagined opening his flesh and having her drink from him. It made his dick hard and he really hoped she'd let him try.

"Fuck, I hope you're not who I think you are," he whispered, running his hand over her body, deciding she'd had enough sleep. He hoped like hell he was wrong and she had nothing to do with Ebony or Lark so she could be all his.

Shine startled awake and then smiled at him. "Good morning, Granger," she said huskily.

"It is indeed," he agreed, pulling the sheet back and revealing both their naked bodies. His was up and ready to go. She raised an appreciative eyebrow when she noticed. "I've been waiting for you to wake up and thinking of all the things I would do to you when you did."

"I hope one of those things involves my mouth and that cock," she said, grabbing it and giving it a playful squeeze.

He gave a guttural groan and thrust his hips slightly, fucking her hand. "It definitely involved your mouth, but I had other ideas of what I'd put in it."

"Really?" she whispered, crawling down his body and doing exactly what she wanted anyway.

Granger didn't have it in him to argue. He gripped her hair and enjoyed the ride as she took him all the way and swallowed him down.

When she crawled back up his body with a grin on her face, he pulled her in for a deep kiss before flipping them around and returning the favor with her legs wrapped around his shoulders.

"I could get used to waking up like this," she said when they lay satisfied and breathing heavy on the bed.

"Every goddamn day we possibly can," Granger agreed.

She turned and propped up on an elbow, gazing down at him with dark eyes that drew him in. He hated to think she'd be putting her contacts in again soon and she'd be covering her pretty face with that stupid veil. He reached up and ran a hand through her blonde hair. Then an idea struck him.

"What if we dyed this and you just left out the contacts? It would probably be enough to keep anyone from knowing it's you. The eyes themselves would probably do enough, no one looks too closely at eyes that dark. But if we were to also hide the hair. You'd be passably disguised to anyone who only knew you from television."

Shine bit her lip and touched her hair, sitting up fully. "My hair?"

"Or we could just cover it, put it up and throw a hat on. I'd hate to see you go around in that veil in this heat."

"And I don't really want to sit in here all day, either," she agreed.

An hour later they were showered and dressed, ready to meet the others downstairs. He hadn't been able to bring up the question of blood needs while she'd distracted him with her delicious body, but he didn't want to take her out of the room without it being resolved.

She sat on the bed with a fresh face and hair up in a tight bun looking beautiful, no need for makeup. She was in the same clothes as last night; he'd have to take her shopping as soon as possible. He didn't want her to feel a lack of anything. She smiled at him but there was a worry in her eyes as he put a hat on her head and pulled it low to shadow her face and cover all her hair.

"I wonder how mad my father is. He'll know by now that I'm not at home being watched by Nurse Reagan."

"But he won't know you're so close to him. Probably will think you're hiding in DC somewhere, don't you think?"

She looked down at her hands and rubbed them nervously. "Probably," she agreed. "It seems so odd to be away from home and the schedule I'm so used to."

"Away from the nurse," he nudged.

"Yeah," she said, not meeting his eyes.

"Shine," he said quietly and waited until she raised her dark gaze to meet his, he liked the rawness he saw in them without the contacts. "Do you need blood?"

Her cheeks reddened and she looked away. "I don't know," she gritted out. "How dumb is that! I don't even fucking know what it takes to keep myself alive. All I know is that they gave me three shots a day and I didn't consume much else. I could and did, especially around others, but it wasn't necessary." She looked back at him, and her eyes were filled with anger. "He kept me helpless."

Granger nodded. "And he'll pay. But I want to give you what you need."

She just shook her head. "I don't know what it is, and I hope I figure it out before it matters, but for now, can you just—" she hesitated, biting her lip and looking down, "can you just stay close. I trust you."

"You couldn't get rid of me if you tried," he said with a smile, loving that she wanted him around.

CHAPTER TWENTY

Ebony woke with a familiar ache in her chest and an unfamiliar ache between her thighs. One made her smile with memories of passion beyond anything she'd ever imagined, and the other reminded her of why she shouldn't be letting Lark develop feelings for her.

"Good morning, love," Lark said, rolling over and pulling her in for a kiss.

They were both nude and he was very happy this morning. "Woah, you're insatiable," she teased.

"Apparently when it comes to my soulmate, I am."

"I'm not sure I can handle any of that," she said motioning vaguely at his lower half. "I'm feeling a bit weak from last night," she admitted, and her cheeks burned.

"My soulmate needs sustenance," he said with a laugh. "I guess I'll tell the guys to meet us for breakfast. They brought Shine back from DC and I'm anxious for you two to meet."

"Shine Buchanan?" She couldn't fathom why that would be necessary.

"Yeah, apparently she wants to confront her father on some illegal business he's been involved with," he said vaguely.

Ebony wasn't sure what that could mean but it didn't surprise her. Just seeing the man on television had always given her the creeps and her mother would practically hiss at his image whenever it came on. Ebony stood up and hurried to the bathroom, trying to ignore the fact that Lark was watching her naked behind the entire time.

She managed to avoid looking in the mirror as she prepared to shower and wash her hair. She hated to see the harsh reminder of the time bomb in her chest. She stepped under the hot spray of water and let it soothe her and wake her up. As she soaped her body and washed away the residue of Lark between her thighs, she couldn't help but grin. She'd gotten to experience something that most people never had a chance to. Not the sex, anyone could have sex, legal or not, but she had gotten to have sex with her soulmate. The knowledge of that was warming and she wished she could pick up a phone and gush all about it to Taylor. They'd spent many a night talking about what a soulmate might be like and although Ebony didn't have anything to compare it to, Taylor assured her that not all men were good in bed and if a soulmate was better than the best she'd ever had, he would be amazing.

Ebony could now attest to the accuracy of that.

She was feeling renewed when she stepped out of the shower, even if the ache in her chest hadn't eased. Then she froze, a hand pressing against her chest, but not over her scar, not where she knew cancer grew. This was different she realized. This was a pull in her soul.

"Fuck," she groaned as the weight of what it meant settled over her. It was everything she'd hoped for and feared finding. Her soulsister was near.

"Ebony, are you okay?" Lark demanded. He was standing in the doorway staring at her, completely nude still and unashamed.

Ebony turned to him and gave a half smile. "She's here."

Lark stiffened and crossed to pull her into his arms. "Shine, I think it's Shine."

"No, she's—it can't be," Ebony gasped pulling back in his arms far enough to look up into his face. She expected to see that he was joking, but his face was deadly calm.

"I met her last night when they arrived. She's not what everyone thinks she is. She's more like you, but also not at all," he said with a shake of his head.

"Did you," Ebony swallowed back a flare of jealousy. "Did you spark with her?" She asked with a tight voice. Images of Lark and Shine in a bed together filled her mind and she wanted to throw something. She pulled her towel tighter around her body, trying not to think about how perfect, unmarred and healthy Shine's body must be.

Lark's eyes softened and his lips pulled up into a small smile as he shook his head. "No. But I must say I like to see you jealous." He pulled her to him and kissed her deeply, easing some of her jealousy and fear, but not all of it. "I didn't feel anything when I was near her or shook her hand and I don't want her. No matter what, I will never want anyone but you, Ebony." He ran his hands down her arms and up her front to brush over her breasts then to her face. "This body, this face, your piece of soul is all I'll ever want. No substitute will do, no addition needed."

Ebony pulled back and shook her head. "You know that's not true," she whispered and turned to the mirror. She stared into her own eyes, searching for the pieces of her soul, the thing that recognized its missing slice. Was she about to meet her death, her savior, her chance at dying with a purpose, her chance at living a full life? What did she even want anymore?

She met Lark's gaze in the mirror and drew in a sharp breath. She saw bloodlust there, an eagerness for her to take everything from another living human so that she could perhaps beat the death sentence in her chest.

She looked away. She couldn't breathe under that pressure. "I am going to brush my teeth," she whispered, her voice husky with emotion.

He touched her back gently and for a moment she thought he was going to say something, but then he walked out quietly and shut the door. When she heard the click, she crumpled to the floor and let silent tears fall from her eyes.

She'd known it was stupid to let herself get involved with Lark once she'd realized what he was, but she'd convinced herself that it would be okay. Now she was paying the price. A deep dread filled her and a fear of death she hadn't had since she was first diagnosed settled over her. She didn't want to die, she didn't want to give someone else a chance to be happy with their soulmate. Not just anyone... Shine Buchanan, a woman she had hated from afar. And not just some random guy who may not exist... Lark, a man she now knew intimately.

Everything had changed, and it was all her fault, why hadn't she been stronger, why hadn't she resisted his advances?

Nothing had changed, she reminded herself. She was still dying and she still wanted to give someone else a chance at something better, and if Lark was right, Shine was ready to come out against her father. Maybe the woman wasn't all bad. Ebony had always assumed that her soulsibling would be a decent person, seeing as she had half the soul that Ebony did, and Ebony had never wanted to do anything terrible in her entire life. The soul likely had something to do with morals, Ebony assumed.

Ebony knew she couldn't let herself wallow for long. She picked herself up and brushed her teeth, then walked out of the bathroom to dress. Lark was already dressed in a pair of dark jeans and a black T-shirt, it seemed to be his preferred look. His hair was shaggy, and he was scowling at his laptop.

She didn't like seeing him upset and she made an impulsive decision. "What is it?" she asked, dropping her towel and posing provocatively.

He looked up at her and grinned. "You have no idea how much I want you to stay just like that," he groaned. "But I told the guys to meet in here for breakfast and if they see you like that, I'll have to gouge out their eyes or kill them." Lark chuckled. "Also, I don't want you to meet Shine in public, just in case things get weird."

"Oh," she said quietly. "Yeah, that's probably good." Ebony bit her lip and walked over to where her clothes from yesterday were thrown on a chair.

Lark was suddenly behind her, his hands running up and down her sides and his mouth hot and wet on her neck and shoulder. He grunted and bit lightly at her skin before pulling away and lightly tapping her bare ass.

Comforted by his obvious desire she smiled as she pulled on the clothes then brushed out her hair and put on some mascara. When she ran out of ways to distract herself with primping, she made the bed and picked up the few things littered about the room.

A knock at the door froze her on the spot and she stared at it, holding her breath.

"Room service!" A voice called, following a second knock.

"I ordered for everyone," Lark explained and went to open the door. A waiter pushed in a cart loaded with trays and cups, followed by Stone looking bright and cheery.

"Good morning, love birds," Stone called out and poured himself a cup of coffee from the cart.

"Morning," Ebony said and accepted a cup of coffee from Stone.

They settled on the couches with the food laid on the table and as soon as the door closed behind the waiter, Stone started talking.

"Granger and Shine should be here soon, and we'll have some answers there I think, right away," Stone motioned at Ebony meaningfully. "But I did come up with a couple interesting items last night in my research that I think we should discuss before they get here."

"Talk," Lark ordered. He'd settled on the couch close to Ebony and she laid a hand on his leg for support. How had he become her safe place so quickly?

"Ebony's mother had a rather large chunk of change in a bank account when she first got to LA. She opened it with Glick as a signee because her residential address was listed as the halfling camp, she couldn't get an account on her own. She registered Ebony at five under the name Henrietta Long, hiding her identity from, well, everyone essentially."

"She knew Glick before she got there?" Lark asked, confused.

"It would seem so."

"My mother didn't have money, she worked every day of her life," Ebony said, shaking her head.

"Yes, but she never used her rations. She never scanned anywhere. She was definitely hiding."

Ebony tried to think about that, was Stone right? Had she ever actually seen her mother scan or had she always used cash? It was strange for a halfling to use cash, Ebony knew that but her mother had always done it that way. Why? "Was she hiding from my father?" Ebony wondered aloud.

"Perhaps, but what if it was more?" Stone said with a knowing grin.

"She grew up here in Vegas. You know this is where she met

your father and got pregnant, right? Well she was raised right here, daughter of two born fullsouls."

"Okay, so her family had money, she had an inheritance to escape with," Ebony reasoned. "I guess that all makes sense, though I don't know why she didn't tell me."

"Maybe. Everything points to her hiding and Buchanan was after her, *is* after you," Stone said around a mouthful of muffin.

Ebony blinked and shook her head, this was all too much. "Whoa, wait, where do you make that connection?"

Lark cleared his throat and she looked at him, he had a contrite set to his mouth that she'd never seen before. "There was a letter in your employee file, it was from Buchanan to you but sent to the hotel so Glick intercepted it. It could have simply been that he was interested in hiring you, but even Glick didn't seem to think that was all on the up and up. It's what sent us on the lead to DC."

Ebony's mind spun at this new information, why the hell had senator Buchanan been looking for her, and why had Glick kept it a secret? Before she could ask any questions Stone continued on.

Stone set a file on the table. "Buchanan had a file on your mother in his home office. It details her life up to her disappearance from Vegas, pregnant with you."

Ebony gasped and darted her eyes from Stone to Lark, expecting it all to be a joke. "Does it say who my father is?" Not that it mattered, not really, but she'd always wondered about him. She supposed it was natural to want to see where you'd come from, who had made you. She wanted to see some kind of care for her mother in the eyes of the man that had risked her mother's life for a night in bed. She didn't want to be a lust baby, she desperately wanted to have been made in love.

"No, I'm sorry, it doesn't reveal that. There is only an address for your father. I looked it up last night, but it seems to just be an office building. So another dead end maybe," Stone explained with a frustrated shrug.

"Perhaps he works there? Maybe she had too. They could have met at work and fallen in love," Ebony knew her voice was high and strained, desperate for a happy memory for her mother. "I want to go there. I want to see it I—I just want to see even if it's nothing. It's all I have of her now."

Lark rubbed her back comfortingly and nodded at Stone.

"The building is owned by Buchanan," Stone said to Lark. "It could be dangerous."

"My life is over. I'm dying. The police are after me and my soulsister is coming into this room any minute. I want to know what my mother was hiding from. Who my father was and who I am."

Lark pulled her to him and grasped her chin, forcing her to look at him. "You are my soulmate, you are not dying, you are not going to jail, and I don't care who walks through that door when. Those are the facts." He spoke with such fierce sincerity that Ebony almost believed him.

Ebony put her hands on Lark's face and smiled into his eyes. "You're good, but I'm not sure you're that good, searcher."

He growled and a knock at the door stopped any further discussion.

Ebony shot to her feet and so did Lark, putting himself between her and the door.

"Come on in," Stone yelled when no one spoke or moved for several moments.

The door opened and Granger walked in with narrowed eyes and scowling lips. His gaze was locked onto Lark and the two men seemed to be having a silent standoff.

"Fucking move," a voice snapped from behind Granger and then the small woman that Ebony had seen a hundred times on television, pushed around him.

The flame inside of Ebony was instantly vibrating and she stepped around Lark, only to have him grab her arm and pull her back.

"Is it her?" Lark whispered in her ear.

"She's my soulsister, I can feel it like nothing I've ever experienced," Ebony confirmed.

Shine rubbed at her own chest. "I feel it too, like a little pulse. I guess that's because I'm not as souled as you," she said with a shrug. "I got the short end of that stick."

"How does that even happen?" Ebony wondered, taking in the darkness of the woman's eyes and the paleness of her skin. If she didn't know better, she'd say this was a nosoul, not just a halfling with less than half a soul. "Let me go," she said gently and patted Lark's hand.

He looked at her and she saw a fear there that warmed her. She smiled at him, this was what had to happen. He reluctantly let go and she stepped forward, so did Shine. Granger was right behind Shine, glowering, and Ebony could feel Lark breathing down her own neck.

"May I?" Ebony asked, raising a hand to touch Shine.

Shine nodded and lifted her own hand. Ebony touched palms with her soulsister.

Ebony groaned with the feeling of completeness that filled her at just that touch. It was like she'd been living with almost-full breaths all her life and this was the first time she filled her lungs to capacity. She never wanted it to stop and she wondered if that's what it would feel like if she killed Shine and took in her slice of soul, would this completeness be permanent? Ebony could understand why people found it an irresistible possibility when faced with it like this.

"Wow," Shine said, blinking. "I've never felt anything like that."

"Well, here I thought Granger was supposed to be good in bed," Stone teased from the couch.

Granger just grunted, not taking the bait, but Ebony appreciated his light attitude in the situation. She dropped her hand but continued looking into Shine's eyes, mourning the loss of contact instantly. Ebony didn't see anything malicious in Shine's gaze, no deep desire to strangle her to death and take her soul. But Ebony knew the thought had to have crossed Shine's mind.

Sure that a fight wasn't about to break out between them, Ebony relaxed a bit.

There was something else that needed answered immediately though. "Lark, I want you to touch her. I need to know if—if you feel it with her," Ebony said. She couldn't go on wondering, she couldn't be around this woman and know that Lark was as attracted to her. It would kill anything she thought she felt for him. It would ruin what she thought they had. He said he had felt nothing when they met last night, but she needed to see for herself.

"No," Granger said, shoving Shine behind him.

"You don't own me, you ass," Shine hissed and pushed around him. "You're good in bed, but I am not your property and I'm so sick of taking orders." Shine reached out a hand to Lark while Granger looked as if he were about to kill everyone and run away with Shine whether she liked it or not.

Lark looked at Ebony. "Are you sure? I don't feel anything looking at her. I don't want to touch her in any way," he insisted.

"You didn't feel anything for me before we touched," she reminded him and took a deep breath because this could change everything. "I'm sure." Ebony stepped away, making sure she wasn't touching Lark in any way as he reached out to take Shine's hand.

It seemed like the entire room held its breath as the two

touched skin-to-skin. Ebony couldn't take her eyes off of Lark, searching for any hint of desire, any spark of recognition.

After a moment he pulled his hand back and frowned. "I felt the tiniest sensation," Lark admitted as if it were a shameful thing. He turned to Ebony, his eyes apologetic. "But it's nothing like what I felt when I first touched you, Ebony. If I didn't know she held a piece of my soulmate's soul, I would think nothing of the sensation at all. There's no way that I'd pick her out as my soulmate based on that touch." He shook his head to emphasize his point. He grinned at Ebony and ran a finger across her chin. "Just you, babe."

"You don't want to..." Ebony gestured vaguely, not wanting to vocalize her thoughts but needing to know.

"Want to throw her over my shoulder and take her to bed?" Lark laughed, gaining a growl from Granger.

"Something like that," Ebony gritted not really wanting to hear the answer.

"No, I feel nothing of the sort for her. Halflings aren't supposed to produce a soulspark remember, and the only reason you and I did was because you have so much of the soul. She does nothing for me. I want no one more than you, no one *except* you Ebony, now and forever."

"It's enough to make you sick, isn't it," Stone said with a mock gag.

"What about you?" Granger asked Shine. "Did you feel it?"

"No, I didn't notice anything at all," she shrugged. "So, now that's settled, I would love a cup of coffee."

Shine pulled Ebony to the couch and settled in next to her. The feeling of relief she got by being near the woman was something she'd only ever gotten from a shot, and she was scared to admit how close she'd been to accepting Granger's offer of blood in the hotel room. Her body had felt weak, on edge, and sensitive. But the thought of taking blood had made her stomach churn.

Stone served up coffee as Lark and Granger whispered near the door.

"Where did you grow up?" Shine asked, her mind going a mile a minute with questions, concerns, and wonder at their situation. She wanted to know everything about this woman she felt so connected to. She wondered briefly if she'd have felt a similar connection to her own mother, or her real father? She'd never felt anything from the senator except duty and she'd been fairly young when she stopped trying to feel love for the man. Was this what family felt like?

"LA."

"And your mother?"

"Dead now, but she grew up here in Vegas, I guess. I don't know my father."

"Me neither," Shine said with a laugh.

"How is it that you, or, how do you..." Ebony trailed off, uncomfortable.

"Everything was hidden from me for a very long time. Obviously, I knew as soon as I was old enough to reason, that I wasn't like the other children. I wasn't even allowed to play with them until I was old enough to wear the contacts, stay out of the sun, and keep my mouth shut about things. I was given shots three times a day. I was kept in DC, and I don't even have a chip." She held up her hand.

"No chip?" Ebony gasped and grabbed her hand, feeling around where the chip should be.

"No."

"And no mother, what happened to her?"

"She died right after I was born, some kind of complication from birth."

Ebony nodded. "As with most parents of nosouls," she said

then gasped and covered her mouth. "Not that you're, I mean obviously you—"

Shine laughed. "Don't worry, I'm not offended. I have come to terms with what I am. Whatever it is. Not a nosoul, not really a halfsoul though either, just like you aren't. You are a little more, I am a little less." She shrugged. It didn't matter, couldn't change, it just was. "It's weird being next to you, I can feel a comfort in it," Shine said and grabbed Ebony's hand, wanting more closeness.

"Me too," Ebony said with a smile, not pulling away.

Stone just watched them with curious eyes, seeming to take in everything the two were saying and doing. Shine wondered if he was waiting to see if one of them was going to attack the other, to try and take the rest of the soul for themselves. She had no such desire, and she hoped Ebony didn't either.

Granger and Lark joined them then, neither looking particularly happy.

"What do you know of Buchanan's facilities here in Vegas?" Lark asked.

"Not much. I wasn't allowed to be a part of anything that he didn't specifically want me to talk to the media about. Which pretty much only consisted of the orphanages."

"And you found out they are not quite what he said they were," Lark prompted.

Shine nodded. "Which is what I want to expose. He's been experimenting on them, trying to figure out what makes the soul tick, I think. Maybe he was after a solution for me," she shrugged. The idea that anything the senator did was for her benefit was laughable, the man was beyond selfish.

"There's a facility here in Vegas that your father owns," Lark explained. "It's listed as the address of Ebony's father."

"Coincidence?" Shine asked, though she didn't think it could be.

Lark shook his head. "Your father had records of Henrietta, Ebony's mother in his home office and he tried to find them both. I think he may have had Ebony's boss killed to keep him silent."

"Silent about what?" Shine asked, not at all surprised to hear the senator could have been involved in a murder.

"That's what we need to find out. Ebony disappeared the same night that her boss died, which makes her a prime suspect. I can keep her hidden but it would be easier if we could prove someone else had a motive."

"Oh! Yes, that would look pretty bad," Shine agreed.

"They want you to help get us into that facility to look around, but I told them it's too dangerous for your father to know you're here," Granger snapped, his protectiveness warming Shine.

"Dangerous, yes, but isn't that what I have you for?" she said with a smile for the big man. "He won't come at me publicly. So maybe I shouldn't be trying to hide." She pulled off the hat and let her hair flow around her face. "Maybe I need to make a statement."

CHAPTER TWENTY-ONE

"Fuck you, I'm coming too!" Ebony snapped as she faced Lark with her hands on her hips. Everyone else had gone to their rooms and they were supposed to meet in the lobby in fifteen minutes.

"You can't be seen," Lark said again.

"No, I can't be recognized, so as long as no one scans me, I should be fine. We are going in with Shine Buchanan! No one is going to be scanning her entourage, Lark. They are going to be scrambling to kiss her feet and alert her father to her unexpected presence."

"We don't know what we are going to find there," Lark said with a soft tone that grated on Ebony. She was no child and she wouldn't be treated like one.

"We might find my father there." She poked a finger into his chest for emphasis. "We might find out what my mom was running from, we might find out why I have more than half a soul and why Shine has less," she whispered the last. "This is my journey and I hired you," she pulled the cash from her old purse and shoved it at his chest. "I am going."

"I don't want your money, soulwife," he growled.

"And I don't want to be told I can't be a part of whatever this turns out to be," she snapped back.

They glared at each other, neither wanting to back down from their stance.

"Fine," Lark finally consented. "But you will stay close to me."

"Of course," she said and stood up on tiptoes to kiss his lips. "I like being close to you."

He just grunted and led her out of the room and to the lobby. They sat in a small waiting area with a view of everyone coming and going. There was a lot of traffic this time of day and it made her a little nervous.

Ebony tried to ignore everyone and take the few moments to think, and since Lark didn't want to accidentally reveal anything to a passerby. He was sitting quietly too. She appreciated the forced silence that being in such a public space gave her. Meeting her soulsister was not the experience she'd feared and she wasn't sure what she was doing anymore. Shine wasn't what she expected, not of her soulsister and not of the famous daughter of Senator Buchanan. Ebony had really thought that as soon as she met her soulsister there would be an undeniable urge to fight, to kill, to take what was missing. But there was none of that. Just a feeling of home, a comfort. How did people get past that to kill? Or was it only because she'd never planned to kill the woman and take her soul that she didn't feel the urge as soon as they were face-to-face? She couldn't say what she would have done if Shine had attacked her immediately. She probably would have defended herself instinctively, though she had no idea how to fight.

Shine didn't seem hellbent on taking Ebony's soul either, though. It sounded like she just wanted to take down the senator and disappear. But did she really want to live the rest of her life with just a sliver of soul? Did Ebony still want to give up her soul to Shine? Somewhere deep inside she'd never thought it would happen, never thought she'd actually meet her soulsister. She had hoped that the effort would have been enough to prove herself and be reincarnated into a fullsoul body for the next go round. A life and family with all the privileges, all the opportunities. She'd thought when the cancer finally took her, she could die thinking she'd done all she could to give a full soul to someone else so they could live a full happy life this round.

But what was she supposed to do when her soulsister didn't want to take it? Neither one willing to make that move? Did they just go their separate ways as if they didn't know about each other? That seemed kind of weird, and she had to admit it felt like a loss to perhaps not see Shine again.

"You're very fidgety." Lark put his hand on hers where they clenched in her lap atop her vibrating legs.

"I know this is what I wanted, but it's not what I expected," she admitted. "What happened when you met your soulsibling?"

Lark's face darkened. "It wasn't anything like this, that's for sure. I was the first of our little group to find his soulsibling, though we were all searching together at the same time. I found him in a small community of halflings North of Salt Lake. He was expecting me. I'd felt him strongly as we made our way and he'd obviously felt me coming. He was waiting in the town square, prepared for the battle. He was older than me, but still in good shape. The town surrounded us, not to interfere, but to witness. It was a good match, and I didn't come out unharmed, obviously. But in the end, I won, I stabbed him through the heart, and I felt his soul enter mine and I knew," Lark paused and cleared his throat. "I knew that I had taken something from the community in that instant. He had been a good man. He took good care of the halfling orphans there, taught them usable skills, helped others when they were too old for the government to care about, and I took his life. For what? So that I could have more?" Lark's voice was rough with emotion and she could see a shine to his bright eyes as if he were holding back tears. He shrugged and shook his head. "It's not easy, no one talks about how hard it is living with the memories of the one you killed. I don't think it's right or wrong, I think it's a no win situation for all of us." He turned then and grasped her chin lightly. Kissed her lips softly. "But then I met you and I realized, this is why. This is what makes it okay and without this, I understand why so many kill themselves after they get their full soul. Ebony, I can't lose you now."

"I don't think I can do it, Lark. I can't kill. I'd rather give her my soul and let her be your soulmate, your wife. It was always the plan, until I met you." Ebony hated how those words felt coming out of her mouth now. She didn't want to resent Lark and Shine for being meant for each other too, but she did, she hated the thought of them together after she died.

"I don't want her," Lark said viciously and slammed his lips to Ebony's again, kissing her deeply. "I'll never want anyone but you, and I'll die by your side if I have to, Ebony. I want to follow your body to the next life; I don't give a fuck about your soul."

"I think I love you, Lark," she whispered.

"I think you do too," he teased and kissed the tip of her nose. They sat close, cuddled and content for a few more minutes. All Ebony could do in that moment was hold Lark close and try to embrace the uncertainty they were in. Perhaps some answer would come along, but if they didn't, maybe she just needed to live in the moment with Lark for as long as she could.

Stone arrived a few minutes before Granger and Shine strode out of the elevator making an entrance no one could miss. Shine had her bright blue contacts in and her white-blonde hair flowing around her. She was dressed in a black pantsuit, and she looked like the woman Ebony saw on the television regularly. People stared and pointed and whispered.

"Well, her father will know she's here in under an hour I bet," Lark remarked.

"That's the plan, I think. Should we arrange for rooms somewhere else tonight, just to be safe?" Stone asked.

Lark shook his head. "I think we need everyone to know where she is, the more public the better. Like she said, he isn't going to go after her with the eyes of the world watching."

"Ready?" Lark stood and offered Ebony his hand.

"I suppose so," she said and took it, enjoying the spark. They met Granger and Shine in the center of the room and walked out together to Lark's waiting car. Ebony and Shine sat in back with Granger, Lark drove, and Stone took the passenger seat.

"How are you feeling about all this?" Ebony asked Shine.

"Surprisingly good. I was never comfortable with my place in this life, but I really did think I was doing a good thing speaking about the orphanages."

Ebony nodded; she believed it. How could Shine have known anything other than what was presented to her, isn't that what the problem was for everyone? Isn't that why things were the way they were? The government presented the picture for everyone to just accept. And they did. Ebony had even bought into most of it, just trying to exist in her little slice of the world.

Now, she was questioning everything.

Ebony reached forward and put a hand on Lark's shoulder as he drove through the city. The soulmate spark jumped through her body giving her a little hum of desire and happiness.

"Woah!" Shine said, rubbing her thigh where it pressed against Ebony's. "Is that what the soulmate spark feels like?"

"What the hell, Lark?" Granger hissed and Ebony scooted

away from Shine, immediately cutting off contact with both her and Lark.

"I'm driving, dude, I am not doing anything."

"I think it sort of passed through Ebony and into me because we were touching," Shine said with a shiver.

Ebony didn't like that Shine had felt it. It was such a personal thing, so intimate a bond between her and Lark, she didn't want to share it with anyone.

Apparently, Granger felt similarly because he pulled Shine over his lap to the other side of the car and settled himself between them.

"Handsy beast," Shine said with a smile.

"Possessive bastard never did like sharing his toys," Stone chuckled from the front seat.

Granger punched Stone's arm, but Stone only laughed more.

They soon arrived at what looked like any other basic office building, outside the main streets of the city, but not so far it would seem suspicious. The parking lot was half full and people dressed in suits as well as lab coats were coming and going from the front entrance.

"What is this place?" Ebony asked.

"BaneCore is all it says officially. No description of what type of business, it was originally leased out as office space under the corporation's name. With a little digging I was able to uncover Buchanan as the owner of BaneCore, but it was buried so no one who didn't know how to follow a paper trail would find it. Nothing has changed, no renovations listed, it was built by a private company that went out of business after. There is no record of blueprints, probably because it was built so long ago nothing was digital then," Stone explained.

"Seems very unusual," Lark said.

"It is, I don't have any idea what to expect when we walk in there, we need to be ready for anything," Stone said.

"So what's the plan then?" Ebony asked.

"I walk in," Shine said with a confident smile. "You four follow, and once inside we try and figure out what the place is really doing and get access to whatever files they have on hand. If there's something here about Henrietta, that's what we want to find but also anything against my father will be helpful."

"Let's do it," Lark said, getting out of the car and opening the door for Ebony.

She accepted his hand out of the car and soaked up the soulmate spark that was all hers.

"Are you certain I can't convince you to wait here in the car?"

"Very," she said with a smile.

"Let's do this," Stone said enthusiastically. "No one will harm either lady. Buchanan isn't even here so I am guessing the danger is low. His official schedule has him meeting with the governor and walking through an orphanage this morning."

"He won't miss that P.R. opportunity," Shine agreed.

Shine took the lead as they headed across the lot, and they all followed at a short distance. Ebony was sandwiched between Stone and Lark, Granger was in front of them, a half step behind Shine. Eyes were on them as soon as they got close to the entrance, but no one approached. Shine knew how to play the part of rich and entitled. She paused outside the front door and Granger hurried to open it for her, they all went through, then he took his place again right on her heel. Playing the part of bodyguard well.

Silence met them as they walked across a very clean and sparsely furnished lobby to a large white desk where a secretary sat looking horrified and not covering it well. There were at least ten others in the room, and they all stood frozen, staring at the group as if they couldn't believe what was happening, and as expected, they didn't know how to react.

"I am here to tour the facility," Shine demanded, not introducing herself and not asking. She had to expect obedience, it was a trick to throw off the workers.

Ebony hoped it worked.

"Ms. Buchanan, we weren't told to expect you today. Your father isn't here."

"I know he isn't," she huffed and fluttered a hand. "I am here to tour, so are you going to get someone, or am I going to be left to wander on my own?" she snapped.

The poor secretary's eyes went wide, and she looked like she might cry, but she picked up a phone and requested someone named Marty to come to the lobby immediately. "He'll be right out," she said as she hung up.

"Cameras," Lark whispered. "No doubt everything happening here is being recorded."

"We may only have a few minutes before Buchanan is alerted and one of his lackeys shows up to take Shine," Stone whispered back.

"That may be enough," Lark said.

A man hurried out of a hallway. He had on a cheap suit and the look of someone who would happily sleep at his desk rather than go home to face his lonely existence. Ebony felt instantly sorry for the man.

"Max," Shine said before the man could speak.

"M-Marty," the man corrected. "And Ms. Buchanan, what exactly did you hope to tour here today?"

The secretary hadn't said why the man needed to come to the lobby when she'd picked up the phone, which meant that he'd been watching on security cameras that had sound as well. High tech stuff. Ebony realized they needed to be very careful.

"Everything," Shine said and started walking the way the man had come from.

He jumped and hurried to get to her side and cast disapproving looks at the rest of them. "Perhaps your security can wait here?"

"No," she said simply and kept walking even though she had no idea where she was going.

This girl was good, Ebony had to give her credit.

"Of course," Marty said, then motioned to a doorway. "This leads to the main offices."

"I want to see the labs," Shine said.

"Of course," Marty said stiffly.

They followed a bumbling Marty further down the hall and Lark grunted at Stone who took the door through to the main offices.

Divide and conquer was the plan, then.

They followed Marty to an elevator that had buttons indicating at least three levels of underground floors. Ebony felt a moment of panic when the doors slid shut and Marty hit the lowest level. She gripped Lark's arm and looked up at him questioningly. Were they making a huge mistake? Anything could happen to them underground.

He just nodded slightly; it wasn't reassuring, but she also knew this may be their only chance to figure out what was really going on. They had to risk everything, at least she, herself, wasn't risking a long and happy life, but the others... they quite possibly were.

"Weren't there more of you?" Marty asked suddenly.

"No," Shine said without a moment's hesitation, and Marty looked immediately unsure of his own memory.

The doors dinged and every muscle in Ebony's body tensed. Beside her she could feel Lark tense up too, though he didn't show it in his face.

She heard it before the doors opened and knew exactly what they were about to see.

Stone peeled off from the others and waltzed into the office area of the building as if he owned the place. He was ready to charm and talk his way around and into whatever files he could. His eyes took in the completely normal and dull looking office space full of cubicles and chatter, quickly picking out his mark.

She was short and dressed extremely professionally with her dark brown hair in a tight bun and cat-eyed glasses on her pert nose. She had bright green eyes and plump red lips and she looked like she would fall for his particular set of charming skills quickly. She was standing at a file cabinet off to the side and frowning at whatever it was she saw there.

"I am hoping you can help me, love," Stone said cheerily.

"Doubtful. If you're here for the interviews, they aren't until this afternoon and being this early is not a point in your favor." She talked without looking at him, so he just stood there smiling until she finally did lift her gaze to him.

He knew the moment she felt an attraction and he knew he had her. It was the slight widening of her eyes and parting of her lips, it told him everything.

"I'm here to retrieve some files for the senator," he said conspiratorially. "He told me to find the prettiest piece in the office and she'd be able to help me."

"Oh, well, what exactly are you looking for?" she asked, a little breathless and reached up to finger the star charm hanging from her necklace.

"It's a file on a woman, Henrietta Landry."

"Breeder or placement?"

"Breeder," Stone guessed and hoped he was right.

"We keep all the breeder files over here," she said quickly, leading Stone through a short hall and into an office filled with filing cabinets. His mind was reeling around the word, *breeder*. "When was she here?"

"About twenty-five years ago I think."

"Okay, that would be one of the originals, here in this one." She opened a file drawer and started thumbing through it. "That's weird."

"What's wrong, love?"

"Well there's a file with that name but it's empty."

"He's not going to be happy if the file was lost," Stone said with a frown, trying to decide how far he might be able to push this woman for information. "Are there backups anywhere?"

"On files this old? No, we didn't start inputting stuff into computers for backup until fifteen years ago. Honestly, I don't know why we even keep the hard copies anymore," she said with a laugh.

"You've been a huge help," he assured her, then gave her a wink and leaned forward. She was too startled to respond, and he kissed her as his hand snaked around to grab whatever file he could reach. Whatever was in Henrietta's would be in the others, at least in a general sense and tell them what the women had been in here doing. He stuffed it down the back of his pants under his jacket before pulling away.

She was too dazed by his kiss to notice or care that he'd stolen something. Then he held out his arm gallantly. "Escort me back through the office?" he asked sweetly.

"Oh," she said shakily, "of course, Mr.—"

"Soren."

"Mr. Soren, please tell Mr. Buchanan that I am sorry I couldn't have been more help."

"Certainly will," Stone said then paused and frowned down at her. "Actually I'll tell him it was some fat guy who tried to help me and couldn't. That way if he gets mad you won't get fired," he said with a wink.

She blushed and smiled, nodding approval and he knew he'd just sealed her lips. She'd never mention this interaction for fear of losing her job.

As he left her at the door he stroked his hand down her arm enjoying the way she shivered slightly. "Enjoy the rest of your day, love." He emerged back into the hallway, there were the elevators that he'd heard the others get into at one end and in front of him a set of doors. He decided more exploring was necessary as the others hadn't seemed to have returned yet.

He walked with confidence across the hallway and tried one door, locked, then the other. It opened easily and he stepped into a breakroom.

"Well why the hell not," Stone muttered and sat at a table, grabbed a cookie out of a box sitting there, then pulled the files out to examine as if it were the most normal thing in the world.

They were for a woman named June Person, sounded like a made-up name to him he mused as he read on. He nearly choked on what he found inside.

June Person had entered the facility of her own free will.

Now why the hell had they needed to specify that?

She had sold her uterus to the corporation. A fullsoul with no family listed and no personal resources. She had been impregnated by a donor and given birth to a son. The son is listed as having been placed in an orphanage after tests came back negative.

"What tests?" Stone mumbled and ate another cookie.

June was then impregnated a second time, same donor. She birthed a daughter and the tests were positive. Daughter was placed with a family for observation. Third pregnancy was stillborn, and June was disposed of.

"What the fuck are you doing, Buchanan?" Stone mumbled.

CHAPTER TWENTY-TWO

Ebony bit her lip as the cries of babies reached her through the closed elevator doors. When they opened she was faced with a reality she never could have imagined. It looked like a hospital nursery with beds and beds of babies crying out for love and just a handful of women dressed in nurse uniforms interspersed with others in lab coats. They all walked among the babies doing the bare minimum to keep them alive.

"We have a full house right now." Marty explained. "This is the most our facility can hold at a time. All pregnancies have been fruitful this round. Usually we have more infant deaths per cycle," Marty added. "As you can see, we give them all what they need and care for them before placements. We will have them all tested before the week's out."

"I see," Shine said, and for the first time since they entered the building, her façade faltered.

"I know the noise is unsettling. Come this way, we can walk through the women's wing."

They followed Marty. Granger moved to offer Shine a supportive hand to her lower back and Ebony gripped Lark's arm tighter. She wasn't sure what she'd expected, but this wasn't it, and it was horrifying.

"What are they testing them for?" she hissed in a whisper.

"No idea," Lark whispered back.

Ebony tried to look at the infants closer as they passed and she saw they looked like fullsouls, but then a dark eye caught her attention and she sucked in a breath. Were they breeding nosouls down here?

They went through a doorway and into a lounge area where women sat around with various activities. Some were reading, others watching television. They all turned to stare as Marty walked in and a few visibly shrunk back as if he were the harbinger of doom in their midst.

"As you can see the ladies have the best facility in which to spend their time with us," Marty said as if it couldn't be truer. He had a wide smile on his face and he swept his hand around to indicate the sterile, cold room.

"Nice," Shine agreed quietly.

"Would you like to see the birthing wing? It's empty today."

"Um, no, thank you, I think we have seen enough," Shine said, and Marty nodded curtly then led them back the way they'd come. Before they went through the doorway into the infant area Ebony looked back at the women.

The deep looks of emptiness in their eyes was terrifying. It wasn't a lack of soul, they were all fullsouls, she was certain, it was a lack of will, a lack of hope. Ebony shivered and pressed closer to Lark. She couldn't wait to get out of there, she needed air and sunlight and maybe a good cry.

"I'll show you the labs if you'd like," Marty said as they entered the elevator.

"Please," Shine said, and Ebony couldn't help being impressed with the impassive way she responded to the situation, she was a real professional at hiding everything.

The elevator went up two floors and opened to reveal a high-tech looking laboratory that was bustling with activity.

"This is where we run all the tests, find the best matches and assess the results. I assure you we take every precaution to make sure our samples are clean and true and everyone who works here knows what they're doing." Marty explained as if Shine were here to judge him.

"I see," Shine said, walking forward.

All of them took the opportunity to look around, reading everything they could see to try and get an idea of what was going on. Shine couldn't ask outright; it would blow their cover. They would have to compare notes when they were back in the car.

"This is where we chart our progress," Marty said proudly, pointing to a large graph. "As you can see, we are getting closer and closer to the goal."

The goal, as Marty put it, was stated in big red letters: *Artificial Soul Passed through DNA.*

"That's great," Shine whispered, then cleared her throat and looked at her watch. "Oh my, look at how much time has passed, this has all been very enlightening. We have a lunch date with Daddy though, so we must get on our way."

"Oh, yes, let's get you out then, and do tell him I send my best," Marty said eagerly.

"I will," Shine said brightly as they loaded back into the elevator and headed up.

They stepped out into the same hallway they'd first been in and as they walked behind Marty toward the lobby, a door opened, and Stone slipped out to join them once again.

Marty stopped at the front desk to wave them on out the door and gave a little startle when Stone passed, but he didn't comment. It was hard for Ebony not to run as soon as they hit the front door. She wanted to get as far from this place as possible. Only Lark's hand on her arm and Granger's imposing presence in front of her held her back. They were still playing a part, making a showing of their lie. But as soon as they were all loaded back in the car, Lark didn't hold back, squealing his tires and blowing out of the parking lot like the devil was on their tail.

"Fuck" Granger hissed when they were on the highway and headed back into the main part of the city.

"Yeah," Stone agreed. "Let's go somewhere we can drink and compare notes."

Everyone was silent as Lark drove.

Lark took them to a dark bar off the strip and they took a table in a corner. Shine put on a hat and kept her eyes down for this venture and they didn't draw more than a passing curious look as they hurried to the booth still not talking.

Lark ordered beer and burgers for everyone, and no one spoke until after they were all served.

"What was downstairs?" Stone finally asked.

"Fuck," Shine said, shaking her head and taking a long swig of the beer. She immediately started to gag, and the entire table went ridged as she sputtered and finally spit it back in the glass. "I—I uh, don't drink beer."

"You don't usually drink anything," Granger said with a frown.

"I'm fine," Shine snapped back. "Trade me places," she demanded and crawled over his lap before he could answer and settled herself next to Ebony. "I hope you don't mind. The connection soothes me." She grabbed Ebony's hand and squeezed.

How could she say no to that? It was comforting for her but she imagined it did a whole hell of a lot more for Shine. "Oh, no, it's fine," Ebony said. She would never deny Shine this kind of comfort just because it was a little weird.

"Don't touch either of them," Granger growled at Lark.

"She's my fucking soulmate, I'll touch her whenever I want," Lark hissed back.

"Not when it affects Shine too. *She's* not yours," Granger said.

"Whoa, settle down boys," Stone whispered. "People are starting to look."

"Just scoot over a bit, Lark," Ebony said calmly, not liking the idea of Shine getting any sparks through her from Lark either.

Lark grunted but did as she asked.

"Thank you," Shine said, looking at him with an embarrassed smile. "I usually get shots, three times a day and it keeps me normal I guess."

Lark shared a look with Granger but didn't comment.

After that they talked over what they'd seen and compared that with the information in the file Stone had stolen. It was obvious what was going on in the laboratory and why Buchanan was keeping it hushed, but they could only guess at what it meant for Ebony.

"I want to confront him. I want to hear the whole truth from his mouth," Ebony said. "I want to know what he did to my mother, where I was made, and how, why." She shook her head. "Am I just a science experiment that ran away?" Her throat tightened and she had to take a gulp of beer to push back the tears.

"He was after you. Did he know that you were going to be born with a dominant soul?" Lark wondered aloud.

"Is it an artificial soul?" she questioned back quietly, voicing what everyone had to be thinking.

"An artificial soul, but you still have a soulsibling and a soulmate?" Stone pointed out. "Seems unlikely. If it wasn't a real soul, wouldn't it act different?"

Everyone exchanged confused looks, no one had any answers.

"I feel like all we found were more questions," Ebony said in frustration.

"There's only one way we're getting the answers," Lark said.

"Which means we need to prepare for an event," Shine said. "I'll need a dress and I bet Ebony will too. Do you boys all have a tux? It's black tie."

Granger and Lark groaned a bit dramatically, but Stone smiled wide. "I look great in a tux."

"I'll need another beer before shopping," Lark said, raising his hand to call over the waitress.

"I can't go shopping," Ebony said, a little panicked. She imagined being arrested immediately and it didn't sound like the way she wanted to spend her last few months on this earth.

"Oh, we don't need to shop," Shine said with a smile. "I know all of the senator's connections and I plan to use his money as usual. We'll have a selection of dresses sent to the hotel and we can pick in private."

"Handy," Granger said.

Shine shrugged. "Or just another way to make sure no one ever found out what I really am."

No one spoke for a while as they all chewed on the possibilities. Not only was Ebony likely an experiment of Senator Buchanan's, but it was also feeling more and more likely that Shine was too. But what didn't make sense was why the senator would have kept Shine and raised her up like his own, especially after his wife's death. Why not pick up a baby from his factory that wasn't almost a nosoul? Why not just scrap the whole idea of a child? He could have gained a lot of sympathy for losing a wife and child.

What did it mean that Shine had the little slice of soul that Ebony was missing?

"Did you know that you had a soulsibling?" Ebony asked Shine.

"No, I couldn't feel anything until you were right in front of me. I guess it makes sense because mine is so small."

"So your father, or, well, the senator, he didn't know that your soulsibling was alive?"

"I don't think so. When I was a young teen, I figured out what I was. I know I should have sooner, but you have to understand how secluded I was. I just thought I had a medical condition, probably something my mom also had, and she died from it. It all made sense in my mind. Then he took me to a doctor who ran some tests and asked me all kinds of questions about sparks and pulls and stuff that I didn't really understand. I was dead inside, or at least that's how I felt, and I told the doctor that. He looked at me with so much pity I knew then what my father had tried to keep from me. I wasn't a fullsoul with a medical condition. It was a few more years before I figured out that I was even less than a halfsoul."

"Do you think Buchanan knew that he was giving his kid the other part of your soul?" Lark asked Ebony.

"I feel like anything is possible at this point. I can't believe what we saw today, what he's doing. Did you see those women? They were... dead inside and not because they didn't have souls. They must be put through hell there and all because they probably had no other options for survival... no family or soulmate," Ebony said.

"We're taking him all the way down," Shine insisted.

They all mumbled agreement and finished their meals. The ride back to the hotel was quiet and Lark circled the place once before parking, looking for anything suspicious.

"I'm sure Buchanan knows you're staying here, we can't guarantee he won't try something stupid," Granger pointed out.

"It would be stupid, with so many people watching," Shine

said, but everyone looked around and wondered about every person they saw. Was there a spy here for Buchanan? Were there police here looking for Ebony?

Nothing looked out of the ordinary, so Lark pulled up to the valet and they all stepped out.

"Ms. Buchanan!" The front desk woman called as they crossed through the lobby.

"Shit," Granger hissed.

"Do we keep walking?" Ebony whispered.

"Everyone is looking," Shine pointed out as she turned on her heel and walked to the waving woman.

"Yes," she asked with an air of importance.

"You have a message." The woman handed Shine an envelope then looked uncomfortable.

"Is there something else?" Shine prompted.

"No, it's just that, well, you aren't registered as a guest."

"So?"

"I understand the need to be careful when traveling, but we really need to have such an important guest registered, especially if you're going to be receiving messages at the front desk."

Ebony bit her lip, this is where everything fell apart.

"Of course, tack me on with Mr. Duport's set of rooms." She raised an eyebrow at the woman, daring her to say something about the propriety of it all. "A message for me could go to any room and I'd get it," Shine added.

"Of course, your security," the woman said carefully.

Shine just stood silent, stoic and the woman shifted uncomfortably on her feet. "Is that all?"

"Yes ma'am," the woman said quickly, probably thankful to have them gone.

"We'll be having a clothing delivery. Don't send it up. Call for one of my men to collect it," Shine added with a frown.

"Yes, of course."

Shine spun and started across the lobby at a fast clip, and they all followed.

"You're impressive," Ebony said when the elevator doors shut.

"Lots of practice. Most people don't question you if you act like you're in charge."

"It helps that you have a famous face," Granger added. "What does the note say?"

They all looked at the envelope in Shine's hand. She opened it and pulled out a small paper. She paled a bit then handed it to Granger who read it out loud.

"Darling Shine, I am disappointed. See you tonight. Love, Daddy."

"What does that mean?"

Shine pulled out some tickets from the envelope. "I think he's expecting us to go to the event."

"Daring us, more like," Granger said as he looked at the tickets. "This one says Ebony Duport."

"Fuck," Lark hissed.

"How much could he already know?" Ebony whispered.

"And why isn't he scared?" Shine asked.

CHAPTER TWENTY-THREE

Shine was lost in her own thoughts as she followed Granger's prompting hand to the room they were sharing. Was the senator bluffing? Did he think he could scare them off so easily? Or was there something that they weren't seeing, some important piece that gave him so much confidence?

"Maybe we shouldn't go," she said, settling onto the small couch in their room.

"Do you really think that's best? To let him keep what he's doing hidden?" Granger sat on the table in front of her so their knees were touching and grasped her hands.

Shine looked up into his face and met his gaze. "I think I want to tell everyone what he's doing, no matter the consequences."

Granger grinned and nodded. "Me too. The bastard doesn't get to play God and hurt people."

"I need to make a phone call, arrange for some things to be delivered. Dresses and such, I could really use some clean underwear," she added, and her cheeks heated a bit.

Granger smiled and slid his hands up her thighs. "My dear, what has happened to your panties?"

"Someone keeps getting them wet," she said, a little breathless as he leaned in and kissed her.

"I really hope you're talking about me and not Lark."

She giggled and kissed him back. "Definitely you. Lark's not my type."

"Tall, dark and soulmate is not your type?"

"Obsessed with another woman is not my type. Want to help me out of these damp panties before I make a phone call?" she asked against his lips.

"Yes, but first we need to talk about this," Granger said, pulling back and holding up her hand which was shaking. "As much as I'd like to think my kisses were making you shiver."

Her whole body was on edge, her stomach was clenched, and her head was starting to hurt but she wanted to ignore it all.

"I think I just need to be with Ebony," she whispered.

"For the rest of your life, stuck to her side? That is going to make our sex life a little awkward," Granger teased.

Tears stung Shine's eyes. "What do you want me to do, kill her and take her soul? She's an innocent life, Granger. I can't, I never wanted to. I just—I just wanted to do something right and disappear," she whispered as tears started to track down her face.

"Is that all you want now?"

She was afraid to say what she really wanted so she just attacked him. She pressed her lips to his, ripped at his clothes and demanded with her body that he make her forget for a while all the things stacked against her.

He growled deep in his chest and gave her what she wanted. He stripped her quick, buttons were lost but she didn't care. Once they were both naked, he pushed her down onto the floor, kicked the table over and away then pushed her legs apart and moved forward with a vengeance.

It was hard and fast, but it was what she needed and when

she came with her legs wrapped around his hips and her back pressed into the hotel carpet, she cried again for all the things she wanted and couldn't have.

They lay together, trembling and breathing heavy. Granger leaned over her and kissed her cheeks where the tears flowed. "Babe," he whispered.

"I know, it's so stupid to cry. I just never expected to find someone who could really see me and want me. Granger, no one has ever known me, not really, but you make me feel like I'm enough."

"You are enough," he said fiercely. "I promise to take care of you, Shine, if you just give me the chance, I know I can make you happy."

"What if I don't want to do what it takes to survive?"

"Will you try?"

Shine frowned up at him. "It's not fair to ask me that while you're still inside me. It makes it hard to think."

Granger smiled mischievously and shifted his hips. She bit her lip to keep from moaning.

"I think all's fair when we're talking about changing the world. You can't do that if you aren't strong, and you can't guarantee Ebony will always be next to you. She's going to be dead in a couple months if Lark's doctor can't fix her."

Shine pushed him back and sat up with a gasp. "What?"

"She's got cancer, it's pretty bad and the doctor says he may not be able to help her, especially since she doesn't have her full soul."

"Oh my god, she is going to want to kill me and take it." Shine wasn't sure how she felt about that. Was it why Ebony was with Lark in the first place, he was supposed to find her soulsister so she would have the strength to survive the cancer?

Granger shook his head. "I don't think so. I think her plan was to sacrifice herself to her soulsister, but that was before she met Lark and felt the soulmate spark. There's no way he'll let her do that now even if she still wants to."

Shine's head spun and she pulled her legs up, wrapping her arms around her knees. "Why is every option so terrible?"

"Because this is Hell," Granger said with a shrug.

"Sex helps," she said with a grin.

"I agree."

Shine laughed.

Granger pulled out a knife and pricked his finger and held it out to her. "Take what you need."

"That's so gross," she said with a frown.

"Grosser than semen? Because you sucked that down like a champ this morning."

"Woah," she laughed. "Fine, but if a couple drops doesn't do it, I give up, and hand me that water to wash it down."

Granger handed her the water and then she wrapped her lips around his finger. She met his eyes as she flicked her tongue around the cut. An involuntary moan escaped her, and she dropped the water bottle as she reached out to clutch his hand, holding it as she sucked and pulled what she needed from him.

"Oh my god," she gasped as she pulled away. "That—was—amazing."

"Women always tell me that," Granger said with a wink.

"If I didn't feel so good right now, I'd hit you for that."

Granger just chuckled and settled next to her, both leaning against the couch. "See, I can take care of all your needs." He opened the water and offered it to her. She waved it off and he downed half of it in one swift gulp.

"Are you okay?" She imagined sucking him dry and ending up with a husk of a human on the floor, and that terrified her. How much had she taken, how much did she need? Fuck, she hated how little she knew about taking care of herself.

"I'm a big strong man, Shine, it'll take more than a few drops of blood to hurt me."

She frowned at him and inspected his face for any sign of weakness, any paleness, any shake to his body. Damn, he was a fine specimen, and so strong.

"Okay, so what if this doesn't work?" She leaned her head against his shoulder and sighed. A happy future was almost as terrifying as what she'd been planning for herself.

Granger put an arm around her shoulders and pulled her closer to his side. He pressed his lips to her hair in a gentle kiss. "What if it does?"

"I guess we'll deal with that when the time comes. For now, I need to get some dresses sent over, and some makeup."

"I want to do some reconnaissance before the event. But I won't leave you alone."

"Ebony needs a dress too. You and Stone go check the place out. Lark can stay with Ebony and me."

Granger frowned. "Lark can come with me; Stone will watch you two."

Shine couldn't help smiling brightly at his jealousy. No one had ever shown that toward her, it felt unbelievably good to mean so much to someone just because—not for money, not for influence. Just for herself and she didn't even have to give credit for their connection to something as ridiculous as their souls, it was all them.

"I never imagined I'd wear something like this," Ebony squealed as she held a white sequined gown against her body. "I wish I could show Taylor, she'd shit."

"That's a great color for you, really nice with your dark hair," Shine agreed as she slipped out of a red satin dress with spaghetti straps and a low neckline. "Blood red for me I think."

They'd tried on multiple dresses, but Ebony had to agree, the white really looked great on her.

"Now sit, I'll do your makeup and hair."

"Oh, I don't usually—"

"I know, that's why I'm going to do it. I know what I'm doing," Shine laughed and pushed Ebony to sit and accept the treatment.

"Being close to you makes my soul happy and calm," Ebony said as Shine got to work on her hair first.

"Mine too, it's weird. I bet no one else has stood next to their soulsibling this long without trying to kill them," Shine laughed awkwardly.

"I was never going to try and kill you, I—" Ebony's voice broke.

"I know," Shine whispered. "Granger told me about the cancer. Maybe just being close to me will help? The way being next to you keeps me from shaking without my, uh, shots."

Ebony thought about that as Shine combed and curled her hair. Could proximity be enough? Had humans jumped to killing without ever trying another way?

A crazy thought occurred to Ebony, had the gods intended them all to live in foursomes, two soulsisters with their soulbrother husbands as one happy unit? No, that wouldn't result in fullsoul children, would it?

Ebony had to admit it was likely just a mistake in their grand plan. Anything other than death, carnage and suffering, the gods were not interested in.

Half an hour later Ebony barely recognized herself and when they emerged from the bathroom dressed and ready to go, all three men were waiting there looking amazing in black tuxes.

Granger had a red bowtie; Lark's was white, and Stone had chosen a light blue.

"Wow," Stone said first, then Lark and Granger stepped forward to kiss and compliment.

"Do we really have to go?" Lark whispered against Ebony's ear.

"Only if you want to confront Buchanan and possibly get some answers," Ebony whispered back, pecking a kiss on his cheek.

"Not as much as I want to peel that dress off you slowly and kiss every inch of skin I reveal."

Ebony's cheeks bloomed with embarrassment, and she stepped away from him as Stone chuckled.

"What did you boys find when you went to check the place?" Ebony asked to change the subject.

"Looks pretty standard for a political press event. He's hired locals for outside security, inside he'll have his own men around him. They'll be well trained and loyal. There's going to be over two hundred people in the ballroom plus the wait staff, plenty of room for us to stay hidden in a crowd if needed. There's a small stage where he'll make his speech and ask for donations then pose for pictures."

"That's where I'll step up," Shine said.

"And we'll have your back," Granger said.

"What should I do? I want to question him, I want answers," Ebony said.

"I think you'll get the chance. He wants you, if he sees you, I don't think he'll be able to resist getting close. I say we use that to our advantage and invite him to meet privately before he can try and get to you, catch him off guard maybe."

"And while he's distracted talking to you two, no one will be watching the stage," Shine smiled.

"The big reveal," Stone agreed excitedly.

It had to work because Ebony didn't think they'd get another chance. She knew that she was risking being arrested, but the hope was that Buchanan would value her alive and with him more than having her in a jail cell. No one else in the room would be able to pick her out as a person of interest in an LA murder. It was a lot of ifs, but it's what they had.

Before they left the room Lark handed her a small blade. "Just in case."

"And where exactly do you expect me to keep that thing?" she scoffed. The dress was skintight and slit up the right leg.

He just dropped to his knees in front of her, lifted her dress making her squeal, then he proceeded to tie the thin knife high on her thigh between her legs. It was so thin she could almost ignore it, almost.

"Okay then," she said when he stood back up. "I guess I can get used to that."

"Not used to something so big between your thighs?" Stone joked and earned a glare from Lark.

"Okay boys, let's go, cars are waiting," Shine said.

They took two cars to the hotel where the event was taking place, just in case they got separated in the aftermath. Stone rode with Granger because Lark said he was an idiot, and no one disagreed. Ebony appreciated the moments alone with Lark, she had a feeling tonight was going to be a turning point for all of them.

CHAPTER TWENTY-FOUR

"Try not to look nervous," Lark said as he put a hand to her lower back. They were following Shine and Granger in as a valet sped off in their cars. Stone was at the back of their little group, and they all had a ticket in hand thanks to the senator. People were everywhere, dressed in such extravagance, Ebony was sure the cost of clothes alone for this event could feed everyone in the LA halfling district for a year. It made her uncomfortable to think of how much her own dress was, although knowing it had been charged to Buchanan helped ease that guilt.

There were lots of looks and whispers and a few greetings to Shine, obviously many of these people had met the daughter of Senator Buchanan before. Shine smiled and waved and greeted back, but she didn't stop to chat. They walked right up the steps and into the main lobby. There was a man there waiting to take their tickets with a look of disdain for the men. Ebony didn't breathe until they had all handed their tickets to the man and had been allowed to enter the ballroom.

"That was too easy," she whispered to Lark.

"The senator is confident, that will likely be his undoing," Lark assured her.

Ebony couldn't help thinking that Lark sounded pretty damn confident too, so what did that mean?

The luxury and extravagance inside was shocking. So many people with glasses of champagne, food being brought around by wait staff. Live music was being played on the stage and the overall feeling was one of joy and indulgence.

"This is supposed to be a fundraiser for his orphanages?" Stone commented.

"The wealthy like to bathe in their wealth while giving tax deductible donations to the poor," Lark grumbled.

"There he is," Shine gasped, and their entire group froze as Buchanan approached with an entourage of security.

"My daughter," Buchanan exclaimed as he embraced Shine, whispering something harshly in her ear that Ebony couldn't hear, but she didn't miss the way Shine stiffened.

The man looked the part of a smooth talking and relatable politician. Grey hair and wrinkles didn't detract from his overall handsome face, and in fact made him look wise. He wore an expensive suit with a silver bowtie and there was a pin on his lapel that said, *VOTE* in red, white, and blue. When he pulled back and looked beyond Shine, dismissing the men in a quick glance, his eyes settled on Ebony and his lips curled in a hateful smile.

"I've been looking for you," he said, but made no move to get closer to her. Lark grasped her waist tightly and Stone stepped up on her other side.

"I would love to have a chat," Ebony said, feeling her confidence waver under his intense scrutiny.

"I imagine you would. Well, I think that can be arranged. My daughter can entertain the men, it's something she's good at," he spat. All the while his smile remained, a practiced look that gave away nothing to the onlookers. To those too far to hear his words it would seem as if he were merely greeting his daughter and her friends.

"She's not going anywhere alone," Lark said darkly.

"Of course, the hired muscle. By the look of that hand on her waist I think I know how she's paying for your services."

Lark made a move forward and Ebony shot out a hand to stop him at the same time Stone grabbed Lark's shoulder.

"Careful, there are a lot of people here. You wouldn't want to make a scene; your girlfriend is already one of LA's most wanted," Buchanan said with a sly grin. "But please, join us." He motioned his hand and suddenly two large men were flanking Ebony and Lark. "Follow me." Buchanan turned and walked swiftly through the crowd.

Ebony looked at Shine who just stared back with unease. She turned to look up at Lark who shrugged, apparently it was her choice what they did next. She was terrified of going anywhere private with this monster but she wanted answers that only he could give, so she started to follow with Lark at her side and two goons behind.

They followed Buchanan to a private room with a few chairs around a coffee table. The goons stopped at the doorway, but Buchanan walked in and sat down as if he couldn't care less about what Ebony wanted to do. She knew she was making an impression on him with every move she made, and didn't want to seem afraid, so she walked in with head high and took a seat. Lark stayed standing behind her and Ebony imagined he was glaring at Buchanan.

"I want to know everything," Ebony demanded.

He smiled and nodded, crossed his legs and leaned back in the chair. His hands were casually laying on the arms of the chair and he looked intimidating. "Well, you know a lot, don't you. But you don't know enough, or you wouldn't be here risking being arrested."

"I know that you've been doing horrid things, but what I want to know more about is my mother's place in it all. Why was she in your facility? What did you do to her? And why were you looking for me?"

"My dear, why wouldn't I look for my daughter?"

Ebony stared, dumbfounded at the man as he grinned at her in satisfaction. He'd been going for shock, and he'd succeeded. She couldn't comprehend, didn't want to.

"What do you mean, *daughter*?" Lark finally said and she was thankful he'd gotten the words out that were stuck in her throat.

"Henrietta came to me when she was young and alone, in trouble because she had no family and no money. It happens a lot. Her father had lost everything at the casino and killed himself. Her mother couldn't handle the shame, the social downfall, and took too many pills one night. I offered Henrietta a chance to be a part of something great. She came to my facility when it was just starting and I was using my own, uh, samples in creation. Your mother was fertile, she took to the first implant right away along with a group of others, but they all spontaneously aborted." Buchanan frowned at the memory.

Ebony was horrified by what she was hearing, but she wanted to know it all even if it threatened to give her nightmares. Lark's comforting hand on her shoulder gave her strength. "So you tried again," she prompted.

"Yes, I adjusted the strength of the artificial soul my lab had come up with. Your mother and about half the women agreed to try it again. Your mother and one other were the only ones whose pregnancy took that time. She carried you in my facility for three months before she disappeared, taking my property with her as well as a good chunk of money she managed to get ahold of from my office safe." His voice had gone dark and his eyes narrowed on her. "The other woman gave birth in the facility both she and the child died a short time later. For a while I assumed the same fate had occurred for you."

Ebony couldn't hold back a shiver.

"So you're the father of how many unfortunate souls?" Lark asked.

"Only one living. I found that my own seed was lacking an important ingredient to get the full desired effect. My offspring would never be able to hold a full soul because I have no soul."

Buchanan dipped his head and swiped a hand across his eyes. When he looked back up Ebony didn't even try to hold back her gasp. His eyes were deep black and soulless. "Oh my god."

"Yes, I am. At least just as good," he said with a bit of a maniacal laugh. "I have given souls, I have given life, and I have figured it all out on my own. I am a god as good as any other, better! Because I am helping to heal the shit hole the others left here. I may not have a soul but I'm the only one who can guarantee a fullsoul baby to those whose soulmates are never born. And who come from supportive families," he added with an evil grin.

"But you had a soulwife," Ebony said with a shake of her head, trying to fit this information with what they already knew.

"I had a wife," he corrected. "You'd be surprised to know how many soulmatches are nothing more than show. How can another look and see a bond like that? They can't. It's a political and social status decision that's made. To live like they are soulmated and come to me for a proper child."

"Why aren't you impregnating the women themselves? Why are you breeding babies in that facility? Are those women who hire you just pretending to be pregnant and then walking out with one of your babies?" Ebony was trying to understand, her mind spinning with everything he was revealing.

"That's the trick, isn't it. You can't fake that many pregnancies well. They have to get pregnant for real, but when they have the child, we make a switch. And as for why I don't impregnate the women themselves? Well there are some unfortunate side effects to the process, many of the women die birthing in my facility, something about the artificial soul doesn't mesh well with their bodies and their organs start to fail." He shrugged as if he couldn't care less about the risks he was putting on those poor women.

"Oh my god, and the orphans are born from the married women," Lark gasped.

"Yes, the orphans," Buchanan said with a wicked grin.

Ebony was dumbfounded. These people were giving up their children, putting them in orphanages to live terrible halfsoul lives and taking the genetically perfected models that Buchanan was producing at the risk of other women's lives, all for what? Social status? Government funding? It was insanity.

"How can you guarantee that the children won't look too different?"

"That's easy enough. I take the man's sample for the fertilizing, and I make sure I've got enough of a variety in women to use for the eggs."

"But there were so many down there," Ebony whispered, trying to understand how so many people could be in on it with him. So desperate for a child that was what they thought perfection needed to be.

"Each couple breeds a child or two, we always have deaths, mistakes and those born... not quite right."

"Like me," Ebony said.

"Yes, you weren't born whole, but so damn close. I could tell when you were in the womb, just three months of development and I could tell you had almost an entire soul. You were what got me to keep trying actually, I knew I was so close to perfecting the soul."

"And Shine?"

"My wife's mistake, an indiscretion. When she was born, I felt a kind of kindred spirit in her and decided I would raise her with the same kind of regimen I'd found worked well for myself. The shots were my first experiment that was successful actually. I had to find a way to live in society, I wouldn't accept the place of a nosoul and I gave Shine the same chance, ungrateful though she may be now."

"Because how could you guarantee she'd do everything you told her if she wasn't bound to you for those fucking shots," Lark hissed.

Buchanan shrugged. "No chip meant no travel. Why she is able to stand in there and not be sick means she has figured out more than I would have liked."

Ebony pursed her lips, unwilling to tell him that by some twist of horrible fate, Shine was her soulsister and Ebony was able to provide a bit of ease to Shine's curse. Let him assume it was all blood related, but if Ebony's soul was faked, how did she have a soulsister at all? It didn't make sense unless her mother hadn't actually gotten pregnant by this horrid man's methods, that was a very comforting thought and Shine just might be the proof of it.

"I'm not your daughter," Ebony said firmly. "My mother stepped out on your little experiment. That's the only reason I survived. Your dead sperm never procreated successfully."

Buchanan's face went red with anger, but he held it back from his voice, a practiced politician. "Perhaps. I could so easily test you to be sure."

Lark put a hand on her shoulder. "You will not touch her."

"You won't," Ebony agreed. "And Shine doesn't need you anymore. She won't do your bidding any longer."

"Won't she?" Buchanan said with a smile that put Ebony on edge. He stood then, and so did Ebony, moving so that he wouldn't get too close to her as he walked to the door of the room. He paused and turned to look at her. "Oh, and before you think you'll go out there and start spouting on about things. You should know that your dear friend, Taylor, is currently at my facility. What happens to her there is on your head... daughter. I'll be in touch for those tests."

Buchanan walked out, his goons followed and they left the door open as if he had no fear. He held all the cards, Ebony realized and she could do nothing to him right now.

Lark gripped her shoulders, and they stood staring at the open door for a time, trying to wrap their heads around all that the senator had revealed.

"We have to stop Shine from doing anything. We have to get Taylor out first."

"You're not his daughter. Not if Shine is your soulsibling and I'm your soulmate. Your soul is real, not whatever he's cooking up in his freaky lab."

"I know. I just wish my mother was here to tell me what really happened."

Lark pulled her in for a comforting embrace. "She did tell you. She fell for a man's charms and then he went and found his soulmate, happens all the time and there's no shame in it."

She brushed a tear from her cheek. "My poor mother must have been so scared that Buchanan would know that she'd cheated on his experiment after I was born, it must be why she left."

"I'm glad she did," Lark said, bending down and pressing a quick kiss to her lips. "She was so brave to do what she did for you."

"She was," Ebony agreed. "And now I need to be brave. I need to save Taylor."

Lark nodded sharply and they left the office.

Shine watched them walk away and the world spun around her. She wasn't processing what Senator Buchanan had just said and she grasped Granger's arm for balance when they were gone. A waiter passed with a tray of champagne, and she reached out for one, downing the liquid in one go.

"Damn girl, are you okay?" Stone asked as he sipped his own glass.

"No," she whispered and grabbed Stone's glass, downing the rest of it.

"Talk," Granger demanded softly.

"He said that my mother is alive."

"What? That's good news," Stone said cheerfully.

She looked at him and blinked back tears. "If I go up there and say anything against him, he'll kill her." Fear slid up and down her spine.

"Shine! So nice to see you outside of DC." A somewhat familiar man came up to her and started chatting on and on, but she couldn't really pay attention to anything that was coming out of his mouth. She just smiled politely and nodded every once in a while. It didn't take long before he moved on, never once noticing that she wasn't paying attention. These people just liked to hear themselves talk; they didn't really care about anyone else. That was a lesson she'd learned long ago.

"I need to get out of here," she whispered to Granger.

"Go on, I'll wait for Lark and Ebony, and meet you guys back at the hotel," Stone offered.

Granger grabbed her arm and guided her back out through

the crowd. A few people tried to engage her in conversation as they went but a quick scowl from Granger was enough to stop them in their tracks.

When they were in Granger's car and on their way out of the parking lot, Shine let herself feel. Her body trembled, tears filled her eyes, and she punched the dashboard. "Fuck, ouch," she squealed and held her hand to her chest. "Why do guys do that shit?"

Granger laughed. "Mostly we don't," he said gently and reached out for the hand she was cradling. He pulled it to his lips and kissed her bruising knuckles. "Most men know that punching hurts."

"He's a monster, Granger."

"Yes, he is."

"Maybe we shouldn't have left Ebony and Lark alone with him."

"They'll be okay, Lark is very capable and I don't think Buchanan will want to make a scene there. Hopefully they get some answers we can use."

"He thinks he's untouchable," she whispered. "Maybe he is."

"No one is that far above everyone else, Shine. We will find your mother and we will bring him down."

She wasn't so sure, and it hurt.

They didn't speak again until they were in the hotel room. Granger started a bath for her and helped her undress. Once she was settled into the hot water, he stepped out of the bathroom, and she could hear his voice humming in the other room as he made phone calls. She closed her eyes and let the hot water soak into her, let it ease the tension a bit.

"Stone just messaged, said he's on the way back here with Lark and Ebony. They want to meet and tell us what they found out. He told them why you didn't make your announcement."

Shine nodded. "Okay, give me another minute and I'll get out. Could you run downstairs and get me something to wear from the giftshop. Some sweats and a T-shirt would be great."

"Sure."

She drained the tub, washed her face, and wrapped in a towel. When he got back with a bag from the gift shop, she gratefully pulled out the tacky hotel emblemed sweats and T-shirt proclaiming *Vegas is for Fun*.

His lip quirked as he took in the sight of her. "Cute," he said.

"I look ridiculous, but at least it's clean and comfortable."

"They are waiting for us in Lark's suite. Are you ready?"

"Yeah, let's do this."

CHAPTER TWENTY-FIVE

Ebony stripped out of the dress as soon as they were back in the hotel room. She washed the makeup off her face and put on a pair of sweats and T-shirt Lark had grabbed at the gift shop for her. She felt more herself this way and thankfully accepted a cup of tea from Lark when she emerged from the bathroom.

When Shine and Granger arrived in the room there was a silent moment and then lots of laughter. Ebony and Shine were dressed exactly the same.

"Can't even blame it on the soulsister thing, I picked out the damn clothes," Granger said and Lark agreed, but it lightened everyone's mood and they all sat with cups of tea as they told their parts of what happened with the senator.

They sat around full of shock after, each one trying to figure out what their next move should be. Or if they even had one.

"Did you know?" Granger asked Shine after a moment. "That he's a nosoul?"

"I had no idea he was a nosoul," Shine admitted. "But it makes sense, doesn't it. How else would he have kept me alive from birth if he didn't already have the shots figured out."

"Where could he be hiding your mother and why?" Lark asked Shine.

"I have no idea, maybe he always saw it as a last way to control me? Certainly worked tonight," Shine grumbled.

Ebony reached out and set a comforting hand on Shine's knee. "No one blames you for not speaking up tonight after that. I'd do anything to see my mother again and I'd never do anything to endanger her if she were possibly alive."

"I just hate that he won." Shine's lips thinned and her fists clenched. Ebony was sure that this woman would do what it took no matter what. The senator may have delayed his downfall but Shine looked ready to regroup and still take him down.

"He bought himself time, that's all." Ebony said.

Lark nodded agreement. "He wouldn't have taken Taylor if he didn't feel his control slipping. He's scared and we have him on the defensive which means he's still worried that he'll lose everything if his business becomes public. No matter how *godly* he thinks he is, he knows that the majority of people will not agree," Lark said.

"So, how do we expose him and his despicable business without him harming Taylor or Shine's mother in retaliation?" Ebony asked with frustration. It felt like they were talking in a circle.

"We need someone on the inside, someone who won't want to go down with the ship and might be convinced to help us," Lark said with a grin, obviously having someone in mind.

"Who would do that?" Shine asked.

"Marty," Lark said with a grin.

"Marty?" Ebony asked doubtfully.

"He runs the facility and labs; he knows it all and has probably had his hand in some really shady shit. If we can offer him a clean getaway, I bet he'll turn on Buchanan in a heartbeat to save his own ass," Lark explained.

Ebony couldn't deny it sounded reasonable. A man with such low morals wouldn't think twice about double-crossing his boss to save himself.

Stone stood up and cracked his knuckles. "Give me fifteen minutes on my laptop, and I'll have an address."

"We don't even know the guy's last name," Ebony said in surprise.

"As if that's ever stopped me," Stone huffed, then pulled his laptop out of his bag and started clicking at keys.

"Can I sit with you?" Shine asked Ebony with a shy smile.

Ebony patted the seat next to her on the couch and Lark moved from Ebony's other side at Granger's glare. Shine sat on the couch and leaned against Ebony with a little sigh.

Silence filled the room aside from the click clack of keys as Stone went to work figuring out where Marty lived. Soon Ebony's eyelids were feeling heavy, and she found herself drifting to sleep.

She woke when a blanket was settled on top of her, Shine was still curled up next to her, breathing softly. Ebony looked up into Lark's face.

"Go back to sleep. Stone's still searching."

Ebony nodded and let herself drift again.

Lark watched the girls sleep peacefully and envied Shine getting to curl up with Ebony like that. He wanted so badly to pick Ebony up and carry her to bed, ignore the world around them, and just enjoy each other's company.

"Got an address," Stone said with a triumphant whoop.

"Shh," Lark and Granger growled.

"Sorry," Stone said, eyes on the sleeping women. "Found

Marty Taison, employee at BaneCore. Has to be our guy. He's a fullsoul without a wife, no living relatives, and a degree in genetics."

"Sounds like our guy. How close is he?" Lark prompted.

"Fifteen or twenty minutes from here it looks like. Should we pay the bastard a visit?"

"Someone needs to stay here," Lark said, looking at the sleeping beauties.

"I'll stay," Granger said. "If Buchanan tries anything, I'll happily put a bullet in his head." Granger pulled a gun out of his waistband and set it on the table.

Lark nodded, confident that his soulwife was safe. He leaned down and kissed Ebony's forehead.

Shine let out a contented sigh.

"She's not yours," Granger hissed quietly.

"I don't want her to be," Lark assured his friend. "But I don't think either of them can live without the other. If being close to Ebony helps ease Shine's body, then being close to Shine might help Ebony's body fight the cancer." It was something he'd been thinking about and wondering at the implications, not only for Ebony and Shine but for all halflings.

"Soulsiblings don't just live together peacefully," Granger said.

"And no marriage is recognized by the government unless it's a soulmate match. If you don't have a fullsoul you are destined to live a terrible lonely life." Lark shook his head at Granger. "Lies from the government. What if soulsiblings can heal each other? Imagine what a difference that could make."

"And what if we all live in a nice universe instead of hell," Stone snapped. "Let's go get Marty."

Lark knew they weren't about to solve the world's problems tonight, but he couldn't shake the feeling that they'd stumbled on something massively important. One thing at a time though, and right now, they had a man to threaten.

When Lark and Stone arrived at Marty's small home, they sat in the car watching for a while. It was completely dark which meant the man was probably in bed, sleeping. There was only one car parked out front which meant he was likely alone. This would be too easy.

They quickly unlocked the front door and crept through the house with only the light from the moon and nearby streetlamp to guide them. The first room they checked was an in-home office. Lark was tempted to check it for files on Buchanan, but doubted it would contain anything incriminating. The second was Marty's bedroom and as expected, he was snoring away in his bed, alone, as if he didn't have a care in the world.

Stone stood on one side and Lark the other. It was a familiar routine.

"Wake up, dumbass," Stone said loudly.

Marty's eyes popped open, he snapped up in bed and Lark punched him in the face. A spray of blood hit the bedding and the man laid back down with a howl of pain.

"We have some questions. You can help us, or you can go down with Buchanan," Lark said.

Marty's eyes darted from one of them to the other and Lark saw the moment he recognized their faces.

"Yes, we toured your facility today and although it was very enlightening, we seem to have a few more questions before we go ahead with our plans," Stone explained.

"You'll never bring him down," Marty said, shaking his head, eyes wide with terror. "The man has support high up, all the way up."

"We aren't worried about the high ups, it's the low downs that will revolt when they discover what he's been doing," Lark said, leaning down close to the man's face. "And trust me when I say, there are far more of us than them."

"You'll start a war," Marty gasped.

Lark shrugged. "Sometimes that's what it takes to make things right when the people in charge are assholes."

"So," Stone said, pulling out a knife. "Whose side are you going to be on?"

"What do you want to know?" Marty said quickly.

Lark held back a smile. This man was as weak as expected. "Where is Shine's mother and the girl Buchanan took from LA, Taylor?" Lark demanded.

"Second floor, the one we skipped. I knew as soon as I saw Shine in person that her mother was the one he keeps there. I don't know for sure about Taylor, but there was a girl brought into the facility this evening, could be her. She'll be downstairs with the other breeders."

"You're taking us there, tonight," Lark said matter-of-factly.

"He'll kill me if he finds out," Marty sputtered.

"We'll kill you if you refuse," Stone said with a shrug.

"Help us and I can make sure you get somewhere safe to disappear. You'll be long gone before Buchanan figures out your deceit. It's your only real chance, Marty," Lark explained.

Marty gave a shaky nod and Lark stepped back. Stone did the same. "Time's ticking," Stone said and pulled the covers off the man.

Marty shook his head and sputtered. "The place has tighter security than DC at night. We can't go in until morning. It will set off alarms everywhere otherwise."

A ringing phone had them all stopping and staring. "Who would be calling this late I wonder," Lark said darkly.

"Answer it, dumbass," Stone said and handed the phone to Marty. "On speaker."

Marty's face was pale, but he answered it as instructed. "Hello."

"Marty, get your ass to the facility. I have two girls I need to drop off."

Lark met Stone's gaze over the bed, fear flowing through him. That was Buchanan's voice and he had no doubt about which two girls he was talking about.

"Sure thing boss, be right there." Marty's hands were shaking as he hung up the phone and dropped it on the bed.

"If he's hurt either one of them, I'm going to kill you," Lark growled.

"He's going to kill me as soon as he sees you two," Marty whined.

Stone had his phone out already and was dialing Granger. "Not our problem," Stone hissed at Marty.

Stone's phone was on speaker and they all listened to it ring loudly, each time it seemed to get louder, the sound pierced through Lark's heart, worry filling him beyond anything he'd ever known.

"Pick up, you ass," Stone snapped at the phone as it rang on unanswered.

"Get ready to go," Lark demanded. Fear and anger was coursing through him, he wanted to run, to kill and he didn't even know for sure that it was Ebony and Shine who Buchanan was talking about, but who else would he have? If Lark lost her, he would burn down everything that belonged to Buchanan before he jumped off a cliff to join her in the next life.

Marty jumped to obey. Lark kept one eye on the man rummaging around the room and pulling on pants and a shirt and one eye on Stone as he hung up and dialed again, this time he had the phone to his ear and Lark wasn't sure if he was glad he didn't have to hear the ringing or not.

"What the fuck happened?" Stone demanded, apparently

Granger had picked up finally. Stone hit the speaker phone and Granger's voice filled the room.

"I had to piss. I was out of the room for seconds and the girls were asleep. When I walked out of the bathroom, I was bashed on the head. I just woke up and they are gone." His voice was frantic and angry.

Lark could imagine him pacing around like a caged beast ready to kill.

"Buchanan is taking them to the facility. Meet us there, we've got Marty," Stone said and hung up.

Lark met Stone's eyes and knew all his emotions were showing on his face.

"We'll get them back," Stone assured Lark but they both knew that wasn't a guarantee.

CHAPTER TWENTY-SIX

Ebony was pissed. Not only was she being dragged out of the hotel at gunpoint, but she hadn't been allowed to put on shoes. Shine was equally annoyed at her side, but they could do nothing other than follow along and hope for an opportunity to escape. They didn't know where the boys were, Granger was lying on the floor bleeding and passed out, and Buchanan and his goons were giving orders.

Ebony and Shine were shoved down a back stairwell and out into an alley and directly into a waiting car. Once the car was driving away and Buchanan hung up with Marty, Ebony was glad they at least knew where they were headed. It also seemed likely that it would be the first place Lark would look for her, so her confidence grew and she glared at Buchanan.

"What's the plan? No one may notice me being gone, but Shine can't just disappear off the face of the earth," Ebony said.

"No, she can't, but I think Shine will agree that our little arrangement is for the best. She's got a lot to lose," Buchanan said, giving Shine a harsh glower.

Ebony looked at Shine and she wasn't sure what the woman was thinking. Her face was passive, almost as if she were going to do whatever Buchanan asked. Ebony hoped Shine was just playing along, because Shine deserved so much better than what Buchanan wanted to use her for.

"And you," Buchanan continued, turning back to Ebony. "After you all left the event tonight, I had a slight change of heart. A realization, perhaps you could say. That I didn't like the idea of you out there, Ebony, a loose end to worry over. So no matter how sure I am that you'll want to keep your mouth shut in order to guarantee your dear friend's safety, I am going to have to keep you closer to home."

"I'll never breed for you," Ebony hissed.

"No, you can't, you're not whole. It would never work; I've tried with others. It just ends up like me, or her," he said motioning to Shine. "The only way to get the artificial soul to present in the child is for the mother to have a full soul." He shrugged.

"So I get to just live there, rot there?" Ebony scoffed.

"Oh no, you get to die there." Buchanan gave her a wide wicked grin and his eyes lit up as if he were relishing the mere thought of killing her.

Ebony shot a look at Shine, terrified that this maniac might be able to do just that with no more thought than someone else might give to buying a pair of shoes. A new wave of fear flowed over her and she started to lose what little hope she'd had for surviving this ordeal.

"That won't put me on your side," Shine said, voice shaky.

"No? Watching your friend die before your eyes isn't convincing enough to be a good girl? Well then how about her death at your hand? I'll make sure your prints are all over the weapon and her body will be found somewhere very public, oh say like your hotel room. Plenty of people have seen you two together, maybe you got into a tiff over one of those men you were with and you shot her out of jealousy."

Shit, blackmail. As if holding Shine's mother somewhere under lock and key wasn't bad enough, he was threatening Shine with life in prison. This guy was next-level insane.

"You wouldn't want me in jail, then everyone would know my secret, *your* deception," Shine spat.

Buchanan looked annoyed as if he hadn't considered that bit. "Well, I can put your mother's prints on it. She'd never last in jail. She's quite delicate after all." Buchanan sneered at Shine.

Ebony could see the very real fear in Shine's eyes at that statement. He'd have her with that threat. Shine may be willing to sacrifice herself, but not her mother.

"Why take me to the facility to do it? Why not kill me now, or back at the hotel? This seems like a waste of time," Ebony said.

"I need a few pints of your blood to test before I spill the rest of it and your men are currently on their way there too, with that traitor Marty. I have his house watched, I knew the moment they pulled up outside and he's too much of a weak link to deny them when threatened. I plan to take out all my enemies in one shot." Buchanan smiled. "And I imagine Granger will arrive as well, as soon as he wakes up from that little bump on the head."

They were all walking into a trap! Ebony's throat tightened, her heart sped up and panic started to fill her. Would the guys be expecting it?

"Oh, and I brought this along for you, dear." Buchanan pulled out a syringe filled with red liquid and smiled darkly at Shine. "How badly do you want the relief? It's hard to be away from, isn't it. To be honest I didn't think you'd have what it takes to get yourself a fix the old fashioned way, but you've proven me wrong on a few accounts the last two days."

"I don't need it enough to go along with murder," Shine said but her eyes filled with longing as she gazed at the syringe.

Ebony could tell she didn't want to need it, but it was a safety net she must crave.

"Oh, don't be silly, you know I don't want you to be uncomfortable. Frank, hold her arm," Buchanan insisted and one of the goons grabbed Shine's arm and held it steady as Buchanan injected her.

Shine didn't fight the hold, just closed her eyes and sighed as the red liquid entered her body. When Buchanan pulled the needle out, she wrenched her arm out of Frank's grip.

"There now, you always were a bit of a brat about it. Nurse Reagan complained about you constantly."

"Maybe she shouldn't work for such an asshole," Shine mumbled and rubbed at the spot where she'd been injected.

Buchanan laughed. "She's been with me for a long time. She understands what I'm trying to do, what service I provide to the world. I'll be responsible for the survival of our country you know. Do you have any idea how few fullsouls are born naturally?"

Ebony just stared out the window. She didn't want to hear anything Buchanan had to say to justify the horrors he inflicted on others. She needed to figure out a way to survive the night, and she needed to make sure Shine took her soul if she didn't.

That's the thought that struck her with an idea, a way to put a wrinkle in Buchanan's plan. The man thought he had everything figured out, but there was a kink that she knew he wouldn't expect, and it might get him to wait long enough for the guys to show up.

"It's too bad you're wrong," she said with a laugh.

Buchanan glared at her. "Wrong about what exactly?"

"Shine and her mother could never go down for my murder," she said, looking him straight in the eye. "Because I'm her soulsister and it's not illegal to kill your soulsibling or to help your child claim their full soul."

Buchanan's eyes widened and he looked from one of them to the other in astonishment. "Artificial souls don't have soulsiblings."

"Oh yeah, and did I mention that Lark is my soulmate? We sparked." Ebony grinned and felt a bit of her power and survival instinct come back to her. "I told you I'm not your daughter, asshole."

"But you're still not a fullsoul, how did you spark to Lark?" His eyes lit up and she knew she had him. He was a scientist at heart, and he wanted to investigate, wanted to test. He would keep her alive, at least for a time so he could see why her soul was acting different. "Is it because you have more than half, because Shine is barely a soul at all?"

Ebony shrugged and let a little satisfaction soften the smile on her face. She could play his weak point long enough; Lark would save them.

The car pulled into the familiar lot of BaneCore, and they were once again prodded and led by gunpoint. This time into a dark, quiet, building. They went through the lobby, straight to the elevators, and down a level to the laboratory.

"I need blood, and a scan on both of you. When Lark arrives I'll need his too. Get me the information on Lark. He's an orphan, I know that much, is he one of our castoffs?" Buchanan shouted the order to a man in a lab coat who didn't look at all surprised by their sudden appearance, or the obvious unwillingness of her and Shine to be there. "No, couldn't be, they never have soulsiblings, they wouldn't spark," he mumbled as he moved around. "Tie them up," he told the guards.

The guards did as ordered, strapping Shine and Ebony to some chairs, then Buchanan sent them back upstairs to apprehend Lark and the others when they undoubtedly arrived.

"Why did you tell him?" Shine hissed. "Now we are lab rats."

"Better than dead already," Ebony hissed back. "Look how distracted he is, like a kid in a candy store. We need the time so Lark can save us."

"Blood," Buchanan mumbled as he walked over and shoved a needle in Ebony's arm, drawing out blood.

"Ouch" Ebony hissed but Buchanan didn't even look at her face just grinned at the vial and moved over to Shine.

She didn't even react to the poke, so used to needles apparently. He walked away and a woman in a lab coat with an apologetic face came up to them and asked them to hold still while she scanned them with some kind of handheld device.

"Now touch please while I scan you both again," the woman asked softly.

"Sure, just untie me," Ebony said with a smile.

The woman frowned and looked back at where Buchanan was mumbling over a microscope. She obviously didn't want to bother him and she seemed unsure about the whole situation.

"If you ask him, he's going to yell at you," Shine pointed out.

"Fine, but only one of you, and only one hand." The woman untied Ebony's right arm and Ebony immediately reached over to touch Shine as the woman scanned them a second time.

The scanning took just enough time for Ebony to discreetly loosen Shines' bound arm as the woman was preoccupied with whatever she saw on the little device's screen. When the woman retied Ebony and walked away, Shine was able to squeeze that one hand out. After that it was only a matter of moments before her other arm was undone, with both the woman and Buchanan completely distracted by what they were currently studying. The harder part to do unnoticed though was going to be reaching over and undoing Ebony's bonds without anyone noticing.

"Go," Ebony hissed at Shine under her breath. "Find a way out, get to the men before they're ambushed. Or find a phone to warn them. He's not going to kill me until he figures out what happened with us, he's too curious."

"Lark will kill me if I leave you here," Shine whispered back, her eyes never leaving Buchanan. "I am certain he'd rather be captured and tortured given the option."

Ebony thought Shine was probably right, but it felt risky to wait. "Fine untie this hand, keep as still as possible and if they notice you, run no matter what. One of us should survive this."

Shine slipped her left hand to Ebony's right and together they managed to get it freed then Ebony quickly undid her other. They both sat there, freed but not sure what to do.

"Even if we make it to the elevator, we'll never survive waiting for the doors to open," Ebony pointed out.

"We don't have any weapons, but I could throw a chair or two," Shine said.

Ebony just shook her head, that probably wouldn't buy them enough time. "The elevator is going to open when the boys get here, but they'll be with the goons and Marty, we'll be outnumbered," Ebony said, thinking out loud.

"Stairs," Shine said. "There has to be stairs up or down, right? Otherwise it would be a fire hazard."

Ebony darted her eyes around. There were a few doors but only one looked dark enough on the other side to presume it was a rarely used stairwell. "There," Ebony said, pointing with her chin. Unfortunately it was on the other side of the room, with Buchanan and the nurse between.

"We could try and make a run for them," Shine said.

"Divide and conquer," Ebony said. "When the elevator doors open, you run for the stairwell, I'll run to the elevator. They won't risk shooting you and if I'm running toward them, they'll just grab me not shoot me."

Shine nodded and thirty seconds later the ding of the elevator reverberated through the room. They both bolted as planned. Buchanan yelled, indignant, as the elevator doors opened.

But it was Lark's waiting arms Ebony ran into, not the goons'. Stone was behind him and Granger with a bloody Marty held by the back of the neck.

"Fuck, Ebony," Lark groaned as their bodies touched and sparks of recognition and relief flew through them both.

"How did you get past security?" Buchanan stuttered.

Ebony's gaze swept the room, but Shine was gone.

"Those idiots," Stone laughed.

"Almost as easy to turn as Marty here," Granger said, shoving the man forward.

"Only took a few punches and they saw our way of thinking."

Buchanan's face turned red with rage. "You can't stop me, you don't understand what I've just found, what she means! It's —it's—it's everything!" Buchanan said loudly, pointing a shaking finger at Ebony.

"Yes, she is everything, to me, to Shine, but not to you," Lark said. "Never to you." Then he raised a gun and shot the senator through the middle of the head.

The lady in the lab coat was already cowering on the floor but she let out a scream at the sound and somewhere deep in the facility an alarm started to go off.

Before Ebony could comment, the sprinklers above them blasted on.

"Fire?" she gasped.

Lark looked at her then growled, "The children."

"Where's Shine?" Granger demanded.

"She was headed for the stairwell, I was the distraction," Ebony explained.

Granger took off at a run for the stairwell and they followed, assuming the elevator would automatically go out of commission with the alarm.

It was massive chaos in the stairwell. More people than Ebony ever could have imagined being in the facility rushed upstairs. Women with glassy eyes, men and women in lab coats carrying multiple infants. Ebony was shocked that they cared about the infants at all, but she supposed Buchanan would be upset if he lost all of his investment, and they didn't know the man was currently bleeding out on the lab floor.

"Take Marty to find Taylor. I'm getting Ebony out of here," Lark ordered Stone and shoved her into the swarm of people and up the stairwell. In the chaos no one questioned them or looked twice as they all tried to get to safety.

They burst out of the stairwell with the crowd and into the lobby then rushed out to the parking lot. She was relieved to be out of that place but fear still gripped her. Fear for Shine and Taylor and all the innocent people who might be trapped inside.

Lark wrapped her in his arms and squeezed her tight. "I thought I was going to be too late," he whispered against her head.

"I knew you'd save me," she whispered back. She pulled back and looked around the dark parking lot. The workers were herding everyone as if they had practiced for this. The women and children were loaded into waiting vans that drove away as soon as they were full.

"All the evidence is leaving," Ebony said not sure if they should try and stop them.

"The culprit is dead, Ebony. I don't think the evidence matters anymore."

She supposed he was right, but she felt guilty anyway. Shouldn't they be trying to find justice for those women, those children? "What's going to happen to them when they find out Buchanan is dead? Is someone else going to pick up where he left off? They still aren't free, they are probably headed to a secondary facility."

"I don't know, Ebony. I think the best we can do right now is make sure everyone we care about is safe, then we can make sure no one else takes on Buchanan's project," Lark said. "We can still reveal all of this horror, we can stop anyone from making the same mistakes."

Ebony was comforted by Lark's assurances and watched the front of the building for the rest of their group. "Shine!" Ebony screeched when she saw her soulsister burst out of the building just as sirens were heard in the distance.

Shine was hurrying out the doors with Granger on her heels. He had a woman in his arms. "Her mother?" Ebony guessed. "But where's Taylor and Stone?"

"We need to get out of here," Lark pressed, pulling her toward their waiting car.

Granger shoved the woman he was carrying into the back seat and pushed Shine to follow, then hopped in.

"Where the hell is Stone?" Lark growled.

"He's still looking for Taylor, we can't leave them here," Ebony said frantically.

"We can't stay and talk to the cops, Ebony," Lark insisted. "You're already under suspicion for murder, there's a very dead body in there and I doubt there's a real fire to cover anything up," Lark shoved her into the passenger seat of the car. "Stone will be okay, he'll get Taylor out too."

"I pulled the alarm," Shine admitted, "Seemed like a good idea at the time."

Ebony didn't argue as Lark got in the driver's seat and started the car

"Stone is capable," he reassured her as they peeled out and followed a back road that the vans had taken.

The car was barely out of the paved lot when an explosion

rocked the world. Lark slammed on the brakes and spun the car around to face the facility again. It was an inferno.

"I thought it was a fake fire," Ebony gasped.

"Maybe it's some sort of failsafe, to keep the evidence hidden in an emergency," Shine pointed out.

"Well there goes the research," Granger said with relief. "It'll be harder for anyone to pick up where Buchanan left off, I hope."

"And the evidence of Buchanan's murder," Lark added.

No one wanted to say what they were all thinking. But tears poured out of Ebony's eyes for her friends.

CHAPTER TWENTY-SEVEN

Shine sat in the hotel room staring into space, beside her was her mother, catatonic as she'd been when they found her and Granger looking murderous as he sat silently. Ebony and Lark sat cuddled together, tears streaming down Ebony's face off and on. The television was on a news channel talking about the explosion and the assumption that the great Senator Buchanan was inside at the time and perished in the explosion.

"I will have to make a statement," Shine said quietly as she clung to her mother.

"You don't have to do anything, you can still disappear," Granger said gently.

Shine shook her head. "I think I need to stay present. I think it's important that I keep an eye out for his research popping back up in his circles. There are people out there who know what he was doing, even if they aren't willing to talk openly about it and they may try to continue it. There has to be a lot of evidence in his office at home and downtown DC too. I'm sure I can use it to help. I want to find all of the babies that I can, I want them to know where they came from," she whispered and looked at Granger. "They deserve to know what it might mean for them in this life."

She didn't have to say that it was a likely sentence to lifelong loneliness, no soulmate waiting for a fullsoul that was developed in a lab. But Shine was right, they deserved to know. They could make the decision to find happiness where they could instead of waiting for something that was impossible. She grabbed Granger's hand. She'd found something incredible that didn't involve her soul and she was sure others could too, given the chance.

"I'll help you," Granger said softly and kissed her.

"I think it matters," Ebony agreed. "I'm glad you'll tell them. It doesn't have to change anything, but it is a piece of who they are."

"Just a small piece," Lark said. "We are more than the cursed souls we were given."

A knock at the door had them all jumping.

"Open up, fuckers," Stone yelled through the closed door.

"Oh my god," Ebony whispered as Lark rushed over and opened the door. "Oh my god," she squealed at the sight of her friend standing there with Stone. "Taylor."

Ebony rushed to Taylor, embracing her tightly. "Are you okay, how did you get out, what the hell happened?" She led her friend to the couch and Stone followed with a frown.

"I found her tied up in the lower level. We were only a few steps from the facility when it blew. Threw us out into a field. We had a hell of a time getting back here. No one wants to pick up a couple dirty street walkers in the middle of the night. Even in Vegas it's weird."

"I'm so sorry that happened to you, Taylor. This is all my fault," Ebony said with tears in her voice.

"No," Taylor said with a frown. "It's all Senator Buchanan's fault."

"At least he's dead," Granger said.

"And you're Shine Buchanan," Taylor gasped, finally seeing everyone else in the room.

"I am," Shine agreed.

"You're a bitch," Taylor said, then put a hand to her mouth as if she hadn't meant to say that aloud. "Sorry, I guess facing death does something to your filter."

Shine laughed, she liked this woman. "It's okay. I imagine most halflings feel that way about me."

"She's my soulsister," Ebony said and before Taylor could ask a million questions, she told her that Lark was her soulmate too.

"Okay, did I die in that explosion?" Taylor said with a laugh.

"I died once," Shine's mother said softly, making everyone stop and stare. She just turned her head to look at a wall and didn't say anything more.

"I think we should take her back to DC," Shine said, looking pleadingly at Granger. "I can get her help, undo some of what Buchanan did, hopefully," she said, biting back tears. She was so glad to have her mother, a woman she'd only ever seen pictures of, but she hurt for what Buchanan must have put the woman through.

Granger nodded, "We can go now. Lark, I'm taking the big plane."

Lark nodded. "Go ahead, we'll be heading to Texas in the morning. Ebony needs to see the doctor as soon as possible."

"That all sounds great, but I want to go home," Taylor said. "The new guy who took over for Glick is less of an asshole but if I miss any more days he's going to fire me for sure."

"I can handle that one, we'll rent a car and drive," Stone said. "If your boss fires you, I'll have a little chat with him," Stone said, cracking his knuckles.

Taylor rolled her eyes at his macho display. "Okay, but in the morning, okay? I need sleep first and a shower."

"Sure," Stone said and stood, holding out his hand to her.

It looked like Ebony was about to disagree with that arrangement, but then she snapped her mouth shut. Taylor looked delighted by the offer and that made Shine happy. Shine stood then and Ebony embraced her, they both whispered promises to talk soon and meet up again when it seemed safe. They didn't want to be apart, but they both had things that they needed to do.

"I'm glad I found you," Ebony said as a tear slid down her cheek.

"I'm glad you did, too," Shine said, and wiped Ebony's tear away. "Take good care of her," Shine said to Lark then Granger picked up Shine's mother and they left the room.

Shine sat on the airplane once again with Granger, only this time instead of Stone keeping them from laying a cabin seat back and joining the mile high club in style, her mother was there, staring off into the distance blankly.

"What do you think he did to her?" she asked Granger.

Granger shook his head and grabbed Shine's hands. "It's hard to say, but we will find her the best care once we land. Even without her records, a doctor should be able to evaluate her. I'm sure we can do it all very hush hush, no one needs to know she's alive and back."

"Why?"

"I just figured—"

"That I'd want to cover up for that horrid man? Oh no. I plan to out so much of what he was doing," she said with satisfaction. "I have been thinking about it for the last hour and I think what we should do is call a press conference at my house for the morning. I think we should confirm that the senator is dead, that my mother is alive and what he was doing in that facility." Shine knew she was angry, knew her voice showed it, but she didn't care. She *was* angry, for herself, her mother, Ebony and everyone who had fled that facility. "The world deserves to know what he did, they shouldn't mourn him."

"Babe," Granger said softly. "I don't think you're seeing things clearly."

"What?" she snapped and pulled her hands out of his grip, feeling betrayed.

"You're not his daughter. If you reveal that bit to the world, then someone is going to come after you for everything he owned. You can't inherit it; you're not really related. Not only that but halflings can't inherit from parents anyway so unless he put you in his will, which I doubt, you'd get nothing. The only way to fight what his will might say is if the world continues to believe you are his fullsoul legitimate daughter."

"I don't give a shit about his money."

"I know, but how well can you take care of her without it? How well can you track down the orphans, the mothers, everyone affected by his dirty work without money and the power it brings? I'll give you every penny I have, and I still don't think it will be enough to do what I know you want to do for them all."

Shine sat back and frowned. "Damnit, I hate that you're right."

Granger nodded. "So here's my plan. We sneak back in much like we snuck out. You *do* call a press conference as the grieving daughter. You confirm he had a meeting at the facility late last night and was likely in the explosion. You don't introduce your mother, at least not until we know what he did to her and what we can undo. Then we get to work. We search every file and every computer and find every one of the children he created with synthetic souls. Let them decide what to do with that information. It is better that it's their decision and they can keep it hidden if they want."

"We need to find the women and children who were taken out tonight. I don't want them used anymore."

"Yes, I think that's at the top of the list. Once word is out that your father is dead, they'll be scrambling. We need to know who would step in if he died, there has to be some kind of second in command and I doubt it was Marty."

Shine shook her head and thought of all her father's associates. There were a couple who might be primed to take over. She'd invite them over for a discussion. A few threats would hopefully be enough to get them to back off and keep their knowledge to themselves.

"How do we keep anyone else from doing what he did?"

"We can't."

"So we can't keep it a secret, can we? At least not forever," Shine said.

"I guess not," Granger admitted. "So, back to plan A? Press conference and reveal all? The good, the bad and the ugly?"

"Hey, who you calling ugly," Shine teased and slid across to Granger's lap. She laid her head on his shoulder and let him hold her close, comforting. "We don't have to reveal what I am, or my mother. But we can talk about his research, we can reveal all he did wrong to those people."

"It's a brave path," Granger said as he stroked her back gently.

"I think it's what Ebony would do," she said with a sigh. "I miss her already."

"Do you need something I can give you?"

She shook her head. "No, and that's another thing. If there is a way to at least partially heal nosouls with a shot, that needs to be knowledge, that needs to be shared around the world. Think of all the people we could save." She sat up straight in his lap and her mind spun around the possibilities. They could save so many from suffering, they could open up the world to those who cowered in darkness.

"You truly are a good soul, Shine."

"Better than what the gods designed, I'd say. I never once wanted to kill my soulsister."

"Not even a little?" he asked.

"Not even when she wore the same outfit as me," Shine said with a laugh.

"Do you envy her having a soulmate, the soulspark is supposed to be great."

"I don't envy her anything. She has everything she deserves, and I have everything I want," she said and slipped onto his lap, kissing him passionately.

A shocked sound from her mother had her crawling off with a laugh. "Meet me in the bathroom in five minutes," she whispered and shook her ass down the aisle.

CHAPTER TWENTY-EIGHT

Ebony sat in a hotel room in Texas a few days later. It wasn't Vegas and although Lark continued to insist he be the only one to get scanned wherever they went, and called her wife as often as possible, people still looked and judged. But she was getting used to ignoring it. She probably could never go back to LA without risking getting arrested for Glick's murder, but she figured that wasn't a huge loss, she could have Taylor send her some things from her house once she felt settled somewhere. Lark talked about the options like they were infinite, but Ebony didn't think she wanted to settle anywhere she felt judged. Vegas, the city her mother grew up in, called to her.

"Oh, here she comes!" Lark said excitedly as they watched on television as Shine stepped onto a small platform in front of her house once again. Granger was visible in the background, looking like a bodyguard.

"I come to you today to talk about my next steps in righting some of my father's wrongs," Shine began.

In the last two days she'd been on television more than ever, and each time she let out a little more information about what her father had been doing. The uproar was reminiscent of the great souling, which is what everyone called the time after the war when the gods first cursed them. People were questioning their neighbors and themselves. Families were torn apart, mostly those in higher society when an adult child found out they were a bought baby with an artificial soul. Orphans all over were reaching out, hoping to find their real parents.

Ebony couldn't even feel sorry for the parents, they'd done it to themselves. The big question was, what was the government going to do about the artificial souls? At first it had seemed like they would be pushed down below the nosouls, but then it started to come out that many politicians had children in this group, and they certainly weren't about to banish them or watch them starve.

"I demand the government lift all travel restrictions based on status and chip scanning." Shine had finished her speech and she stood while the crowd shouted questions at her.

"She looks like she's loving this," Lark said.

"She really does well in front of cameras, I'm just glad it isn't me," Ebony said and turned off the television.

"Time to go?" Lark asked and she nodded.

They were on their way to see the doctor that Lark was insisting would be able to cure Ebony's cancer.

She still didn't believe it was possible and held herself back from getting too excited. She'd accepted her lot a long time ago, and although it was harder now that she'd found Lark, she wasn't ready to hope too much just yet.

They walked hand in hand to the office of Dr. Lewis Grey. The secretary greeted them cheerily and ushered them back to a small room.

A nurse came in and drew some blood, and scanned her with a handheld device that reminded her uncomfortably of the one that had been used at the facility.

Lark squeezed her hand when she tensed, and the nurse made a sound of surprise.

"What is it?" Lark demanded.

"The doctor will be right in," she said and hurried out.

"I hate when they do that," Ebony said with a frown.

Luckily it wasn't long until Dr. Grey entered the room and smiled warmly.

"You must be Ebony, I've heard a lot about you," he said, reaching out to shake her hand. "And it's always good to see you, Mr. Duport."

"What did the nurse find?" Lark demanded, not caring about pleasantries.

Dr. Grey took a seat on a stool and stared down at an open file. "Well, I read all of your history, Ebony and like I told Mr. Duport, your chances looked very slim. Very likely that you'd last no more than a year and a tough one at that."

Ebony nodded, tamping down on her fear, holding back her emotions, and trying to concentrate on the words the doctor was saying. Lark was by her side, a hand over hers where they clasped in her lap nervously.

"I know," she said quietly she'd heard it before in LA

"I'm testing your blood now to compare with the last draw you had in LA, it will tell us a lot. The scan did detect cancer of course, but also something unexpected."

"What is it?" she croaked. She didn't want him to sugar-coat anything, she wanted the band aid ripped off.

"Well, when Mr. Duport touched you during the scan it showed an increase in your immune response."

"What does that mean?" Lark snapped.

"Well, it could mean that since you are her soulmate, she's able to borrow some strength from your body."

"To fight the cancer?" Lark asked.

"I think so. Comparing the scan today with the last one in

LA it already seems as if the cancer has started to retreat, the mass is significantly smaller which I would have told you is impossible if I wasn't looking at it right in front of me."

"Oh my god," Ebony gasped.

"I'm still not sure I can do anything for you. This is a very aggressive type of cancer, but, maybe, and this is a really big maybe, if your body can borrow some of Mr. Duport's strength during the process, you could beat this thing with treatment. I've just never seen anything like it. Your body isn't acting like anyone's I've ever met, even fullsouls would have trouble with this type of aggressive cancer."

Ebony looked up at Lark. Tears were pooling in her eyes, and she smiled. "I'm not like anyone else, Doctor." She looked back at him. "I'm a dominant halfling with a soulmate."

He sat back and stared for a minute. "That's true. Very intriguing," the doctor said with a smile. "Ebony, I am very much looking forward to working on your case. I must say, I was nervous about you coming in, sure I was going to get a fist through the face when I gave Mr. Duport bad news," he said with a sly smile that didn't hide the real fear under that statement.

Ebony patted Lark's arm. "He's a bit protective," she agreed.

"Which might be why his body is trying to heal yours. Once I have your bloodwork in hand, I can set a course of treatment but most importantly, I'm prescribing as much physical contact between you two as possible."

Lark pulled Ebony into his lap and grinned down at her frown. It was highly inappropriate.

"Doctor's orders," he laughed.

She couldn't deny that, and she really didn't want to either. She snuggled into his chest and sighed. "I guess I'll take my medicine then."

"Multiple times a day," Lark whispered in her ear, and she shivered with anticipation.

EPILOGUE

Three years later Ebony and Lark left Dr. Gray's office with a clean bill of health. She immediately pulled out her cell and dialed with a huge grin on her face.

"I did it! Well, we did it," Ebony said, looking at Lark. "We beat it, Shine, I know I couldn't have done it without your help and Lark's."

"Just like I couldn't keep my shit together without yours and Granger's," she said with a laugh. "I'll see you tomorrow for mom's funeral?"

"I'll be there," Ebony said and put her phone away. Shine had managed to keep her mother alive for three years, and it hadn't been easy. The woman was completely out of her mind from whatever drugs Buchanan had put her on. When she had moments of lucidity she seemed stuck in the days after Shine's birth, she just kept asking for the baby, saying she was sorry and when Shine tried to explain that she was her daughter it only made her angry and violent.

Her death had been a blessing, but it didn't mean it hurt any less and Ebony was anxious to get to Shine's side and support her through the small funeral.

Lark grabbed her and pulled her into a hug, burying his face in her neck. "I can't believe it's actually over, no more treatments, no more worries."

"No worries," Ebony agreed. "Now we can really put all our energy into Shine's foundation." Shine had started a foundation to support nosouls who wanted to come forward and get help accessing medications and jobs and housing. It was successful, but it took a lot of footwork, nosoul communities didn't trust easy, and they weren't stepping up in large numbers to risk retribution.

But slowly Shine was turning the storyline and Ebony had hope that the world was headed in the right direction. Shine had patented the medication and offered it free of charge to all nosouls in and out of the U.S. She was a real savior and Ebony was proud to share a soul with her.

Lark opened the car door for her, "Stone called earlier and said that he and Taylor have followed that lead to Canada and think they might have a real chance at finding the women."

Stone and Taylor had hit it off on their drive from Vegas to LA and had decided halfway there that they would go in search of the women and infants who had been taken from BaneCore. The infants had been easier to find than the women, but they refused to give up even after multiple dead-end leads. It would be nice to close that one last door on the horrors Buchanan had brought into the world.

"That's great. We should head up there after the funeral," Ebony said.

"Oh sure, and what, have you arrested at the border?" Lark teased. They hadn't been able to clear her name in Glick's murder and she was technically still wanted for questioning. Luckily, Shine had been able to pass some laws that made travel within the U.S. free of scanning necessities, but out of country was still a no go for her.

Ebony stared out at the Texas landscape as they drove to a private airfield where Lark's plane waited to take them to DC,

They were undoing the things that the gods had done, and she worried that it would come back to bite them all in the ass, but she couldn't believe they were wrong in the journey. Equality and opportunity for all living beings couldn't be wrong. Love couldn't be wrong.

She believed with her whole heart that the gods were wrong.

MEET THE AUTHOR

Courtney Davis is an award-winning author of fantasy and romance living in North Idaho with her family and animals. She is a teacher, spending her days instilling a love of books in the youngest students and spends her nights writing or reading. She enjoys time in the sun with her family, traveling, yoga, and coming up with story ideas to explore humans in inhuman interactions. She hopes that readers find joy in her books the same as she finds in creating them.

OTHER TITLES FROM 5 PRINCE PUBLISHING

www.5princebooks.com

Soul Sacrifice *Courtney Davis*
Picking Pismo *Emi Hilton*
Spring Showers *Sarah Dressler*
Secret Admirer Pact *Bernadette Marie*
The Taste of Treachery *Emily Bybee*
The Publicity Stunt *Bernadette Marie*
A Trace of Romance *Ann Swann*
Descendants of Atlantis *Courtney Davis*
Holiday Rebound *Emily Bybee*
Rewriting Christmas *S.E. Reichert & Kerrie Flanagan*
Butterfly Kisses *Courtney Davis*
Leaving Cloverton *Emi Hilton*
Beach Rose Path *Barbara Matteson*
Aristotle's Wolves *Courtney Davis*
Christmas Cove *Sarah Dressler*
A Twist of Hate *T.E. Lorenzo*
Composing Laney *S.E. Reichert*

Milton Keynes UK
Ingram Content Group UK Ltd.
UKHW022156040824
446478UK00001B/39